GRAVITY WELL

Melanie Joosten's debut novel, *Berlin Syndrome*, saw her named a *Sydney Morning Herald* Best Young Novelist and receive the Kathleen Mitchell Award; it has since been made into a motion picture directed by Cate Shortland. In 2016, she published the essay collection *A Long Time Coming*. Her work appears in various publications, including *Meanjin*, *Kill Your Darlings*, *Best Australian Stories 2014*, and *Going Down Swinging*.

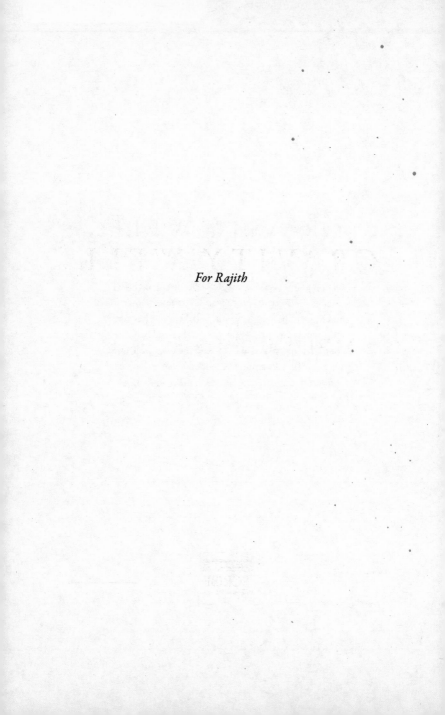

For Rajith

GRAVITY WELL

MELANIE JOOSTEN

SCRIBE
Melbourne • London

Scribe Publications
18–20 Edward St, Brunswick, Victoria 3056, Australia
2 John St, Clerkenwell, London, WC1N 2ES, United
Kingdom

Published by Scribe 2017
This edition published 2018

Printed and bound in the UK by CPI Group (UK) Ltd,
Croydon CR0 4YY

Scribe Publications is committed to the sustainable
use of natural resources and the use of paper
products made responsibly from those resources.

9781911617297 (UK paperback)
9781925322057 (Australian edition)
9781925548228 (e-book)

CiP records for this title are available from the British
Library and the National Library of Australia.

scribepublications.co.uk
scribepublications.com.au

Look again at that dot. That's here. That's home. That's us. On it everyone you love, everyone you know, everyone you ever heard of, every human being who ever was, lived out their lives ... on a mote of dust suspended in a sunbeam ... Our posturings, our imagined self-importance, the delusion that we have some privileged position in the Universe, are challenged by this point of pale light. Our planet is a lonely speck in the great enveloping cosmic dark. In our obscurity, in all this vastness, there is no hint that help will come from elsewhere to save us from ourselves.

— CARL SAGAN

PROLOGUE

The flyscreen door bangs shut as you thump down the steps to the garage. You haul up the roller door, the dust coming alive in the sunlight. The campervan is faded, a memory of itself; the stickers on the bumper describe things people used to care about: *Keep Australia Beautiful. Be Safe, Be Sure. Give a Damn, Vote Democrat.*

Squeezing into the narrow space between the wall of the garage and the van, you ease the driver's door open and pull yourself into the seat. The vinyl is cool against your bare legs, but there's an old beach towel handy to sit on; the seat will burn hot if the van is parked in the sun for a few hours. You don't expect the battery to start, but when you turn the key, the engine coughs into service. Releasing the handbrake, you put the van in reverse. Throwing your left arm over the jump seat, you grab the passenger headrest and look back at the driveway. After the dark of the garage the bright sun flares, and you clench your eyes shut, put your foot to the floor. The van leaps backwards, you don't want it to stall. Give it some more petrol and push out into the day.

And then everything stops.

1

LOTTE

It is the scorpions scuttling across her chest that wake her; her windbreaker whispers and shifts with their movements. She thinks it is rain at first, her half-asleep mind convinced by the sounds of pattering. Wary of the sharp stones digging into her elbows, Lotte props herself up, her eyes on the sky. Not a cloud in sight, just stars popping loud, multiplying in whichever direction she turns, and the moon tossing glare across the desert.

It can't be rain; she is in one of the driest places in the world. Even during the height of what they call the Bolivian winter, no deluge has ever made its way down here, not in living memory. During the day, snow cracks light off the sides of distant mountains crowned with solemn volcanoes; just twelve kilometres away, the Pacific runs far wider than eyes can take in. There is water all around, but not in the air, not here.

That noise again, delicate, sounding now like a bird hopping about in the undergrowth, and Lotte looks around, letting her eyes adjust as she waits for understanding. Watch and wait — she knows it well enough. On a nearby ridge the four squat shapes of the observatory's main telescope are silhouetted like office blocks against the sky. The mountain has been flattened here into a platform, so the units of the Very Large Telescope can move about on their tracks; she isn't as far from civilisation as she might like. Twenty kilometres away, at Cerro Armazones, they are building the Extremely Large Telescope — the unimaginative names never fail to make her smile. As the telescopes get bigger, language struggles to keep up: there is the Giant Magellan Telescope planned for Las Campanas, and the Overwhelmingly Large Telescope, which had proven just too overwhelming to build. Even the radio telescope being erected across the deserts of Australia and South Africa has a requisitely derivative name — the Square Kilometre Array — having, as it will, a square kilometre of collecting area. It is a constant challenge for astronomers — how to comprehend and communicate the immensity of everything they hold dear. Words are not big enough.

Lotte coughs and swallows, her lips tight and mouth dry. There is so little humidity that the air steals whatever it can, wicking away any moisture a body dares emit. It was here that Pinochet built his concentration camps, repurposing old nitrate mines deep in the Atacama Desert: low dormitories hunkering in the sun, alien in the red desert sands. She cannot fathom how anyone survived out here without the humidified enclosure of the observatory residence, though survival was not exactly what was on the Pinochet regime's mind. Those camps sound eerily similar to the old detention centres back home — Curtin and Woomera — places so far from the lights and life of cities that they are just as ideal for holding the unwanted as they are for watching the night skies. Pinochet's political prisoners would track and identify the constellations rolling above; dream of the freedom they might one day attain. Lotte doubts that Australia's asylum seekers, now marooned on island prisons far from the mainland, are even allowed outside at night.

4

She is reaching for her water bottle when she sees them, ruby-edged in the moonlight. Almost a dozen, perched on her chest amongst the hills and valleys of her jacket, and there, further down, on her jeans, each one smaller than her hand, an army of neckless thugs. Not a single scorpion is moving now that they have her attention, seemingly indignant at their exploration being interrupted. Their tails are raised in parentheses, a synchronised swimming team of attack, and Lotte is mesmerised, impressed by their aggressive righteousness. Then, a scratch at her collar.

She scrambles to her feet, abruptly shaking the scorpions off, jiggling at the sleeves of her jacket and dancing about. Are they poisonous? They must be, why the hell else would they have tails like that, pincers at the ready? For holding hands? She stops moving, alert to any possible activity against her skin, her breath sharp in her chest. The air is thin up here. Even after almost five years she still finds herself wheezing if she walks up the road to the control room of the VLT instead of catching a ride on the shuttle. Walking isn't strictly allowed — no one wants any kind of accident, not this far from proper medical help — but everyone understands the need to get out once in a while, to stretch your legs and pretend you have somewhere to go other than the telescope platform or base camp. There is a gym at the residence, and a swimming pool in the lobby, its water feeding the air while the surrounding palm trees sway hopefully, oblivious that the sky they are reaching towards is capped by a glass dome, and covered at night by an umbrella that unfurls to block the residence light so it doesn't interfere with the observatory. They'd held a staff Christmas party there, paper hats and Christmas bonbons strewn about the atrium, the babble of heavily accented English and Spanish hanging in the air, the occasional outburst of laughter or exclamation in any number of languages. Her team had toasted Lotte to send her on her way; five years of service, and she had little to express but gratitude for their dedication and hard work. Promises of meeting again that would be fulfilled by circumstance of employment rather than any genuine attempt at friendship — such was the nature of the job, people coming and going from all over the world. She would miss them; she would miss the work more.

The scorpions disperse, skating camouflaged over rocks and pebbles. It is low now, the moon, skimming the horizon, and if she stays out long enough, another hour perhaps, she'll see it burn deep orange toward the mountains. Dare she sit down, or will the little fuckers come back? Properly awake, she is alert to the sounds of the desert now — the slippery trickle of sand over rock, the hum of the wind crossing the ridge of the dune.

Lotte stamps her feet together, trying to get a little warmth into them; it always seems impossible during the mild, sunny days that it will be so cold at night, but the Atacama is a place of extremes. Especially in one regard. Lotte tips her face to the sky and drinks in the view. Millions of stars fill the vast space above the mountains. She spots the Scorpius constellation easily: riding high, its brightest star is tinged red, holding the place of the creature's heart. Eight hundred times the size of the sun, and it looks like nothing, hundreds of light years away. It seems impossible that the desert scorpions wouldn't know of their colossal namesake, watching over them and chasing Orion through the sky since the beginning of their existence. Its tail curls from the Milky Way, the sting marked by the paired Cat's Eyes stars. At least ten planets have been discovered in that constellation alone, and Lotte is proud of her role in this. But it isn't even a drop in the ocean: a conservative estimate places 160 billion planets in the Milky Way itself. There's every chance one might prove as habitable as Earth, and no chance at all. So much work to be done. But not by her, not right now: tomorrow, Lotte will be down the mountain and taking the bus to the airport at Antofagasta; a flight to Santiago, and then another to Australia. She'd been back just once in five years, briefly, to sort things out with Vin and renew her visa. But she'd avoided almost everyone else, hadn't even told them she was in the country. This time, though, she doesn't know how long she will be staying. And she doesn't think she'll be able to do it alone.

The sky has been her constant companion over the last five years, even if she sometimes forgot it was there — her nights were spent in the fluorescent-lit control room, comparing data and plotting the following night's observations; her days were spent sleeping in one of the comfortingly austere rooms at the residence. Odd how little time astronomers actually spend looking up at the sky — just *looking*, not measuring, or plotting, or reading.

Slung between two hills and buried underground, the residence building is a bunker by any other name, and if it weren't for the internet, a person could spend months in there unaware as to whether the outside world was collapsing entirely. Since she's been here, it feels like every time she goes online, the planet is reaching for its endgame: Ebola breaking out across Africa; airplanes disappearing or being shot down; schoolgirls being abducted en masse. Not to mention the bushfires, earthquakes, and floods, as biblical as any gospel writer could hope for. All of it happening within 40,000 kilometres, yet somehow seeming so much further away than the celestial bodies her work is concerned with.

Until recently, Lotte had spent less and less time on the internet: the voices increasingly histrionic, the world both despairing and incredulous as events seemed to spin out of control. Yet to an observer like herself, nothing substantial had changed. Like other planets, the Earth's history could be understood in chunks of thousands of years, its current period one of unremarkable stability.

Much of her time is time spent looking at objects to confirm there has been no change, so that when there is change it can be accurately measured. Each observation holds potential significance, the possibility of a great uncovering. Over the years, her team has predicted with confidence that every red dwarf in the Milky Way hosts at least one planet, and that a quarter of these are likely to be habitable. Recently, they'd identified an Earth twin. Only slightly larger than Earth, and inhabiting the elusive 'Goldilocks' zone: not so close to its sun that all life would burn up, not so far away it would freeze. This discovery of a possibly liveable planet had lit up Twitter for twenty-four hours: *how long might it take to get there? What would be found when we did?* Fleeting dreams that promised a future once the human race had finished trashing Earth; musings about alien life forms and colonisation. It was nonsense, of course: all the team hopes to find is water, in some recognisable form. And they doubted even that was achievable, guessing early on that the planet's makeup was most akin to that of Venus — scorching hot with a thick, soupy atmosphere. But Lotte cannot deny that she loves it when the public gets interested; when they can see, however briefly and selfishly, the worth of her work. It justifies all the hours she spends contemplating distant, barren worlds when, arguably, there are more pressing things to be doing for this world.

A fox looms out of the desert, disappearing as soon as Lotte moves her head to look at it. She turns slightly away and stares towards the ridge, relying on her peripheral vision in the dark.

The fox reappears, a grey skeleton of a creature, the moonlight fraying its fur. The sound it releases is guttural — a purr almost, deep in the throat — and Lotte interprets it as a warning, taking a quick step back. What the hell is she doing out here all alone?

•

It was Lotte's mother, Helen, who'd told her that retrospect works like a telescope: looking back in time to predict what will come — but never soon enough. The job that took Lotte to the Atacama Desert wasn't really the beginning of the end; she is not that naive. The map of the end is always present, right from the moment of conception. A star's lifespan is determined by its original mass, expanding as it runs out of hydrogen then helium, eventually collapsing and exploding, a neutron star or a black hole left in its place.

Knowing this — the inevitability of everything — as Lotte sat in the car park of the Siding Spring Observatory five years earlier, she wondered how the air could be so indifferent to what it wrapped itself around that it barely bothered to rustle the leaves of the languid gum trees. The few vehicles that were left in the visitor's area crouched in flickering shade; dry leaves sidled up against each other beside the tyres. The children had gone mad, running and leaping at the treated-pine fence posts, kicking at the hardened clay ground and stomping on the ants that trailed, panicking, from one hole to another. The children's faces were smeared with icy pole. Having spent too long trooping about the observatory, looking and not touching, they grabbed at anything they could reach, peeling strips of bark from the trees, kicking at exposed roots. Two or three of them were hanging from a broken bough, clowning, jerking at the branch, which clutched its leaves like a cheerleader's pom-pom. The parents were squinting at their phones. Tapping. Swiping. A playground of boredom, the children unimpressed, the parents unaware, the observatory dome a disapproving matryoshka ghost looming over them.

Lotte sat in her car with the heat building, the key in the ignition. She'd just finished a week-long stint at the observatory and she didn't *want* to turn the key, put the car in reverse, manoeuvre her way out of the car park to drive home to Canberra — it was too long to comfortably do in one day, too short to bother stopping overnight. But the university in Canberra ran and staffed much of the observatory, sited up here in the far reaches of New South Wales, so, first as a PhD student and later a researcher, it was a trip Lotte had made many times. And this would be the last for a while. Her car, a beat-up maroon Alfa Romeo, was eighteen years old. The air-conditioning only worked when she got above sixty, and the radio aerial had been snapped off the same night the badge had been prised from the hood. Twisting to check that there were no rabid children behind her, she turned the key. Best to get it over with.

She was coasting down the winding road, past the billboard of tiny Mercury, and onward towards Venus, when her phone rang. Vin. And with the thought of him came that all too familiar feeling of happiness tinged with something else she had refused, so far, to identify.

I just got your message, he said. I'm so glad you'll be home tonight.

I will. The clouds are already massing, so we won't get a clear view tonight. Luckily, I've already collected enough data; I can be home a day early.

That part wasn't a lie. In the photo displayed on her mobile, which was mounted on the dash, Vin was smiling at her, but she could almost see the disappointment that would wash across him when she told him her news. She glanced at his perfect teeth, the cowlick that made his fringe either stick up or flop down, and which he kept threatening to shave off. His eyebrows that curved upwards like the Golden Gate Bridge, leaving him looking constantly quizzical. Maybe it would be easier to do by phone, to give him a chance to hide his true emotions. Which she was counting on him to do; she wouldn't be able to go through with it if he pressed her, they both knew that.

Lotte pulled into the parking bay beneath the billboard of Earth, to let a LandCruiser travelling in the opposite direction climb past her up the narrow road.

Where are you at the moment?

His reply was garbled as his words bounced up to the satellite and back down again, distorted by the hundreds of kilometres between them. It was mid-afternoon; most likely, Vin would be sitting on the edge of his desk, one arm across his body, the other holding his phone. He would have kicked his shoes off as soon as he walked into his office; he'd be flexing his toes as he dialled her number. She knew him so well; surely he would understand.

I found a house we can look at, it's got an open inspection tomorrow, said Vin, his voice clearing the static. It's three bedrooms, with a study, and it's probably only a twenty-minute drive for each of us because I could take the Parkway.

Lotte jerked the handbrake free, continued rolling down the hill. She would tell him tonight, in person. Right now, she needed to be moving, to feel like she was actually going somewhere. Vin kept talking at her; she picked up speed, and his words were lost beneath the glockenspiel of the gravel flicking up from the road, pinging against the car's undercarriage.

That sounds great. Sorry, you keep cutting out — I'm going to have to go, I've got to get some petrol.

That's okay, we can talk about it when you get home. What time will you be?

Hopefully by around ten.

Alright, drive safe. Love you.

Love you, too.

And if he heard the sigh in her voice, she hung up before he could say anything about it. The sun stepped behind a bank of cloud, and shadow lumbered across the national park. Lotte turned left at the T-intersection toward Coonabarabran, the jumbled topography of the Warrumbungles retreating to the horizon in her rear-view mirror. She would tell him about the job offer tonight, over a glass of wine. Or maybe it would be better left until morning.

Out on the flat, Jupiter thrust its portly belly towards the road, its festoons faded from years of relentless sun. Lotte noticed for the first time that its stripes were like a cat burglar's shirt: fitting for a planet known as a stealth body, hiding from any radar courtesy of its lack of surface. There were nine of these in all, billboards with 3-D models protruding, haunting roadside rest stops at measured intervals all the way from Pluto at the Visitors' Centre in Dubbo to the observatory at Siding Spring, where the main telescope represented the sun. Lotte had always felt disappointed by this. To have come so far and then be greeted by what was, essentially, a large white shed, rather than a massive yellow globe? It was something of a let-down, even with its domed roof.

Her own mother had been part of the group who'd created this series of billboards, prosaically named the 'solar system drive'. All over the country, amateur astronomy groups raised money through sausage sizzles and raffles, passing a hat around at the end of talks at the local observatory, and earnestly pleading on local radio, and to anyone who might listen, that it was important to nurture children's bona fide curiosity in the universe. Lotte had already moved away to university when the project started, and she recalled sketches strewn across the dining table when she came home to visit, detailing what each planet billboard would look like, how big they would need to be, what they could be constructed from. In the beginning her mother was adamant that the model would be an exact replica, thirty-eight times smaller than the real thing — the diameters of the planets, their location in orbit, everything had been calculated to a precise scale. By the time local-council regulations and the road authority had intervened, arguing over who'd be responsible for maintaining the recycled-plastic picnic furniture, and ensuring it wouldn't distract drivers, the model had become skewed, more representational than scientific. At the time, Lotte had been embarrassed by her mother's fanaticism for the project, the way she treated it as though it were serious scientific research when it was basically an overblown school-project diorama. Now she wished she had paid more attention.

She drove into Coonabarabran, turned right at the clock tower, and drove out again, the small town traversed in under a minute. And to think, she wouldn't be back here for at least twelve months. The excitement built in her gut — a position at the International Astronomical Observatory; it was what she'd been working towards all these years. It wasn't that there was anything wrong with being in Australia; on the contrary, Australia had some of the clearest skies and most useful equipment in the world. But to be in Chile at the IAO, and to be working on the newly launched planet-hunting project? It would put her right in the thick of things, give her a basis for all the other research she wanted to do. Surely Vin would understand.

Anaemic-looking, Uranus clung hopelessly to its billboard background of midnight-blue sky as Lotte drove by. She could guess what was in the pithy description printed beneath the fibreglass model: something about Uranus being the only planet tipped on its side, its axis running almost horizontal so it seems to trundle about the Sun, rather than gracefully twirl. These were the kind of descriptions her mother used when she gave talks at the local observatory, animated and passionate. Lotte remembers sitting in the back row, both proud and slightly embarrassed by her mother's zealous delivery. *Uranus's vertical ring system is so dark it's unable to reflect the meagre sunlight the planet receives, thus remaining near invisible*, Helen would tell the audience with awe, her enthusiasm impossible to resist.

A position at the IAO: her mother would have been proud.

•

Five weeks after leaving Siding Spring, and only a few days before Christmas, Sydney's streets were overrun with anxious shoppers. She had sailed into the waiting room that morning full of confidence, only to be told that her appointment had been delayed until four o'clock. Anger and a curt manner had not helped: in the kindly-yet-firm tone for which she had surely been hired, the receptionist told Lotte to come back later. Lotte had tried to reason with her: she'd come all the way from Canberra, what was she to do all day? Not to mention, the information she was there for would already be sitting in her medical records. The receptionist could even glance at it if she wanted, she could give Lotte a little hint — positive or negative — and she would be on her way. The receptionist had turned back to her computer, lips pursed, and Lotte had slunk out of the room, defeated.

In a department store, she bought a new pair of shoes as a gift for herself; she liked them very much. The heels of the shoes unfurled beneath her own, nudging her hips forward, an invitation. She pictured Vin bending down to unbuckle one strap and then the other, his delight infused with serious intent. They were lipstick red, a small buckle on the ankle of each, and she wore them out of the store. On the street, the glass-fronted shops blasted their chill at the passers-by.

Snatches of frenetic electronica sailed over the crowds, scrapping with the Santa-hat-wearing Salvation Army choristers stationed at the entrance to a mall. The smell of cinnamon drifted from a churros shop, followed too quickly by the cold reek of salmon, sushi rolls laid out on a cushion of frilly lettuce. Her stomach clenched and revolted, scrambling at her ribs. Feeling faint, Lotte lunged toward the curve of a metal bench, but a doughy woman who already sat there heaved her shopping bags onto the only empty bit of seat.

Can I sit for a moment?

But the woman rifled through her bags, determined not to see or hear Lotte, who paused, swallowing down her sudden nausea, and then walked on. She had no reason to be nervous, she told herself. Whatever she would find out in the appointment would be simply information; it wouldn't change what was already inside of her. Her ankles were tentative in her new shoes, forcing her to mince when she wanted to stride. Suddenly, it was all too much. The tears came on without warning, her face tense and teeth clenched as she tried to keep from sobbing. Searching for sanctuary, Lotte veered into the lobby of a large hotel, catching a glimpse of her own startled face in the revolving door. Dropping onto a couch, the impetus to cry left as swiftly as it had arrived. Why could the day not go as planned? How was she to get through the hours of not knowing until four o'clock? She was supposed to get her results and drive back to Canberra. All the information at the ready — and then, finally, she would tell Vin about the job.

It had been over a month since she had accepted the position at the IAO, but still she hadn't found the right time to tell her husband. Every Saturday was spent at auctions and open-for-inspections, Vin determined to take advantage of those vendors who wanted their property decisions settled by Christmas. To Lotte, the houses all looked the same. Bedrooms, bathrooms, garages. All of the necessary and much of the superfluous; nevertheless, Lotte managed to ask the right questions, share due considerations. She would only be away twelve months, she reasoned. She found herself leaning toward the houses that needed renovation — the more complicated the better, as if Vin could be distracted from her absence with a torrent of tradesmen and visits to Bunnings.

In all the years they'd been together, Vin had only ever been supportive; yet that didn't stop Lotte from swallowing the words down, and failing to even hint that by the end of January she'd be halfway across the hemisphere. He'd be insulted to think she was 'asking' him for permission, she told herself. Which she wasn't, of course — she was simply telling him she'd been offered a prestigious twelve-month position that happened to be in Chile. He could come over in the middle; they could travel to Machu Picchu, and the salt plains of Bolivia. Hike in Patagonia; he'd love that. And still, she hadn't told him.

Lotte pulled out her phone, but it wasn't Vin she called.

Hello!

Hi! How's things?

Good. Guess what? I'm in Sydney for some Christmas shopping. What are you up to? Lotte blinked away her tears, and settled back into the couch. She watched an older couple scurry out of the revolving doors into the hotel lobby, looking startled by the wheeled suitcases that chased them.

You should have told me you were coming, said Eve. I would have taken the day off work.

It was a last-minute thing. I thought there might be a few things I'd need before I go overseas.

I'm so jealous. I've heard there's some excellent mountain biking in Chile. Down south, I think.

As long as you're not thinking about that road in Bolivia that all the tourists go down. Hundreds of people have died there.

Amateurs! Eve laughed. So, what did Vin say about it all?

Lotte didn't answer. She watched the couple advance to the service desk, lean over their luggage to talk to the concierge. As one man spoke, the other rested his hand on his partner's shoulder.

You haven't told him, have you?

Lotte could hear Eve's disapproval, imagine her steely-eyed gaze.

What are you waiting for?

I don't know, said Lotte. He's just so intent on this house-hunting thing, I feel bad telling him I won't be there for the next year.

He'll be fine. He's always fine. It's only for twelve months.

I know. I will tell him. Look, do you want to grab a drink tonight? I've got a thing at four, but it should only take half an hour. We can have a Christmas catch-up.

Sorry, I can't, said Eve. I've ... I've already got plans.

A date? Who? Tell me!

No one you know.

I'd hope not! I want to hear all about it. Are you sure you don't want to come to Vin's parents' for Christmas lunch? You know you're always welcome.

Thanks, but no, I'm going to take the van, head out of town. When do you leave for Chile?

End of January. Lotte watched the couple head to the lift, now liberated of their luggage. Come and stay with us before then, okay?

That would be great. Just make sure you tell Vin, alright? Tonight.

Promise, said Lotte. Talk soon.

When she hung up, the ill feeling returned. She considered her reflection in the mirrored column opposite. Straightened her shoulders, lifted her brown hair off her shoulders and tied it up with an elastic from her wrist. She had been eating badly, working nights to avoid Vin, and it showed in her skin, too pale for summer. What sometimes, to her eye, looked voluptuous now looked heavy, dragging. She really should do some exercise, but even the *thought* of those endless, repetitive hours bored her.

•

Four years ago, the summer her mother was dying, Lotte had given up making any effort with her own health. Helen had been admitted to hospital after her final round of chemotherapy, fatigued and nauseous, her body telling her what her mind already knew: this time, the treatment wasn't working. It was the middle of summer, the accumulated heat of each day lingering into the next. Lotte's dad was working mornings at the council offices while Lotte slept in her childhood bed, willing the day not to start. After breakfast, she would walk up the town's wide main street, the thick northerly wind buffeting every surface so that breathing was like drinking. When Lotte came into the hospital ward she would count the heavy, nodding heads of the roses outside her mother's window, noting any casualties that had occurred since her previous visit. At the base of each bush was a brass plaque, the hospital beautification committee unperturbed by the thoughts that might haunt a patient looking out the window and seeing a roll call of names and paired dates.

As her mother's body had shrunk, Lotte's had grown. She could see her choices reflected in its sway and give, her waist soft and seemingly limitless beneath her own curious fingers. She'd gone up at least two dress sizes since her wedding six months before. She knew exactly what was to blame: hastily racing across to the shopping-centre food court and eating hot chips and dim sims, so as to avoid sitting down to lunch with her father. Cheese-and-salami panini in the hospital canteen, mugs of sweet and foamy chai lattes and, most of all, the odd, firm coolness of the protein-enhanced puddings that were tucked onto her mother's tray with every meal. Lotte had acquired a taste for these puddings, unsure whether they actually dissolved or simply dispersed around her mouth. The pastel strawberry and banana flavours reminded her of childhood, a place she would rather be, even as her ballooning thighs and belly took her further from it.

One morning, squashing spoonfuls of pudding against the roof of her mouth and counting the roses, Lotte didn't notice her mother was crying until a nurse appeared by the bedside, dabbing at Helen's cheeks with a tissue.

Is it the pain, Helen? asked the nurse. Would you like something more for it? Just let me know if you do.

No, no.

Helen attempted a smile. She bared her teeth, loose in their gums, and Lotte watched, horrified, afraid that her mum might fall apart in front of her. Every part of her body was rickety and rattling, with too many empty spaces.

The nurse did not comment on Lotte's silent presence, nor on Lotte's seeming inability to wipe away her own mother's tears.

Are you uncomfortable, is that it?

The nurse tugged at one of the three pillows her mother was leaning against, jammed in so tightly they seemed poised to catapult her from the bed. A plastic sheet crackled beneath the starched hospital linen, reporting on every movement.

I just …

Lotte looked away, not wanting to watch her mother scrabble about for words. So often Helen started a sentence only to trail off, unaware that she was leaving it unfinished, growing irritated if prompted to continue but upset if no one seemed to be listening. Lotte had taken to waiting silently, seating herself just out of her mother's direct line of sight; she was having trouble masking her boredom. Taking tiny spoonfuls, she concentrated on her pudding, following it around her mouth with her tongue as it disintegrated.

Or is your mouth dry? Just take a little sip, dear, you'll feel better.

The nurse held a plastic cup with a straw to her mother's lips. Lotte looked back just in time to see the water, mixed with whatever else was in her mother's stomach, splash over her chest as she spluttered and vomited.

Whoops! A little too much, maybe. We'll just clean you up.

Sorry, sorry.

Helen's face crumpled as she looked down at her chest then up at the nurse. She had become meek in front of the nursing

20

staff — apologising for any inconvenience she was causing, prefacing every comment with: *when you have a moment*. You've never been so kind to us, Lotte had joked, after her mum had simpered at a nurse who'd brought an extra blanket. I never needed to be, remarked her mother, showing for the first time just how defeated she was.

It's okay, these things happen, said the nurse. She turned to Lotte, nodding at the cupboard.

Can you just grab one of your mother's nightgowns?

Lotte found a nightgown, then helped by holding Helen's slight body forward as the nurse changed her, staring at the wall, not wanting to see the intrusions on her mother's abdomen. *Ex*trusions was more accurate. The wide tube of the colostomy bag and its stent; the stubby opening where the chemotherapy had been delivered once the IV had proved ineffectual.

You can go, said Helen, as Lotte gently placed her back onto the pillows. You don't need to stay with me all day. It's bad enough that your father's been working these ridiculous hours, let alone you coming all this way. You should be at work, you can't let things slide just because you've got a contract now. You've got to keep up with the others.

It's fine, Mum. I want to be here. Besides, it's university holidays — it's always quieter this time of year.

This isn't much of a holiday.

Her mother closed her eyes then, letting her head drop to the side, and the nurse scribbled something in the folder at the end of the bed before leaving the room.

Seriously, Lotte. Just go.

Mum, stop it.

It was yet another version of an argument they'd had many times over the last few years — ever since her mother had been diagnosed with ovarian cancer. From the beginning, Lotte had wanted to move home to help. Not sure that her father could cope, not sure that her mother would want him to. But Helen had insisted that everyone carry on as normal; she didn't want the world to come to a grinding halt, just because of an illness. She'd beaten breast cancer, she'd beat this one, too.

Will you at least promise me you'll bring Vin down to stay? Her eyes opened, showing a tiny spark of eagerness. He shouldn't be up there all alone.

Okay, Mum.

Good. Helen smiled. Now, tell me about your new project. How many exoplanets do you hope to find?

We're not sure. It's hard to find them; they've only found two with this new technology. It relies on the Doppler effect — a planet's gravity will have an effect on its host star, making it wobble. So we watch the stars, and when we detect that movement from their wavelength, we know there's a planet nearby.

I would have thought you had a much fancier way of finding them these days. It seems so old-fashioned.

No need to reinvent the wheel, Mum.

And what do you do when you find them?

We calculate their size and mass by measuring the eccentricity of their orbits: the tilt of their orbital plane, and their resonance, or how they move in time with others in their system. There's a lot to consider.

It's like scoring ballroom dancing, Helen pointed out, delighted. You're awarding points for measurements that could seem arbitrary, but are vital to those in the know.

Lotte laughed at her mother's version: Helen could always make the most complicated scientific concepts graspable. She had a habit of using astronomy metaphors to explain things that had nothing to do with astronomy, and while it had bugged Lotte in the past — it was too whimsical, too quixotic — increasingly, she had found herself doing it. Watching her mother's decline over the last few months, her desperate lurching from one effort to another, had made Lotte think of planets, greedily grabbing at anything that came near — a satellite, a comet, a space shuttle — and turning it into a moon to keep them company. As she became more unwell, Helen dropped and picked up projects at random. She told Lotte that there were certain books she just *had* to read, but then they would be discarded by the bed when her mother picked up her knitting, needles furiously clacking until they, too, were put aside. She was the same with her friends: asking them to come and visit, and then having nothing to say, making it obvious she was impatient for them to leave. Lotte watched with sympathy and despair, unable to change her mother's trajectory, knowing what all these attempts at diversion were trying to conceal.

This would be Helen's last visit to the hospital. They all knew it.

You don't need to be here all the time, Helen said after a long silence. You should be back at the observatory. It makes me feel like you're waiting for something.

Even now, her mother managed to look formidable. She stared at Lotte defiantly, daring her to say it. Since the cancer had returned, it had refused to respond to any treatments. The palliative-care team had come to do their assessment yesterday; they were at the house now, installing a hospital bed and drawing up schedules with Lotte's father.

I *am* waiting. Lotte forced down her annoyance, tossing the empty pudding container into the bin. Waiting for you not to be so bloody difficult.

This, at least, drew a smile; her mother could only ever take 'difficult' as a compliment.

Go on, Lotte. Go outside, enjoy some sun. For me at least. I'll still be here when you get back.

They both ignored the fact that she wouldn't be able to say that for much longer.

•

Sitting in the hotel lobby, Lotte looked at her watch. It was only late morning; she had hours to fill before her appointment. Four years since her mother's death, and what had Lotte achieved? A bounty of publications, but nothing truly extraordinary — that's why she needed to go to Chile. All her work, years of it, would come to nothing if she couldn't discover proof of the planets her research pointed to. To be part of something so big — Vin would understand. And time might be running out. She pulled herself up from the couch and walked back out into the fray.

2

EVE

She doesn't remember if it's closer to Lorne or Apollo Bay. Each time the bus eases around a headland, Eve looks for the familiar dip of the road where cliff gives way to sandy beach. Traffic is sluggish, the road slippery with rain; the bus climbs steep hills in low gear, negotiating hairpin turns almost too tight for its long body. Eve steals another glance out the window, not wanting to invite conversation from the woman across the aisle but unable to ignore the mesmeric pull of the ocean. The afternoon sea is a sink of dishwater, the sky dangling above like limp grey curtains. Last time she'd been here it was summer: the sky was crayon cerulean, the midday sun stripping the landscape of depth, pulling every part of the view onto the same plane.

Makes you feel alive, doesn't it?

The elderly woman directs her comment to the window. She sucks noisily on a mint and offers the bag of them without looking at Eve. She likes her, this woman. Just for that — the not-looking.

I've been watching the waves churning over themselves down there; they'd swallow you up in an instant, says the woman.

How cold it would be: how numbing. The winter sea pulling

itself through Antarctic ice floes to eventually pound onto the shore. In the bag of powdery mints, Eve feels the broken edge of one and drops it for another.

Thank you, she says, putting the mint in her mouth.

Soldiers built this road, you know, says the woman. My father, he worked on it awhile before he got his land. Thirty acres out near Korumburra.

Scrabbling for another mint, the woman's arthritic knuckles fight each other. In the seats ahead, adolescent legs cantilever the aisle; backpacks spill boxes of Barbecue Shapes and soft-drink bottles. Teenagers pass headphones over the seats, yelping accusations at one another, pouting at mobile phones.

They're a bit of a handful, aren't they?

The woman is expecting conversation. Eve has avoided looking at the teens since they boarded the bus back at the station. The prickly sideburns of the boys, new to shaving, angry bumps of acne crowding their necks and cheeks. The girls are slick of any body hair, their ankles decorated with charm bracelets and rainbow-coloured bands, feet bare in thongs despite the season, toes stubby beneath chipped nail polish. There is so much wrong about them, so much still to grow.

Ah, kids, the woman says, still struggling with the mints, the plastic bag crackling at her fist. They'd all have rough lives, those ones; this is probably the only holiday they're likely to get, and it's not their parents who are taking them.

She finally succeeds in extracting a mint from the bag and pops it in her mouth.

A woman wearing a lanyard is kneeling on a seat at the front of the bus, passing a clipboard across the aisle to her colleague. They'd ticked off each child as they entered the bus, friendly demeanours keeping their authority at the ready. Youth workers.

How do they do it? Their charges talk too loudly, aware the whole bus can hear them, refusing to censor their crass conversation, seemingly revelling in the discomfort they unload on the other passengers. The boys cram chips into their mouths; the girls loll against one another, stroking each other's arms. Eve hates them. The unfairness of these children. Their loud, obnoxious freedom to do as they please. To be the age they are. She pulls her gaze back to the window, risking encouraging the woman in further conversation, but the woman says nothing for a while. They both stare out to sea. Eve takes another mint without asking; the first has been ground to sugary spit in her mouth.

Most kids have got no chance these days, the woman says eventually. Not going to be able to afford university, and what can they do without that? Can't buy a house, can't get a job.

It's not that bad, is it? asks Eve.

She marvels at this woman's ability to care for others, these children she doesn't even know. How old must she be? Seventy, at least, maybe eighty. Twice Eve's age. Is that what happens when you get older? You get more time for other people?

It's all relative, I suppose, says the woman. Better like this than sending them off to war. My dad, he signed up when he wasn't even twenty, and when he came back, he was never the same. Well, not that I remember — I was born well after all that. But they all said it later: my aunties and my grandparents. My mum. Said he came back different.

When the woman sucks on her mint her lips purse and release with a sloppy sound; a toddler with a lollipop. *Shut that thought away.*

But they built this road, they did. A couple of miles a month, and livin' in tents. He used to tell us kids that there was a shipwreck one night. Hundreds of barrels of beer and whiskey bobbing about in the ocean and theirs for the taking. I don't know whether to believe him or not, he was a storyteller, he was. But he reckons they stopped work for two weeks then, couldn't get any of the boys off the grog long enough to lift a shovel until it was all drunk.

A murmur of encouragement, and the woman talks on. Her words block Eve's thoughts, like insulation batts squashed into place. It is easy, this listening. A noise here and there. A nod. She tells Eve how cold it could be getting up to milk on a Korumburra morning, the only heat coming from the cows' udders, warm and pliable in her hands, toes cultivating chilblains in her shoes. She tells of picking straw out of her hair before dressing for church, and trying not to fall asleep while jammed in next to her sisters in the front pew. She tells of scorching the back of her school dress while standing in front of the Aga. She tells of fibbing about sunning her legs on the parish tennis court with the other girls when she'd been sent into town to the shops.

Dunes build between the road and the ocean, and the cliffs flatten out. The bus swoops into Lorne, and there is a scramble amongst the teens to pack up their belongings: clothes stuffed in plastic bags, sleeping bags that have seen better days. Eve softens towards them, just a little. Their loud bravado is excitement, not an attempt to annoy her, or to remind her she is no longer so young and carefree.

Are you getting off here, love?

The woman stares. One of her eyes is the colour of milky tea; the other so brown it's almost black.

No. Eve hugs her tote bag to her chest. It fills the gap between her and everything else. Sorry, are you? She stands to help the woman with her bags.

Nope. I'm going on to Apollo Bay. My daughter has a holiday

28

house there. Well, not quite Apollo Bay – Skenes Creek. Do you know it? It's just a little way before.

Eve shakes her head, relaxes back into her seat. A kind daughter to provide such refuge. The bus starts up again, almost empty.

A nice wood fire, a cup of tea, and a good book, says the woman. That's about all you need to be happy. They don't tell you that when you're young though, do they?

It's not always so simple. Eve tries to snap, but the words slide out of her mouth, softer than she wants them to be.

The woman turns to look at her, and nods slowly. Milky tea. Browny black.

Right you are, love. Right you are.

The bus crawls out of Lorne, between the pier and the pub. Eve closes her eyes. Light leaks in around the edges, a world of dark red. This is what it would have been like. Not awake, not asleep. The bus sways; her thighs tense to correct the rocking and keep herself upright. How is it that her body wants something she does not? She wills herself to collapse, but her body remains seated; it won't slump. The bus slows again, jolts her awake.

Cumberland River? calls out the bus driver.

Eve recognises these words; she waits for her body to respond.

Oh shit, sorry. This is me.

Pulling herself from the seat, she stretches to tug her sleeping bag down from the parcel shelf.

Take care, love.

This from the woman. She is facing the window, talking again to the sea.

Eve shuffles off the bus, arms full and catching at the headrests. Her skin tingles in the cold, unwilling to leave the heated bus behind. The bus driver is standing by the luggage doors, socks pulled up on calves the size of roadside bollards.

Which one is it?

I don't have any bags, she says, turning to leave.

I put your bags on the bus, lady. Now I'll take them off. Which ones?

The door is lifted above his head like a verandah. Eve wants to climb into the compartment and pull the door closed after her. It is dark in there, amongst people's precious things. She points out her bag and tent, and he pulls them free, drops them to the ground by her feet. Then he grabs a small blue esky with a Red Cross sticker on the side, and puts it down beside her bag.

That's not mine, she says, accusatory — sharp and sour. She already has more than she should.

Of course it's not. It's for Len's kid. He waits for her response before prompting. The caravan park owner?

Right.

They both wait to see if she will say any more. She doesn't.

See ya then.

The bus eases off down the road. Why did she bring so many things? A family — mum, dad, and three kids rugged up in polar fleeces and beanies — wait to cross the road to the beach. Eve lifts the bag to her back and tries to gather the sleeping bag and esky in one hand, but her finger-span isn't big enough.

Wait up!

The family has crossed the road; the father jogs to her.

Let me give you a hand.

No, it's alright, really.

He takes the biggest bag, picking up the tent in his other hand.

No worries. I'll just help you across and leave you to it.

The three children watch, open-faced stares. The wife smiles with her mouth, but her eyes warn. Yes, I *am* dangerous, thinks Eve. She crosses the road, walks through the car park to the reception.

Bit cold for camping, isn't it?

When he puts down the bags, the tent poles clatter against each other.

She shrugs. He doesn't see it.

Fair enough, then. Well, stay warm.

The door to reception is locked, though the sign is flipped to *Open*. Leaning into the glass, Eve can make out a deserted desk, a bell to ring if it's unattended. She slumps to the steps, jamming her hands in her pockets. Coming here wasn't such a good idea. Running away will only ever be a cliché, not an answer.

We're all booked out.

A bald man comes around the side of the office, black eyebrows like caterpillars clinging to his forehead. He is struggling to pull his right arm into a down vest — he can't seem to bend it enough.

I took a tumble on the pier two weeks ago, the man says.

He gives all of his words to her as though she wants to hear them.

Slid on a pile of fish guts, and landed on my arse. I snapped my rod in two; Jordie cacked himself. My arm hasn't been the same since.

The caterpillars gently nudge up against each other until the arm is through the opening, and he smiles widely.

Did you say you're booked out? says Eve. She looks past him to the camping ground. There are no tents; the lawns are bare, green and lush until they fall away to the swollen river.

Just kidding. We've got plenty of cabins available. Pretty quiet over winter.

He steps around her and unlocks the sliding door, opening it with a flourish.

You're off the bus?

He points at her luggage, and the esky sitting next to it.

Yes.

She gets to her feet and passes him the esky.

Thanks for that, he says. Will keep the little monster going.

He puts it on the counter.

So, how many nights do you want? All the cabins have hot water, a shower, toilet, and TV. Just the regular channels, not Foxtel.

I'm just after a campsite. I've got a tent.

The man sucks air through his front teeth, looking at her properly.

Bit cold for that, isn't it? And the river … well, if we get more rain, I don't know, it might flood.

Tent, sleeping bag, and foam mat — she'd bought them all at once, not listening to the salesman's patter. It was the only way, the only kind of space to be in: small and enclosed, with no view and no comfort.

Is it going to rain?

Well, it's not forecast today. But that doesn't mean much. If it's the price, I can give you a discount on one of the cabins. Not like there's a huge demand just now.

It's not money. I just wanted to camp. I'll be fine — it'll just be a couple of days.

Pause.

Well, fair enough. Until Thursday, then?

Yes. I think.

Thursday must not be tomorrow; maybe it's the day after. Her body lurches, reaching for the counter. Both Eve and the man look at her hand, clinging there like a lost sea animal.

Well, is it just you?

What do you mean?

Are you by yourself? Is there anyone else with you?

Just me.

Still not used to saying those words.

There's a spot tucked up the back, it's a little bit higher than the rest, he says.

They watch her hand unclench.

It's a fair hike from the facilities, but it won't flood. And it's not under the trees, so I won't have to worry about them dropping their branches on you.

Thanks.

She signs her name in the register, paying three days in advance, and he leads her past cabins with their blinds drawn, gas bottles beneath tarpaulin shrouds, to a grassy patch at the pointy end of the park. Here the hills steeply fold in on each other, leaving just enough space for the river to pass down below. The trees skirt the campsite uneasily, huddled up against the sheer rock face, which goes straight up like a theatre backdrop.

She is back at the reception desk within ten minutes.

You're after a hammer, aren't you?

Beckoned by the bell, he stands again behind the counter. She nods. The hammer is already in his hand; he passes it, and she takes it by its head.

I'm Len, by the way.

Eve.

She waits for the requisite jokes. *Original woman. Bit of a sinner, hey?* He seems the type, but the jokes don't come, and they each shake their end of the hammer, holding it between them like a relay baton. Imagine if you could pass everything on so easily. *Your turn now, I'm taking a break.*

Make sure you use the guy ropes, it can get pretty windy, says Len.

She has to tear the plastic wrapping and price tags from the tent before she can erect it, arranging the head of her bed uphill. As if these things still matter. She piles all of the food into the tent bag and zips it closed before crawling into the sleeping bag and hooking the hood over her head. She tightens the drawstring around her face, not caring that it's only mid-afternoon. She is not cold; she shivers. Closes eyes, tries for sleep.

The reedy voices of children, floating through the nylon walls of the tent, wake her. The scuff of shoes on gravel, a cabin door sliding open, car doors slamming shut. It's dark when she climbs out of the sleeping bag and uses the light of her mobile phone to find a can of baked beans and the loaf of bread. Fifteen missed calls, and the battery is about to go flat. *I'm okay*, she would type into the message box. But they can trace you these days; they can figure out exactly where you are. She left a note, anyway. Explaining what she could.

In the campsite kitchen she tugs on the ring-pull, and the beans slurp out of the can and onto her hand. She eats directly from the saucepan, dipping the soft white bread into the sauce and folding it into her mouth. It's disgusting that she can feel hunger; that she can eat. As punishment, she has bought only this kind of non-food: processed to the point it bears little relation to anything appetising. Food that will fill, not nourish. The sign above the sink tells her to clean her dishes and return them to their places, but she doesn't wash out the pan — she leaves it sitting on the stovetop, the fork in a sticky puddle on the bench. She wonders if Len will come and find her later, his caterpillar face asking why she hasn't followed the instructions.

A cake of lemon deodoriser sits in a tray on the toilet cistern;

gritty sand gathers in rivulets across the concrete, and soggy toilet paper attaches itself to her shoe. She concentrates on these details rather than anything inside of her. She washes her hands slowly, staring at herself in the mirror. She looks the same as she always does; when will her body catch up with events?

Returning to the tent, she crawls back into the sleeping bag. It smells new and synthetic. Clean. It smells full of promise, and Eve knows that she won't sleep tonight.

Light appears from no particular direction; tent walls become a dull green that brightens as the sun rises. Eve's shoulders and hips ache from the hard ground, and rolling over only gives temporary relief. How is it she's so unable to put up with discomfort?

When she can bear it no longer she goes outside, the day fresh and new and already serving admonishments. At the river, water bubbles and tumbles over rocks, unaware it's rushing forward into the salty mass of the ocean, that it will be embraced then promptly dispersed. She bends and scoops, the sepia water becoming clear in her cupped hand, tasting woody in her mouth, trickling down the inside of her sleeve.

Minutes pass. She looks at her watch too often, willing time to slow down. Begging the minutes to expand to hours, the hours to days — for everything to come to a lumbering halt, too obese to move, before changing direction and going the other way. Going back in time. She undoes the buckle of her watch and stands, flinging it into the water.

Red river gums protected by the cliff wall line the waterway. A beautiful camping spot, with the beach just over the road, it has barely changed over the years. Her thoughts chase — if only … if only … — without coming to resolution. And she's not looking for one. Just a few years ago she was lazing on this same riverbank, the trees dripping their leaves to the couch-grass lawns. Families returning from morning trips to the beach and children flopping about on the grass, sucking juice boxes as their mothers made sandwiches and hung towels. Snatches of conversation, fluting voices sure of an audience. She still remembers their names: Ava, Leo, Jacob, Harriet, Maddie. Easy to love, every one of them. At the time, Eve's own belly was taut with pregnancy, being laughed at as she lumbered to her feet, ungainly and exhausted.

Back at the tent she pulls on a pair of runners. She wants to take off down the beach, to pound at the firm sand of the receding tide. Her body aches for the release — how *good* it would be for her: adrenalin flooding her system, blood vessels gorging on oxygen. She won't do it. Instead, she heads inland, walking along the skinny path by the river. She concentrates. Once, she might have attacked a path like this on her mountain bike, but those days are long gone. Now she walks steadily, one foot in front of the other, avoiding tree roots, embedded rocks, anything that could cause trouble.

•

Twenty years earlier, and not knowing a single person in Canberra, Eve had joined the university mountain-biking club. On the weekends they cycled out to Majura Pines, their bikes sluggish on the paved roads, but becoming slick over the pine needles. The first time she headed downhill she felt as if her rigid arms would pop from their sockets. She gripped the handles and clenched the brakes, releasing them in panicked jolts. It wasn't a rock that upended her but a slide of gravel. Her front wheel swooped aside, the back followed, and Eve went the other way. When she hit the ground it didn't hurt; rather, it was like a massive release, and she got straight back on the bike. This time she let her arms and knees sit loose, absorbing the bumps and letting the bike buck beneath her without upsetting her centre of gravity. She got to the bottom of the hill without further incident and let the bike drop to the ground. She had never felt so alive. She bought her own mountain bike second-hand from a guy called Stu, all bandana and skinny legs. She rode with him sometimes, their shouts grabbing at the trees as they ripped by, stop-starting over the rocks. She found her vocabulary whittled down to nothing but swear words, low down and drawn out or screeched to the sky. Found herself thinking of her parents, their relentless assaults on each other.

You've a mouth on you like a fuckin' dunny, said Stu, picking at a scab on his knee.

You fuckin' ought to know, she retorted, laughing.

Her mother had died when Eve was fifteen, interrupting her parents' seemingly endless argument. *It's a fucking discussion*, one of them would say to Eve, when she asked them to go five minutes without attacking each other. In the following years, Eve's father's face sank into itself, fading in the silence — except for occasional outbursts where he would rage at the radio, the world, the neighbours. Never at Eve, but it was close enough. Two days before she was to leave home to study in Canberra, she found her father's body in his armchair in front of the television. *A broken heart*, the doctor said. *He was never the same after Shelley passed.* Eve thought the latter was true, but doubted the former. Now it was swear words that brought her parents back to her, reminding her of the teasing way they would taunt each other. *You silly old bitch. You old bastard.* She relished the familiar words, grunting them as she urged her bike up the hill, shouting them as she skipped it downhill, imagining her parents slinging the insults at each other from where they leant against pearly gates.

By the time Eve had sorted things out after her father's death, the university semester had started and student accommodation was hard to come by. She moved into a single-room bungalow at the back of a house in O'Connor. It was advertised as a granny flat, but it was just a room up on stumps, with flimsy French doors that opened to the garden. She wore gloves and a beanie to bed in winter. The bathroom and the kitchen were in the house, which her housemates called the mainland; the bungalow was known as 'Tasmania'.

Four others lived in the house; they all seemed much older than Eve, though it was only a matter of years. A potter, a musician, a sculptor. And Nate, with his student politics and PhD. A giant beanstalk of a man, lumbering and inelegant, who drew people to him, moths to flame. There were unfinished projects in every room of the house; in the living room, a clotheshorse covered in woollen tassels looked like an overgrown Highland cow had crawled through the window and given birth to a fall of painted terracotta tiles. Slabs of clay were stacked in buckets in the bathroom; they had to be swung out of the shower when someone wanted to use it. When Eve went to her housemates' art exhibitions she always expected their work to be transformed by the white-walled gallery, but each piece still looked like a child's homemade art project.

They frightened her, these brash artists with their performative laughter and self-congratulatory talk, but they didn't seem to mind Eve skulking about, hiding out in her room and emerging to cook only when she knew the kitchen would be empty. Her wish to fade into the background seemed to infuriate Nate, though, who would stride out to the bungalow at least once a week to demand Eve's presence in the house, or that she accompany him and a dozen others to the pub. Sometimes he would lounge on her floor, leaning against the bed, telling her about all the places he had travelled to while doing volunteer community development work: building wells in small villages, and fixing solar panels to corrugated iron roofs. Other times he would invite her into his bedroom, pull her down beside him on the bed and demand her opinion of some band he'd just heard of. He peppered her with questions, and — perhaps because he didn't mind if she answered or not — on those evenings, Eve's words came out without getting tangled and running into one another. As long as she didn't look directly at Nate, she found she could say things — interesting things, sometimes things that even drew his laughter — without examining them first for unintentional points of provocation. It wasn't like talking to her dad had been, when she was always wary of inciting his rage, whether about some hurt he had long nursed, or some imagined slight his memory had magnified. After those evenings, though, Eve, alone again in the bungalow, would wonder if she had embarrassed herself. Spoken too much or too little. Whether Nate thought her strange or, even worse, felt sorry for her. And her resolution to seek him out of her own accord, to ask to borrow some of the CDs he particularly liked, would quiver and retreat.

That first year, she was studying law. It had seemed the surest way out of her small hometown and away from her father's misery — but after all the effort to get there she couldn't find her way into the course, the dreary subject names managing to dull any intrigue the law might have held: *Constitutional Law. Torts. Legal Institutions. Law of Obligations.* In the evenings, she would close her curtains and turn on her desk lamp, trying to focus on her textbooks and not the sounds of her housemates smoking on the back deck. When Nate came knocking, she would half-heartedly refuse his invitations before giving in and following him on whatever expedition he had planned. Nate was all rhyme and no reason. His enthusiasm shot out in every direction at once, a radar signal of possibility and goodwill; he just sat back and waited to see what it would bounce off. He was always making plans and carrying them out: inviting random people on adventures to plaster Civic with posters calling for the government to apologise to the Stolen Generations, or building a raft to paddle the length of Lake Burley Griffin.

One afternoon, Nate borrowed a friend's white Corolla and drove Eve out to the national park so they could go bushwalking. As he led the way along the track, Nate explained the detail of his PhD in micro-financing and international development; how the greed of capitalism had to be embraced in order for it to be tamed. His research was laden with theory and discourse, and he explained it to her carefully, confident of her interest.

He told her the names of plants and explained how they all worked together, the smaller plants huddling for protection against the trunks of the eucalypts. He pointed out the size of the trees that had survived the most recent fire in the area, the way their growth was stunted but still assured. Nate walked ahead, and Eve looked at the tightly spiralled hairs on the back of his legs, wondering if she found him attractive. His T-shirt rode up beneath his backpack and a soft roll of skin squeezed over the waistband of his shorts, surprising on a man so slim.

When they stopped to eat, Nate lay down and put his head in Eve's lap. She wasn't sure where to put her hands and wondered whether she should cup his ears. Instead, she leaned back and put her hands on the ground.

I feel so relaxed when I'm with you, Eve. You're an excellent listener. Most people aren't. Most people are just waiting for a break in the conversation so they can start talking.

He had his eyes closed and a half-eaten apple in his hand.

I suppose it's because you've got a lot of interesting things to say.

She cringed as she said it, even though it was true. The conversations she had with Nate were nothing like those she used to have with her friends at school. There was an urgency to all the things he told her, and the presumption that they really mattered.

Well, let's talk about you, Eve. Do you think you'll end up as a defence lawyer or a prosecutor? I can see you working for the Crown, locking up those crims.

And she let him talk on, surprised to think he spent any time imagining anything about her.

In the mid-semester break, when most people had gone home to see their families, Eve rode out to Majura Pines. Without the other club members watching she went harder than usual, taking the more difficult forks and larger jumps, wishing she knew of a track that wasn't as well defined. The air was cold and sharp, the ground damp. She wasn't sure what made her fall, but she came to staring up at the spindly pines. She moved her legs, then her arms; nothing appeared to be broken. When she sat up, she gingerly shifted her weight from side to side. Just bruising. She heard her feet slipping about on the pine needles, and the wind batting at the trees. Somewhere a pinecone fell, rattling through the branches and landing with a thump. Hardly anything was moving, but in every direction was a busy syncopation of sounds, and as Eve wheeled her bike along the track, she found herself straining to hear a level of detail she had never before paid attention to.

Later that week she bought a minidisk recorder, enthralled by its smallness, the coloured disks snug in plastic cases. She carried it with her everywhere, sometimes sitting the microphone out beside her on the bench as she filled in time between lectures, listening back later to the chatter of students walking past, their voices rising and falling with distance; the sharp swoosh of fingers on paper as she turned a page. Once, she clipped the microphone to her bra, capturing the beating of her heart as she ran up the stairs to the back of the lecture hall, the racing thump when the lecturer asked her a question, the unexpectedly deep rumble of her own voice, amplified by her chest, when she answered. At night, as she lay in bed, headphones on, the laughter and clank of cutlery from the kitchen across the yard would be banished, replaced by the thwack of Converse sneakers on brick pavement, the hurried clatter of high heels accompanied by a whisper of synthetic fabric against stockings. She would keep some of the disks as they were and record over others, marking out timed segments that could be filled with new sounds until the tracks were dense, some describing familiar journeys of her day, others a medley of commotion. She listened to them until they became emphatically familiar. Later, she bought a computer and loaded it with editing software, teaching herself how to edit and splice the audio, layering her sounds into pillowy landscapes, entranced by what she could achieve by nurturing a single sense.

Nate would disappear for days on end. She wasn't sure if he was sleeping elsewhere or if their paths just no longer crossed. Twice she sought him out, only to find his bedroom empty and the other housemates unhelpful. When he next turned up, he told her he had been visiting his parents on the farm.

It keeps me centred, he said. I'm a country boy through and through. I just can't concentrate here; at this rate, I'm never going to get my thesis written.

Eve invited him to come mountain biking. He turned her down.

This? On a bike? He had laughed, gesturing at his body. I'd have to fold myself in half; my knees would be up over the handlebars.

She put together a recording for him, trying to capture the heaviness of winter as it sank into the bush: eucalyptus branches wheezing in the damp wind, the sodden weight of ferns rotting in the undergrowth, the playful trill of currawongs. She left it on his bed, and for days it lay undisturbed on his pillow; Eve pushed aside her disappointment and tried to concentrate on her assignments. It was late when Nate came pounding on her doors, the glass rattling in the frames.

This is great! I love it; it's just like home. He made her listen to it with him, eyes closed on her bed, and they fell asleep like that, side by side.

She thought she saw him once, cycling down Constitution Avenue, a helmet jammed over his curly hair. It must have been someone else.

One day when Nate parked the Corolla, the sky was herding disappointments — clouds had been replaced by the grey resentment of an ongoing winter.

Let's not walk too far today, Nate said over his shoulder. Just far enough to be sure the mic won't pick up any of the four-wheel drives.

He wanted another recording; he was tired of the first.

By the time they stopped, the rain had set in and Eve's trousers were soaked through. She set up in an open space, wrapping the unit in cling wrap, leaving the microphone free.

We'll see how it goes. I don't want to get the sound of raindrops hitting the plastic, but we'll see.

She watched the rain gather on her jacket, the creases forming rivulets that rushed to her wrists. When the equipment was set up, they crouched against a tree and listened.

After ten minutes, Eve noticed she could feel Nate's thigh against her own. She glanced across at him; he was staring at the microphone with a confused look, as though worried it might run away. She shifted her weight a little, not wanting to topple onto the soft ground. He was just cold, she reasoned, knowing that this wasn't really true. She wasn't cold. And he wasn't just touching her leg, he was pressing against it; if she moved away, he would unbalance. She rocked forward a little, tried to judge where his weight lay, giving him a chance to move away. When he didn't, she leaned away from him and let herself go. He fell against her, and for a moment they lay, Eve buried beneath Nate, her arms pinned and useless.

Sorry, I lost my balance, I …

Nate fumbled, tried to lift himself from her. Eve managed to get her arm out from underneath herself, haul herself back to her knees. When she kissed him, she was surprised by how thin his lips were; his face went from skin to teeth; there seemed to be nothing in between. She could hear her pulse swirling in her ears, amplified by the hood of her rain jacket. He kissed her back, his tongue pushing her teeth apart as he let her pull him down on top of her. Small rocks poked at her back; she could feel the rain seeping through her trousers to her underwear. She found it difficult to breathe with the weight of him, the way his nose squished hers against her face, first one way and then the other.

They had sex with their trousers around their knees, their hiking boots still laced up. Their raincoats as bed sheets, the smell of wet hair, wet dirt, wetness in the air. It was just as Eve imagined it would be — uncomfortable and a relief all at once — and when he was inside of her she knew she had never felt as far away from someone as she did just then. She clutched at his shoulder and his hair. She could see his dandruff; she would like to wash his hair in the bathtub, massaging the shampoo into his scalp while she recorded all of the sloshing sounds. He pushed inside as though there were further to go, and she squirmed, trying to tell him that there was not. He pulled out, and when he came he let out a little yelp in her ear, the hot air sending a shiver down her neck. It was only then that she realised all of this would be on the recording. She wondered whether he knew this, whether that was what he'd wanted.

He moved off her, pulling his trousers up as she struggled with her own. He gave her a wry smile and then his hand as he pulled her to her feet.

Alright then? he asked, and she nodded.

He held her face in both his hands for a moment, bringing his thumbs to her eyebrows and smoothing them out. Then he nodded and let her go, turning to begin packing the sound equipment away. Eve thought he was humming, but she couldn't be sure because the wind whipped the notes away as fast as it brought them to her. She did up the fly on her trousers, straightened out her jumper. Her legs were covered in mud; she could feel it drying and tightening on the skin of her lower back.

Ready?

Nate hoisted his backpack onto his shoulders, and she did the same with her own. He hesitated, as though he was about to ask her something, and it was that hesitation that made her stride out. Eve took the lead; it was Nate following her, and she knew that he would be looking at her the whole way back.

Looking at the mud smudged down the back of her legs, and thinking whatever it was he thought. As she walked, she listened to the forest in the way that he had taught her, and, above it all, she listened to her breathing. She felt as though her lungs were larger, they were reaching a little further into the world, drawing more in.

•

The walk to the swimming hole from the campsite had seemed much longer the last time she was here, in the hot stillness of the summer: Eve had also been carrying the weight of Mina — it was only three weeks before her daughter would be born. The tail-end of the school holidays, and the swimming hole had been crowded: children with their floaties and legionnaire caps; mothers watching from picnic rugs laid out in the small patches of sun, everyone enjoying the cool of the narrow gorge while the beach was burning hot. Fathers and older children swam a little further upstream, where rock ledges formed gentle waterfalls. Back then, water ran thin across the rocks, and in the shallower recesses it was only a muddy trickle. Now, mid-winter, the river is replete with rain, gushing and tumbling over itself. Blue gums march by the stone walls, their fallen leaves and twigs caught in a multitude of tiny dams that gather scummy bubbles; an undersong of roar and splash is amplified.

It must have been the pregnancy: Eve recalled, at the time, being so aware of every child she came across, in awe of their independence and tenacity. A little girl standing in the shallows, absorbed in the appearance of her own feet, wobbly through the water. She'd worn a Dora the Explorer rash vest, her stomach unabashedly round. A running boy who'd pulled up short of the swimming hole's edge, jogging his feet to carry him into the air, and, gathering his knees to his chest, falling smack to the water. Years have passed; those children would have grown. The girl in school, the boy a teenager by now.

In winter, without the families, the swimming hole is calm. Climbing over the rocks, and avoiding the damp moss, Eve sits down by the water's edge and unlaces her shoes. Cold, so fucking cold. The clench races from her toes right up through her back, and her body wants her to withdraw, to pull her foot out of the icy water. Each of her toes is screaming at her and she tries not to move them, knowing it's impossible to keep any feeling in them at this temperature. Within minutes they have tingled into a warm numbness. Relief.

3

LOTTE

Leaving the hotel, Lotte turned corners and pushed uphill, away from the shopping precinct, walking fast lest she fall backwards into the aggressive mess of the city.

She had only once been to the Sydney Observatory, for an award ceremony years ago; some of the names on the badges pinned to rumpled cocktail attire were recognisable enough that Vin and Lotte had kept a running tally of those she'd cited in her thesis. It had been summer then, too, and Lotte had to pick her way through the crowd, her heels sinking into the lawn, to collect her award from the professors standing like a line of patient groomsmen beneath a swarm of fairy lights. Three of four awarded researchers that night had been women, and the head of school had nervously licked his lips and thrust out his hand to Lotte as he congratulated her, before stuttering out a speech that tried to positively highlight the increasing number of women involved in astronomy, but only managed to make it sound like the death rattle of an obsolete profession.

Coming upon the observatory now, Lotte saw purple banners strung across its walls: *Give the ultimate gift this Christmas ... give a star*. It wasn't ever enough to just look — everything must

48

be owned. Perched on the top of the hill, the old observatory building looked too small to be of use, its sandstone walls marking it as a relic from the past. From here, only the time ball — balanced on a four-storey tower and dropped every day at one o'clock in the afternoon — gave away the building's function. Lotte pictured an ancient astronomer, hidden away in the tower, reading the time from the position of the sun and the stars, and heaving the ball to the top of its pole in readiness. The reality was much more likely to be an automated process: a little motor to lift and drop the ball, its accuracy checked every now and again by googling *current time Sydney*. She walked a slow lap around the perimeter wall, welcoming the sight of the observatory's two copper domes, tarnished to green. It was her mother who'd told her that the first was built to house the equatorial telescope, and the second had to be built soon after, when it was discovered that the time-ball tower obstructed the telescope's view of much of the eastern sky.

Turning her back on the observatory, Lotte crossed the lawn, her gaze drawn to the harbour: the squat yet elegant bridge of steel girders, the chomping mouth of Luna Park. Taking a seat beneath the low branches of a Moreton Bay fig, she reached down and unbuckled her new shoes, putting them neatly to one side, her feet grateful for the cool of the grass. She still had hours before her appointment.

In June, Lotte had felt a small lump in her breast. Two lumps, in fact, snuggled up against each other like a peanut. Considering Helen's illnesses, a tiny bit of her was relieved that this had finally occurred. But it couldn't have come at a worse time: her first paper on potential exoplanet locations was about to be published, and she was head-down wading through the most recent data. Without giving it much thought (nor wanting to), Lotte had made an appointment with her doctor, had been referred to a specialist and then to a surgeon — all within a week. Just one of those things, she said, repeating the specialist's words when she asked Vin if he would be available to pick her up after the surgery the following day. She ignored his anger at being told so late in the piece, just as she ignored the hastiness of the process, the guarded expression of the doctor when she'd detailed her mother's illness. A fluctuation of hormones, perhaps, the specialist had said when the growth had been pronounced benign. He suggested she take a lower-dose pill or go off it all together, just for the time being. Having children sooner rather than later was something she should be thinking about, he said, considering her mother's medical history. Lotte hadn't told Vin that. Just as she hadn't told him about her referral to have genetic testing.

At the initial genetic testing appointment, the counsellor had spoken carefully, laying out each possible outcome as softly as a mother covering a sleeping baby.

Some people prefer the certainty of knowing, the counsellor had said. But it's important to recognise that when the answer is positive, that when you *do* have the gene mutation, this certainty might not feel as comforting as you hoped.

Lotte had barely listened, concentrating instead on the fabric panel that hung above the counsellor's desk. It was natural linen, stretched on a frame and screen-printed with the trunks of white birch trees. It was a repeating pattern, Lotte was sure of it, yet she couldn't quite see where the break was: the point where the same trees appeared again. It was the bird, she finally realised. A small wren appeared by two of the trunks, but not in the same position. Had it been printed with a different screen? The counsellor talked on, and Lotte nodded. Of course she wanted to know; of course she expected the result to be positive. She would not be shocked. She had let the nurse take her blood, reciting her name and date of birth again and again to avoid a case of mistaken identity, irritated by the solemnity of all the staff.

The roots of the Moreton Bay fig pleated out on either side of the bench, forming a gentle buttress. She was her mother's daughter — it was improbable that she would not have the gene. All she had to do this afternoon was go to the appointment so the counsellor could divulge the news, and then Lotte could do what needed to be done. One step after the other. The ferries trailed ribbons of white, frothy wake across the harbour, stout matrons caught with lengths of toilet paper attached to their sensible heels. The sun set without fanfare; the lights of the city came on well before dark, lest anyone take fright at the night closing around them. The street lamps mapped out their own constellations; the spectacular lights of the bridge and Opera House denoted far-off galaxies; the dark matter of the harbour was cut through by water taxis barrelling across like comets, booze-cruise pleasure crafts proceeding at a more stately pace. Venus appeared low and bright near the horizon, then Jupiter — a little higher, warmer and bigger. Finally, the moon showed itself, a tipped crescent reclining on its bottom. Only then did Lotte pick up her shoes and walk barefoot back toward the city.

•

Despite her mother's protestations, when Helen was moved home from the hospital, Lotte took indefinite leave from her job, determined to be the daughter she no longer had a lifetime to be. She busied herself with tedious and repetitive tasks: bundling up soiled bedsheets and clothes; scheduling nurses; searching out recipes on the internet, following their instructions to the letter, and scraping them into the bin without complaint when her mother refused to eat. Sometimes she had to scour at the carpet in the places her mother vomited so suddenly, the baking soda creating lighter patches on the ash-grey wool, like dappled sunlight thrown across the floor.

Every time she was crouched over some task, she would promise herself that as soon as it was done she would join her mother in the front room where they'd installed the hospital bed, and ask her one of the hundreds of things she must surely need to know soon. She saw the years stretch ahead, a blank, motherless expanse. But when one job was finished there was always something else to do, and the conversations went unspoken.

Do you think she reads it? Or does she just like to have it there?

A bottle of wine sat between Lotte and her father. It was an awkward routine they'd fallen into after Helen had gone to sleep: usually, one of them would pour the other a glass and they'd escape to different parts of the house or switch on the television, taking relief in the mindless distraction. But that night, Lotte had asked her father about something that had been bugging her — the Bible she'd noticed on her mother's bedside.

I don't know, he replied. But I know that she prays. Didn't you take her to church a couple of times?

I did, but I guess I thought it was nostalgia. That she was remembering her childhood. I didn't think it was more than that.

God works in mysterious ways, said her father, raising his eyebrows as Lotte groaned.

Bloody hell, Dad. But it is weird, don't you think? Mum could never deal with any kind of authority figure, let alone an all-seeing one. Do you remember the time the council tried to charge her for having one of her star parties by the lake? It must have been to raise money for the planet drive.

An unauthorised commercial gathering on public land — that's what they told her. She was livid. She berated that poor man for twenty minutes, asking him if he had also taken out a controlling lease on each of the stars, and if so, would he be so kind as to let her know which ones she was permitted to point her telescope at.

She wrote a letter to the *Courier* as well, said Lotte. I remember that.

I don't think she ever paid a parking fine, said her father. She managed to argue her way out of every single one.

They traded stories then, of Helen's demanding moods that could just as quickly jolt into mirthful glee. Lotte remembered looking up *bolshie* in the dictionary one night after a comment from a school friend's mother, and asking her father if her mum was a communist. Just contrary, her father had said, laughing. And obstinate. She'd had to go and look that up, too.

Lotte traced the base of her glass with her finger.

Will you stay here, Dad? In the house? In Ballarat?

He didn't answer straight away. Then: Where would I go?

Anywhere. You could move to Melbourne or Sydney. Come to Canberra.

They both knew it was a flippant invitation, but he smiled as if considering.

I wouldn't know what to do with myself somewhere else. I'm too old to start again.

You're only fifty.

Only.

He stood up from the table, gulping down the rest of his wine.

And at the moment, I feel every day of it. You know, I really didn't think it would come so quickly, but at the same time I didn't think it would last so long.

He ruffled her hair as he passed by, and she almost reached for his hand.

Some days, Lotte caught herself thinking that the illness was all part of an elaborate performance: despite the determined ebbing of her mother's body, despite the nurses who came twice a day.

There were times she wanted to ask her dad if he felt the same: helpless and unfit for the task of caring for a woman whose personality had always outshone them all. Lotte forced herself to look at her mother's body, to be reminded that this was real, it was happening. She had always thought that the longer you looked, the more you could understand. But the more she looked at Helen, the less she was certain about.

When the Hubble telescope was first sent into orbit, it sent back flawed images: the precision mirror was 2.2 thousandths of a millimetre out of shape, less than a hair's breadth. Astronauts were sent into space to fix it, a painstakingly delicate task, but four years later its riveting images illustrated the beauty that scientists had been able to calculate but not see. The Hubble peers so deeply into space — or back in time — that one day it may confront the edge of existence. The result of Hubble's persistent staring — the Deep Field — was spectacular. A spill of lollies across a black tablecloth; a slice of fairy bread; the pattern printed on a child's pyjamas; a field of wildflowers in full bloom. It was indescribable. Thousands of galaxies gambolled across the image, whirling dervishes of colour and heat. Every single one harbouring stars, every star lassoing planets.

Lotte was reluctant to admit her mother's ultimate transience, but each day, there was less of her than the day before. Ridges jutted beneath the surface of her body — shifts in the continental plates. Shoulders and collarbones. Elbows and knees. Cliffs and crevices. Bedsores that had erupted on her legs, and bloomed ever larger.

Each day, Lotte watched the visiting nurses move about, sure of themselves as they tugged and adjusted, not afraid to reach for Helen's hand, or wipe the saliva from her cracked lips as she slept. But Lotte was afraid. She was repulsed by her mother's body: the slack skin loose over bones, the brittle hair that wasn't a colour at all familiar. It was her mother's body that had caused all of this, and Lotte could barely bring herself to touch it.

How is she? Eve's voice was muffled — she must have the phone jammed up between her shoulder and cheek while she rummaged in the fridge.

Some days she's good, some days she just lies there. She doesn't even try to get up, just stays in her pyjamas and lies there with her eyes closed.

Is she in pain?

No. Lotte sighed, struggling to keep the exasperation out of her voice. She says she isn't, they give her morphine. She says she's just tired, but she also says she can't sleep. But it seems like she's asleep all the time!

It would be strange to see her so still. Every time I've seen your mum, she was just a blur of activity.

Not any more, said Lotte. It's like she's already gone. Seriously, I try to have a conversation with her and she just tells me she's tired. Every time. As though *I've* done something wrong.

Oh, Lotte.

Lotte felt the tears prick at her eyes. She kicked at the edge of the garden bed, looking back at the house. The lawn had faded to yellow, and the fuchsia bushes around the deck were exhausted, their pods withered. She could see her father in the kitchen, washing something in the sink. She waved at him, but he was already turning away.

She just makes me so mad! Lotte laughed as she said it, knowing how ridiculous it was to feel, let alone say. Can you believe that? I'm mad at my own mother for dying!

Of course you are. It's not fair; it's not how things should be.

But you don't get it, Eve. I'm mad at her. Not *for* her. What the hell is wrong with me?

Lotte tipped her head back, taking in the gentle dusk. Tears ran toward her ears and she wiped them away.

You love her, Lotte. Eve's voice was even and unapologetic.

But she's the one who's going through it all. I'm just watching. I feel so angry, but this even isn't happening to me. It's *her* illness.

It's yours, too. That's just how it is. Besides, if you weren't mad at her, you'd probably feel sorry for her. And that would be worse.

Lotte laughs. Eve is right; Helen wouldn't abide pity.

Why were you crying, Mum? Just now, when the nurse came?

Helen didn't answer immediately. She lay back on the bed, her eyes sunken.

I was thinking about the Golden Records.

The Voyagers. Launched just in time to seek out all four of the giant planets — Jupiter, Saturn, Uranus, and Neptune — when they briefly lined up like coloured beads on a necklace. Once every 175 years, they were close enough together for the probes to swing past one planet and then the other, using each body's gravity well as a force to slingshot the spacecraft on to the next planet.

What about them? prompted Lotte.

They were engaged two days after the launch of Voyager 2.

Carl and Ann. I know, you've told me this before.

Her mother smiled at this — Lotte's usual response — and opened her eyes. It was the year you were born, she said.

One of her mother's favourite stories, Lotte knew all its details. Carl Sagan, the astronomer who enthused the masses, and Ann Druyan, the creative director of the team who chose the music for the Golden Records, thus launching the sounds of Bach, Chuck Berry, and Blind Willie Johnson into outer space for the edification of any aliens who might one day intercept the spacecraft. Classical composers dominated the list, yet it was refreshingly diverse: panpipes from Peru, Aboriginal rhythms, the chanting of Navajo Indians, and a men's house song from New Guinea. The music was etched in binary code onto gold-plated copper discs, alongside recordings of bird calls, cracking thunder, wailing wind, a mother kissing her screaming baby, the drone of crickets, the countdown lift-off of Saturn 5, and the sonic boom of an F-11 — each short track crackling with the dust and static of seventies' sound engineering.

There was a recording of Ann's brainwaves, said Helen. They plugged her up to machines, and Ann thought about the message she wanted to convey to any life forms that might be able to listen. She thought through the history of human life, the organisation of society. About the violence and poverty that makes life hell for so many of this planet's inhabitants. That's what she said, anyway.

It's a dark view of life.

The messages were all like that, said Helen. It was the seventies, the Cold War. They even included a message in Morse code: *per aspera ad astra*. Through hardship to the stars.

Helen had told her about the Golden Records when she was

a child, but it was Eve who had shown her that the digital files were available online in the NASA library. Each message was one of peace to residents of far skies; Jimmy Carter's message expressed a desire to solve the problems of Earth and to embrace what he called the vast and awesome universe. If there was a hint of colonisation in the expression of humankind's desire to survive the present time so that we may come and live in another time, it was excused by the trusting sentimentality of the project.

Ann and Carl fell in love during a phone call, said Helen fondly, as though they were old friends of hers. She called him from a hotel room because, after a long time searching, she'd discovered the ideal piece of Chinese music to put on the recording: a centuries-old song called 'Flowing Stream'. Somehow, in that conversation, they felt something bigger than themselves; they decided to spend the rest of their lives together. And when Ann hung up the phone, she screamed.

Screamed?

Lotte didn't remember hearing this part of the story before. She tried to imagine a grown woman, alone in a hotel, screaming with delight. It wasn't the kind of thing that really happened.

She said she knew, right then, what it felt like to make a scientific discovery. That's how she described falling in love.

Lotte tried not to roll her eyes. As if a feeling like *that* had any resemblance to science. She watched her mother's hands pat impatiently at the mattress before grabbing the edge of the sheet, screwing it up in her hand, her knuckles white.

She put it on the record too, said Helen. At the end of the recording of her brainwaves, of everything that her heart and mind were communicating, she lay there and thought about what it was like to fall in love, because it was what she knew right then. That's what they recorded, and that's what they sent out to space.

What would the aliens make of that? It was a haphazard collection: images of a woman in a supermarket; Olympic sprinters; the Great Wall of China; the Sydney Opera House; a demonstration of eating and drinking; countless diagrams of DNA and the human body. No sex and no guns. An hour-long recording, when played at the speed associated with the fundamental transition of the hydrogen atom. The cover of the record was a diagram for how it was to be played and where it came from: a map of the fourteen pulsars that could be used to locate the sun, and directions to turn the binary code into images. It was a brilliant collection of human futility and naivety. She had not thought about it in years.

So why were you crying, Mum? It's a happy story — a love story.

Helen stared at her as if surprised to find her still in the room.

But it's not my story, she said. And when she turned away, her body was so much smaller than it should be, and Lotte could think of nothing to say.

•

Have you eaten? Vin was lying on the couch, his computer in his lap. I didn't wait, he said. I wasn't sure what time you'd get here, but there are leftovers in the fridge.

Lotte knew that he'd have at least a dozen tabs open in his browser, all real estate. She could picture the houses as they appeared on the site, all the detritus of living tidied away. Rooms folding out from one another; boundaries of perspective stretching as the camera lens distorted the image to show space where it was not. Dining tables set with more places than they would ever need, marooned on a sea of floorboards; furniture oddly small and afraid of the walls. Kitchens of pine cupboards, and Laminex benches made to look like granite or marble; kitchens that other families had lived in, setting an example for all new owners to follow. And she knew she wouldn't argue with his plan; it was Vin's childhood home he wanted to emulate — the one his parents had had to sell when his father had a stroke and could no longer manage the steps up to the front door and down to the split-level lounge. They'd moved into a flat instead, one with an elevator, wide doorways, and handrails in the bathroom, and nobody was really sure what Stan thought of it all. Just as she knew Vin could never quite believe his father was still within the shell of his body, neither could he think of the apartment in Parramatta as home.

I grabbed something to eat before I left, she said. Have you found anything for us to look at?

There's a couple of properties that look okay, but it's hard to tell because they haven't got floorplans, Vin said. Nothing new has come up.

I guess we should wait until February now, said Lotte. No one's going to sell over Christmas.

She imagined the two of them in a too-big house, dining table an expanse between them, empty rooms lined up behind closed doors. That's what she liked about their flat: there were no secrets there. They'd bought if off the plan, and when they moved in, it was exactly as the developers said it would be, right down to the stainless-steel appliances that had been featured in the display suite. But a house with the ghosts of owners past? All that space demanding to be filled? To Lotte, the end game wasn't going to be a three-bedroom brick house in an outer suburb, but a massive black hole. That's what the fish-eye real-estate photographs reminded her of: the house exerting its immense gravitational pull, sucking her and everything she has into its hold. Spaghettification

— the process of being stretched beyond recognition, the pull of the hole's gravity grabbing first at her feet so that they would reach the hole faster than her head, before the inevitable plummet into an oblivion from which nothing could escape.

You're right, Vin snapped his laptop closed, swivelling himself into an upright position. I was thinking I would contact a few different agents in the new year, let them know what we're looking for. Let them do the work.

Lotte nodded. Now was the time to tell him about the job. But when she spoke, it was a different confession that came out.

Vin, I wasn't in Sydney for Christmas shopping. I had an appointment. A medical appointment, with a genetic counsellor.

What for? He bent forward, ready with his sympathy. Have the lumps come back? Why didn't you tell me?

No, nothing like that. It wasn't urgent. A few weeks ago, I was tested for the mutation in the BRCA gene, the one that Mum had which caused her cancer. I had an appointment today to get the results.

She could see him readying himself, his gaze holding hers, but there was a stiffness in his shoulders as he braced himself for the news. This is why it was difficult to tell him anything: he cared so much.

And?

I didn't go to the appointment.

She felt again the solace that had coursed through her as she left the observatory and walked back down the hill to the city, then made her way to where she had parked her car.

Why not?

His tone was incredulous, and she almost laughed, she was so glad to hear it; it was the same response she would have given if the situation were reversed.

I decided I don't want to know. I don't think it's helpful to know.

On the day of the test, the counsellor's explanations had all seemed logical and responsible, the statistics and gentle warnings brushing by her like a breeze. It was similar to the beginning of a new project at work: the quickening atmosphere of two colleagues in perfect agreement, egging each other on. Lotte recalls congratulating herself for being such an easy client for the counsellor; she wasn't going to make a scene, she wasn't looking for the impossible — just an answer based in fact. What she remembered most was the counsellor's furnishings: a low couch covered in grey felt with twin duck-egg blue cushions; pastel-coloured ceramic bottles on the window sill, pink and blue and cream. It was a deliberately serene space with no traces of the clinical rooms down the hall — the nurses' domains, with their trays of test tubes and coded stickers. Lulled by the counsellor's voice, and happy in the knowledge that finding out her genetic make-up was the right thing to do, Lotte nodded and smiled, all the time thinking of what could be put in the ceramic bottles, what they would be suitable to hold. Flowers, perhaps, though it would be impossible to properly clean the bottles of mildewed water afterwards, their mouths too small for a brush or sponge. Milk for tea and coffee? Yet there was no indentation in the lip to assist with pouring. It was unnerving, these decorative objects that pretended to be something useful but clearly were not. Stealing their shape from another, more vital item, and parading it as something to be looked at and admired.

How can you not want to know? Vin's voice, sharpened with urgency, cut through. If you have the gene, you're much more likely to get cancer. You should find out so we can do something about it.

I don't want to.

Lotte stood up from her chair. The moon was bright above the apartment building opposite, a gorgeously luminous crescent lifting into the sky. For the tiniest moment, it appeared to Lotte as an ornament — pure decoration — but all too quickly its beauty shifted, dissolved by her knowledge of its necessity and command. Desert dry, the moon yanks at the Earth's oceans, causing the calendar of tides as it tries to quench its infinite thirst. To want what can't be had — who didn't know this state? But the moon's neediness was not one-sided: the Earth had done its share of tugging, pulling the moon's once molten core off centre, causing the dark, iron-rich plains that scar its face: *Mare Crisium* — Sea of Crises. *Mare Tranquillitatis* — Sea of Tranquillity. There were few *maria* on the far side of the moon, only peaceful highlands; it was the only part of space where radio signals from Earth could not be picked up. In return for this solitude, the far side paid dearly: facing outer space, it received a battering of impacts that resulted in massive craters, giving it a pockmarked appearance. Of all the planets, stars, asteroids — the orchestra of celestial bodies that Lotte had explored throughout her career — the moon was still her favourite.

I've given it a lot of thought, Vin. I've made an informed decision.

She tried to explain that she had thought the test was the right thing to do. But in the weeks that followed that first appointment, she had ignored the counsellor's advice, instead googling every combination of the words she could find, conducting her own literature review. *Breast, ovarian, cancer, prevalence, prognosis, BRCA, intervention, treatment.* She'd answered the self-reporting questionnaires on support-network websites, establishing her place within the high-risk category and noting the alarmingly high prevalence statistics. The results were terrifying: if she had the mutation, it was almost certain she would develop the cancer in one form or another, with the likelihood increasing every year of her life until it was higher than eighty per cent. From a website, she learned that the most effective prevention measure currently identified was a full mastectomy and hysterectomy, which could be performed on women in the high-risk category *after they have finished childbearing*, the emphasis making the latter seem compulsory. *Sooner rather than later*, her own specialist had said, as though it could only be one or the other.

What would it be like to be without so much of her body? The internet obligingly provided diagrams and photographs of reconstructed breasts, nipples created from tucks of skin, areolae tattooed with precision. They looked like ordinary breasts; if anything, they looked more ordinary than her own: buoyant, survivors after a tragedy.

The websites were full of survivors. Message boards of affirmations bumping up against strangers' despair. Women who had lost their mothers, their grandmothers, their aunts. Reassuring each other that they didn't feel any differently after the surgery, that they were no less than the women they had always been. Lotte admired their courage and their pragmatic attitudes; their conviction that it was better to know, because then you could take control. The counsellor's words came back to her.

It's something to give some deep thought to, she had said. *Because considering you're over thirty, and your mother's breast cancer appeared quite early, we would recommend a mastectomy soon. Not immediately, but soon. The ovaries and reproductive organs can be removed later, if you decide to follow that path.*

But the results could be good news, Vin said, his voice polite with barely restrained exasperation. Surely there's a fifty per cent chance you would find out you don't have it? And then we've got nothing to worry about.

Her attention snagged on his use of the collective. *We've got nothing to worry about.* This was the problem — she needed this to be hers alone.

But what if I do have it? All they can do is tell you to have a mastectomy. To have your ovaries out. And it's not even guaranteed to work. You saw what Mum was like when they'd taken everything out of her. What was left? She was literally a shell.

That was the cancer, said Vin. She was already sick. You'd be avoiding that, if you knew in advance. The way Helen died, that's the exact reason to find out. He ran his fingers through his hair. You're a scientist, Lotte, I'd thought you'd want to know?

Is it possible to know too much? she asked.

She didn't want her future planned out for her; she didn't want decisions taken away. How defeated her mother had been in those last few years, understanding all too well the trajectory her body was going to take, the one she had no choice but to follow. Not once did the doctors consider not treating the cancer, even when the treatment made her life worse. *We will beat this,* they said, over and over again, but they only ever managed to confuse its course and force the forging of another route. Was the surgery, the chemotherapy, the radiotherapy, worth the resulting nausea and pain? Were they worth the extra time? How is it that humans still maintain that time is something that can be stretched, pulled, made to fit their purpose?

Look at the moon, Vin. Lotte opened the sliding door, stepping out onto the balcony. It's beautiful tonight. Otherworldly.

He stepped out behind her, wrapping her in his arms, chin resting on her shoulder.

I just want what's best for you, he said. I want you to have every chance.

You know the moon is trying to get away? said Lotte. It's caught in our sky at a cost: as it pulls toward the sun, it's slowing us down, slowing the Earth's rotation.

She felt Vin's sigh, rather than heard it.

So the world will slow down, he said. We won't notice; we don't even notice it's moving. Not really.

It's moving at over a thousand kilometres an hour, she wanted to say to him. We'd notice. It's just that none of us will be alive to witness it.

Maybe *we* need to slow down, he said. We need a holiday, a proper one. It will be easier to deal with everything if we've had some time out. You said this year you'd be spending more time on campus, less time out at the observatory sites.

I did.

Lotte rested her arms on his, happy to entertain the idea that stopping time was so simple. Eventually, the Earth would slow enough for the moon not to run any further: the two would establish perfect harmony. But by then the moon would only be seen from half of Earth: it would never appear in the sky of the other half. She could never look at the moon without knowing this, its beauty tainted by its truth.

On Christmas morning, Lotte folded the cardboard box of the coffee machine flat, and dutifully accepted the coffee Vin had made, admiring the ease of the machine, its handle that pumped down then up, the light that switched from blue to red as the water was heated. They stood together at the pantry door and discussed where it was best to store the little pods of coffee. Each serve came in its own foil container — a different colour for each flavour; a treasure chest of precious jewels.

Vin had given her a bottle of perfume and a photo frame

made from recycled timber. As she sipped her coffee, she looked at the frame propped on the couch.

You didn't put any photos in it, she said.

There were nine blank rectangles cut into the wood. It seemed bad luck; like a set of knives, or a purse given without money. A hint of an absence that was to come.

I thought we would take a bunch of photos if we go on holiday, said Vin. I was thinking maybe Japan — it's so close and neither of us have been.

Your parents will ask why we don't just go to China.

And spend the whole time visiting relatives I barely know? Vin laughed. No, thanks! We should look at flights when we get home from Mum and Dad's today — see what's available in January. It will be freezing, though.

Already his mind was skipping ahead — he'd book the hotels, train tickets, restaurants, everything in advance. He'd have researched the holiday so thoroughly that by the time they got on the plane, it would be as though they'd already been to Japan and she had failed to pay proper attention.

Vin, I don't think we can go on a holiday. Not just now.

Lotte took a breath, putting her coffee cup on the bench.

I've been offered a job at the International Astronomical Observatory. At one of their sites in Chile, in the Atacama Desert. It starts at the end of January.

She felt her face burn with shame as she spoke, to have kept it secret for so long when there wasn't even anything to hide.

End of January? In a few weeks? That's great, Lotte!

His beaming smile disarmed her.

When did you find out? We can holiday in Chile, go to Peru. When does it finish? March? April?

Realisation dawned — he thought it was a regular assignment.

A few weeks, a month at most.

The end of the year, she said. Well, the beginning of next year, actually. It's a twelve-month contract.

His face fell — eyebrows slouching, cheekbones retreating, mouth turning down; every part dutifully giving a performance of the expression.

Twelve months?

She nodded.

It's on their new planet-hunting project, she said. The one the uni is collaborating on. But they want me on the ground there — they need me to coordinate one of the teams.

A whole year, said Vin, shaking his head. But we agreed that this year we were concentrating on Canberra. Buying a house. You didn't have any international conferences; you weren't going to be up in Siding Spring so often. You said you were sick of always being away …

And she realised that he had catalogued every one of their conversations over the last year, stacking evidence and drawing conclusions. Her throwaway comments and aloud musings had become fact, something that she would be held to.

I *was* sick of it — I am. The travel, the living out of a suitcase. But this would be different; it's for a proper period of time. And it's an amazing opportunity, Vin. I'll never get it again. If I turn this down, it's not going to come back. It's everything I've been working towards.

She watched Vin rinse out his coffee cup, jabbing at it with the sponge.

You're leaving at the end of January?

The fifteenth.

She closed her eyes, not wanting to see his reaction.

That's only three weeks away, he said. When did they offer it to you? It wasn't today, obviously.

A few weeks ago.

And you're telling me now.

She opened her eyes. It wasn't a question.

I had to think about it for a while. I had to decide whether or not to take it, consider all the possibilities. I know it disrupts our plans, but I didn't want to bother you for no reason.

You think about everything, don't you? The genetic testing, this, what you want to do with your life. And then once you consider all the facts, you make a decision, and choose a course of action. And then I'm the one who has to follow, or I get accused of holding you back.

I've never said that.

Because I've never given you the opportunity. You were always going to take the job, weren't you?

Yes, she said. She couldn't lie to him, not directly.

And you should take it, of course you should. But you should have told me.

I'm telling you now.

Earlier, Lotte. You should have told me earlier.

He carefully dried his coffee cup and put it away, hanging the tea towel on the oven door.

I'm going to have a shower; we need to get going soon. Mum said lunch was at one, and traffic might be bad.

She watched him go down the hallway, the legs of his navy shorts whispering as he walked, a thread hanging from his T-shirt. On the couch, the photo frame caught the sun, blank and expectant.

Balancing her empty glass on the balcony railing, Lotte contemplated the mark left by the lipstick she felt compelled to wear every time she saw Vin's mother. Sue was always so impeccably turned out: her fingernails lacquered, her hair set in tight curls, except for the neat fringe that bobbed above her pencilled eyebrows. It didn't help that, despite not being particularly tall, Lotte towered over the diminutive Chinese woman, just as she did over Vin's sisters, who always seemed effortlessly svelte. The balcony door slid open and Vin joined her, rolling his eyes at the shrieks of his sisters escaping the room — Janet's husband had bought her a terrier puppy for Christmas, and it was chasing a ball about the lounge room, slamming its body against the skirting boards, unable to find enough purchase on the tiles to slow down. The women were entranced and horrified in equal measure by its destructive behaviour.

Vin leaned against the railing, squinting in the sun even as he seemed to unfold towards it. Sunlight opened Vin up, and, not for the first time, Lotte felt bad that her late-night job meant that they both spent too much time in the dark, sleeping away mornings, starting halfway into the day, always struggling to catch up. Looking out over the rooftops, she could see the green ribbon of the Parramatta River, the yellowing grass of a sports field. It was the sort of day where clear-eyed people could see forever.

I'm sorry, Vin. I should have told you sooner.

It's okay, he said. It doesn't matter. Twelve months isn't so long; you'll be back before I know it.

He gave her a wry smile, which was gratefully accepted.

You can come to visit, you know. It's an eight days on, six off cycle. Plus holidays. You could come mid year, we could have a proper holiday.

Sounds good.

He shuffled closer to her, his arm warm against her own.

Maybe I'll get a dog, he said. Something to keep me company.

Lotte laughed.

Like that little ratty thing of Janet's? It would be crazy after being cooped up in the flat all day while you're at work; you'd be sick of it within a week.

No, a bigger dog. Maybe a Golden Retriever or an Irish Setter. A proper dog — it will have a whole backyard to explore.

He caught her eye then looked away.

I still want to buy a house. I want to stick to the plan, he said, drumming his fingers on the balustrade. Besides, it will be something for me to do while you're away.

Lunch is ready!

Janet appeared at the door, the puppy — which was now wearing a Santa hat — desperately nudging at her ankles.

Don't let him out; I don't think this balcony is dog proof, Vin said.

He ran across to the door, picking up the dog and swooping it in the air.

See, he might go over!

Vin, stop it!

Janet jumped at him, trying to grab the puppy, not knowing whether to laugh or shout.

Give him back!

But Vin neatly sidestepped her, walking back inside, puppy held aloft in one hand.

Come on, Rex. Let's get this ridiculous hat off you.

Stop calling him Rex. It's Cherry!

Inside, the table was set for eight. The smell of melting palm sugar and cooked pineapple mixed with the chillies and spices that had sent Lotte dry-coughing onto the balcony twenty minutes before. As they all took their seats, Vin pushing his father's wheelchair into place, Sue came backing out of the spare room, carrying a highchair. They watched as she wordlessly placed it between her seat and her husband's, a smile playing at her lips. A visiting cousin, a family friend? Who was it for?

The table was covered in dishes. Gems of sweet-and-sour pork, a hotpot of eggplant, nests of dumplings, and soon they were all reaching and passing, filling their bowls. Lotte tried her best not to make a mess with her chopsticks. Sue fed Stan small bites, mopping at his chin and laughing as he shook his head, pointing to the beer. His stroke had robbed him of language, and while he gave little indication, Lotte suspected he still kept up with the volleying conversation of his family. She remembered when she had first met him years ago, when he was running his shoe import business and he'd teased Vin about landing a woman smarter than he was. *And with good taste in shoes*, he had said, looking at her feet in a pair of flocked-velvet kitten heels. They were a pair imported by his own company; she'd gone and bought them specially to wear to that meeting, surprised by how much she liked their elegant point and suggestive shape. Vin had laughed at her efforts, doubting his father would even notice, but Lotte had wanted to do everything right, knowing she was the first non-Chinese girl he'd ever brought home.

Who is the highchair for?

It was Vin's voice that cut through the din, and Lotte saw his older sister Michelle shake her head at him.

I'm glad you asked, Vincent, said Sue, smiling carefully, putting her chopsticks down and placing her hands in her lap. It's for my grandchild.

Lotte glanced at Michelle and Janet, and both rolled their eyes, used to their mother's theatrics.

Who's pregnant?

The question seemed innocent, but Vin's voice was thick with tension.

Well, I don't know, said Sue, with a look of triumph. It seems that you're all much too busy to give your father and me a grandchild, so I thought I might just give you a little reminder. A little push in the right direction doesn't hurt, does it? None of you are getting any younger.

Vin pushed his chair back from the table.

It's hardly any of your business, Ma.

Vin, Lotte said, placing a warning hand on his wrist. She doesn't mean anything by it.

Sue picked up her glass, lifting it in a toast.

You know I just want you all to be happy, she said. And nothing has made me happier than my own children.

Lotte lifted her glass, Vin's sisters and their husbands doing the same. She caught Stan's eye, sure she could see laughter in it.

To family, said Lotte, clinking her glass with Sue's, relieved to see Vin reaching for his own glass.

Merry Christmas.

As they drove back to Canberra that evening, Lotte tried to get Vin to see the funny side.

She was just having a go, Vin. No need to take it so seriously. You know what she's like — remember when she came out in that horrible orange hat and jacket before Michelle's wedding, saying it was her mother-of-the-bride-outfit? She just likes to tease you all.

Well, it wasn't very funny.

I bet she just feels bad for your dad. Having to be at home all day. Maybe she thinks it would be better if there were some grandchildren running around.

Would it? Do you think that would make a difference?

He glanced in the rear-view mirror and changed lanes.

All he does these days is watch TV, said Vin. Though whether he's really watching is anyone's guess.

You know, *you* could spend some more time with him, said Lotte. Why don't you take him to the football?

Despite being the only one in the family to follow AFL, Stan still had a favourite team: the Sydney Swans.

Like you're one to talk, said Vin.

Lotte didn't answer. She loved Vin's family, but having grown up as an only child, she found them exhausting. The quips flew thick and fast as soon as someone opened their mouth, drowned out only by the self-congratulatory laughter. We all get on so well! their body language screamed — the crowding, the absentminded patting of hands. They talked over one another, not leaving space for anyone to disagree, to not get on, to correct a mistake that had been made. On their first meeting, Lotte had tried to emulate this amplified joy, but she soon gave up; it had never come naturally to her.

It had been the same at school: she'd always hated the way the small girls would huddle in the shelter shed, screeching at one another as they skipped rope or played elastics, friendships lauded or discarded at whim. She recalled a time at school camp, when they'd all had to tumble about underneath a billowing silk parachute, students and teachers shaking it high and low, until there were no edges, no sky. As the other students ran about giggling and grabbing at one another, Lotte had frozen to the spot, the thin material of the parachute clinging to her face, threatening to suffocate her. Meals with Vin's family felt the same — all their voices holding fast to one pitch and barrelling across the table, laughter cackling behind and no air left to breathe. Until inevitably — and it happened so smoothly she never quite captured when — they forgot she was there, breaking into Mandarin, the conversation flooding with multiple tones, a river unleashed.

How long has it been since you've seen *your* father? Vin continued, raising an eyebrow. One year? Two? I reckon it might even be more than that.

It's different with Dad.

Lotte stared out the window, focusing on each roadside bollard as it sped past, then flicking her gaze to the next. Someone made those, in a factory somewhere, and someone else installed them along the freeway, high-tension cable twisted tight between them to create a crash barrier. There was something comforting about there being so many specific jobs to be done in the world; how unlikely it was that she had stumbled across one she so enjoyed.

How is it different? He's your father, said Vin. You should spend more time with him.

What would we do together? You know what he's like. We have absolutely nothing in common, and no interest in what the other thinks or does. It's always been like that.

He's your father, Lotte. Isn't that enough? Haven't you thought about how lonely he must be since your mum died? Going to work each day and coming home to an empty house. You should be calling him all the time; he doesn't have anyone else.

You and I both know Dad would find it bizarre if I started calling. It's different in your family — you were always a family, you did things together. We weren't like that. So we don't need to pretend to be something we're not.

You think family is just pretend? Something that can be

thrown away without any kind of consequences? What are we then, the two of us? Imaginary?

Come on Vin, don't be like this. Dad and I were never close; we don't have that kind of relationship. We don't need it.

Lotte let the scenery blur to a muddy ribbon in her vision.

Not in the way I need you, she said.

Yeah, right. Vin let his laugh perform his scorn. Need me so much you're disappearing for a year. Seriously, Lotte, sometimes I wish you would look at yourself even half as hard as you do at those planets. What's going to change if you figure out there *are* other planets out there, light years away? Nothing. And meanwhile, you ignore everything that's going on in front of you.

I could say the same about your work, she said. What's the point of it?

Vin taught maths to students who just wanted to figure out how to play the market, or who would happily let a computer perform any calculation they ever needed.

But I don't criticise you because I know it's important to you, she said. I support you, and the things you want to do. Is that too much to ask?

Do you really, Lotte?

He reached for the radio, punching at the control. They drove the rest of the way home without speaking.

The fastest way to head south from Canberra was to drive north for almost an hour, and then connect to the Hume Highway. Instead, Lotte decided to drive towards the Snowy Mountains; she was in no great hurry. She pulled over on the shoulder and reached for her phone.

Are you sure you don't want to come? You know Dad would love to see you.

Which is exactly why I'm not coming, said Vin. Your dad and me would just hang out, and the two of you would barely say a thing to one another. It's better this way. Go have some quality time.

What are you going to do?

Drink coffee. Lounge about. It's just for a few days, Lotte. You'll be fine.

Easy for you to say.

When she pulled back onto the road, a cherry-red SUV overtook her, reindeer antlers fixed to its side windows, a stick-figure family dancing across the rear.

Maybe she needn't go all the way to Ballarat to see her father; maybe a phone call would suffice. He'd be just as uncomfortable with her visit as she was, so perhaps she should save them both the awkwardness. Spend a couple of days in a cabin in Jindabyne instead, looking out over the lake.

Recently, there had been an experiment in Russia in which six men were put into a mock-up space station for five hundred and twenty days, to simulate a trip from Earth to Mars and back again. The idea of this had horrified Vin: not just the isolation for such a long period, but the falseness of it. To know that outside the walls of the pretend space station were crews of researchers and technicians doing their best to make the situation as realistic as possible for those on the inside, but who were themselves able to go home every night, to drive out to their summerhouses with their families on the weekends, to swim in the ocean. Lotte, though, had been envious of those six men. The responsibilities of the outside world had been removed for them. They were free to concentrate only on the task at hand: putting their lives on hold for something bigger than themselves.

Every aspect of the mission was created as it might occur in space — the twenty-five minute communication lag when radioing through to control, the rationing of resources, the impact of such a confined space on the mind and body. A woman who had been involved in one of the fifteen-day trial simulations was banned from participating in the main event, the sexual tension of her presence having been deemed to jeopardise the success of the mission. Lotte had eagerly followed blog updates of the men's day-to-day activities: their insomnia; their irritation with other crewmates; the lamenting of missing night and day. Disappointingly, the project was unable to simulate weightlessness — the cosmonauts had to trudge around performing their tasks on two feet, including their simulated walks on the surface of the red planet. Her curiosity waned only when she learned about the experiments in cosmic radiation. The researchers, unwilling to expose the crew to the levels of radiation they would encounter on a trip to Mars, instead brought a group of pink-faced Rhesus macaques in contact with caesium-137, and charted the results. She often wondered whether the human crew knew about these monkeys; if there was one named for each of them, and whether they ever met.

4

EVE

AUGUST 2015

From where she sits with her feet in the water, Eve can see that, after crossing a log bridge, the trail follows the river uphill, trees leaning their branches over the path. She remembers grabbing on to a branch when she'd stumbled that summer she was pregnant with Mina; the way it had gracefully followed her fall before pulling tight just as she was about to hit the ground. She'd given herself a fright, and had been glad she was walking behind, that Tom hadn't seen. She didn't ask whether he was as solicitous to his first wife, or if he'd been this concerned with the coming of his first baby. She didn't ask anything about that; it was a different time. When she stumbled, she cursed Tom in her mind, pre-empting his concern and wanting him to know that twelve months before she would have torn down a path like that on her mountain bike, disbelieving that she could come to any serious harm. But since she'd become pregnant she hadn't even considered mountain biking. It wasn't so much to avert the danger of such an irresponsible injury, but simply that, for the first time in as long as she could remember, she'd felt no urge to be so reckless, to test her limits. Having a child makes you afraid. It should make you afraid.

In the water her feet are aching, sending shudders up through her shins. She could do it now, surely. The strength and tense balance would return quickly enough — and the sheer bloody mindedness to throw herself down a hill? She has that back in spades.

Eve leaves her pained feet in the water and leans back. The green buzz of the leaves hangs above, sunlight fighting through, throwing itself at the ground. She closes her eyes; maroon paisley patterns and lazy firecrackers swirl. Water gathers momentum, producing a heavy static as it rushes over stones. Breaking down the sounds' layers, she hears the ripple of wind-whipped plastic bags, the mumble of the sea that rests above the thundering volumes of the river. A bird squawks, another tweets. High chirrups and smooth, fluting calls. She has no idea which bird makes which noise, but she is hearing every one.

For Eve, each second that passes is a distance; each distance both an escape and a torturous reminder. She had a family in her parents, and then she did not. She had a family in Tom and Mina, and then she did not. She has no one to blame but herself.

Would it all have been easier if it had been with Nate? A man who corrupted time … no, he disallowed time altogether, it was a measure he refused to be aware of. He would not celebrate anniversaries, he would not respond to reminiscence. He was, deliberately, a man of the present. Of *presence*, as though time had to step around him, grumbling at the inconvenience. It was no small comfort to Eve that his children would have made his dismissal of time difficult to reconcile. Children grow. They change. They would ask him questions, and one day they would stop asking him questions and start telling him things. Eleven, that's how old his son Jack would be now. And Grace, just a few years younger. How long before his children become aware of time, start to see it spooling out ahead of them and become desperate to embrace it? See it trailing behind them and try to record it so they can play it back?

•

It was Nate who'd encouraged her to give up studying law. She enrolled in a sound-engineering course instead, buying new editing software and better headphones, working shifts at the campus library to pay for it. She realised that all those years of quiet observance of her parents' moods — listening out for how much anger or surrender might be contained in her father's tread down the hallway as he returned from the pub — had tuned her ear to the nuance of sound. She didn't mind that the other students in the course were predominantly boys, or that they just wanted to produce tracks of one another's garage bands. She was drawn to the acoustics of space, how to reduce or direct noise, but she struggled with the physics, a field entirely new to her, and wondered if she had made the right choice.

Nate was little help, dismissing her concerns with a shrug.

You'll get by, Eve, you always do.

She was drawn to him without relent: her hand reaching out to grasp at his wild spinning-top antics, always surprised when he stopped and looked in her direction. She often wondered if he was attractive. He probably wasn't; he tousled his wispy hair to disguise his balding, and his body lacked all definition, straight up and down. It hardly mattered: his inclusivity drew people to him, the way he always assumed the best. Eve experienced her first tugs of jealousy watching him entertain a bunch of his students at an orientation barbecue, noticing the way he invited their gaze as he laughed at one of his own jokes, demanding their acknowledgment and mirth. He was a generous storyteller and a demanding one, wanting conspirators for his tales who would follow him to the end and wait for him to launch into a new beginning. But he always came back to Eve.

Some nights, she would feel her way through the kitchen in the dark, open his bedroom door and slip into bed beside him. Other times the bed would be empty, and she would hurry back to the bungalow before one of the housemates saw her. Their relationship wasn't a secret so much as not spoken about. Eve liked to think of it as something unquestionable rather than taken for granted.

When she moved into a two-bedroom flat, she hoped that he might follow. But Nate maintained that his hours were long and uneven, that he wouldn't be around to share the housework or keep her company. That there was nothing wrong with the way things were now. And he was right, there wasn't. She advertised for a housemate instead, and Nate became a night visitor, arriving in a flurry of noise, bursting to tell her about his day and all the annoyances that had attempted — and failed — to upend him: the smart-arse interns, the finicky senior staff at the NGO where he worked, the ever-changing rota of housemates, and the paediatric nurse who had taken over Eve's room in the bungalow.

Thank God for you, Eve, the eye in the storm, he said once, pulling off his T-shirt and collapsing onto her bed. In the years to follow, the urgency in his voice as he spoke about his most recent thoughts or fascinations would bely a truth he would never speak: he needed her. For sound to carry, its wave needs a medium to travel through. A constant medium to ensure the sound is not refracted or dispersed. Eve was able to provide this, and in return she got Nate. Enthusiastic, irrepressible, confident Nate.

Lotte couldn't see his appeal and wasn't afraid to say so.

He's just so full of shit, she said one morning, as Nate slammed the door loudly behind him and rushed down the stairs. He just tried to explain string theory to me as though I've never heard of it before.

Lotte had answered Eve's ad for a housemate, and when she turned up at the door, forthright and uncommonly beautiful, Eve's instinct had been to tell her the room was already taken. She was hoping for a quiet mouse of a housemate who would offer occasional chitchat and then leave her be. Not someone like Lotte, who came marching in, poked her head in every room, and announced it looked just fine, if a little expensive. As long as Eve wasn't planning on throwing parties every weekend, because she had a lot of uni work to do. Lotte was studying astronomy, and, despite her misgivings, Eve needed not only a housemate but also a tutor in physics. It turned out to be, without question, the best decision she ever made, though looking back all those years later, Eve can see clearly that she barely had a hand in it at all.

Eve and Lotte became firm friends. Long hours of studying side-by-side at the kitchen table; watching *Seinfeld* and *SeaChange* cross-legged on the couch, with dinner propped on their knees; walking round Lake Burley Griffin on freezing winter afternoons. Lotte getting in arguments with Nate, and then allowing him to buy her forgiveness with a six-pack of beers shared on the balcony as Eve cooked dinner. Lotte treated Nate with a wary indifference, asking him so many questions about his politics and theories that he took it as complimentary, never realising that she was making fun of him. Eve would listen to their banter, rarely joining in, and wonder how it was that some people had so much to say. When Lotte turned her insistent questioning on Eve, Eve found herself opening up. It was something in the way Lotte listened so closely, never forgetting what had been said, never letting Eve get away with a glib response. It was as though she was seeking out the truth in every exchange, and, in time, Eve relaxed into the intimacy, relishing the immediate yet slow acquiring of a close friend.

Would she return to that time if she could? Back to when decisions — or a lack of decision — didn't seem to have any consequences? Instead, they grew up. Eve finished uni and took a job as an acoustic engineer, her days spent talking to blank-faced building developers about sound barriers and insulation. She volunteered in the National Film and Sound Archive, updating databases with digital recordings, trying to minimise the crackle of dust on vinyl playbacks. Lotte's mother was diagnosed with ovarian cancer, and Lotte's research, always central, took on a new urgency. When Lotte wasn't visiting her parents or working, she was at Vin's, welcoming his nurturing calm, and eventually they moved out together, apologising for leaving Eve alone, but nonetheless resolute. Nate was there and not there, and when Eve decided to move to Sydney, where there were more job opportunities, Nate thought it a fabulous idea and declared that he would follow. Eve still remembers his loud dreaming of the life they might have together — Sydney cast as an emerald city and the future full of possibilities. But he didn't leave Canberra. He lives there still.

What if *she* had not left? Would she be so adrift now, nothing to live for and no one to care? What if she'd put her foot down and confronted him about what he wanted; about whether he wanted her at all? They had known one another seven years. What had he been waiting for? But one cannot play that game of 'what if?' and win. Because if she had held on to Nate, then there would have been no Tom, no Mina. No family to be lost.

Tom. To meet someone and know that you have been seen,

heard, recognised. To find a person who will go on standing by you, even to his detriment.

•

At the thought of Tom, Eve sits up. Takes her feet from the water and pulls her socks on, their cotton catching on the dampness. She walks back the way she came until she arrives at the campsite and crawls inside her tent, zipping it closed. The walls of the tent offer no horizon or distance. The material has been strengthened with a cross-hatch thread, designed to make sure that a hole does not tear away into a run and cleave the tent in two. Is that what she had neglected to do? Secret reinforcements, pre-emptive efforts to allay future problems? Instead, she has caused this rent, this split, this separation — she cannot point to fate, or anything else that might shoulder some of the blame.

•

Eve had only the vaguest memories of the Eureka rebellion: stories learnt in primary school about hardworking miners and corrupt policemen during the gold rush; an outlaw who would lose his arm to the cause and go on to become a politician. She recognised the flag as that of the builder's union, fluttering over construction sites throughout the city. When she saw there was a position available as the audio curator for a sound-and-light show being developed to tell the story of the rebellion, she knew it was what she'd been waiting for: a reason to leave Sydney and spend time in Ballarat; a chance to see if there was something to pursue with the man she'd met there only a few months before. Tom.

Eve's favourite moment of every Skype conversation was at

the beginning, in the seconds before her own image would have popped up on Tom's computer screen. She knew that the look of concern that crossed his face, a premature disappointment that she might not appear, mirrored her own. But their conversation was always easy: a few times a week they talked long into the night, sometimes with a bottle of wine (he would message in the afternoon, asking what she felt like drinking that evening so that he could buy one of the same). The intimacy of the internet allowed them to consider one another without having to own up to what they were doing.

She didn't tell him about the job. The first interview was by phone; for the second they flew her down to Victoria, asking her to rent a hire car from the airport and drive up to Ballarat. Crossing the dry plains and dipping into the cutting where the landscape dropped into more fertile ground, she considered stopping or turning back. She tried to tell herself that this relationship was inconsequential — if things didn't work out with Tom, she could just head home. But they both knew there was more at stake.

The sound-and-light show was a larger project than she'd ever taken on; the majority of work at her current firm was acoustic management: making sure museum displays didn't drown each other out, or that office workers who needed to actually work weren't distracted by their colleagues lounging about in the now ubiquitous breakout spaces. It could be monotonous work even when complicated, its worth only recognised when it failed. But over time she had also established a profile as a sound artist, occasionally exhibiting in small galleries and collective shows. The openings reminded her of her student days in Canberra — she found herself timidly looking over her shoulder, waiting to be found out as a fraud — but she liked to go back to the galleries during the exhibition run and watch the audiences interact with the work. That was when it became art: not in its creation but its reception.

One of her shows was entirely comprised of the sounds of bridges: the wind snap of taut suspension wires; the hoot of a northerly winding through metal trusses; the regular repeat of car tyres over a loose plank of wood. She had made the recordings on her camping trips to small towns, as well as on various overseas holidays, stalking cities with her recorder in hand. In the galleries, she would watch as people fitted headphones to their ears, their expression moving from suspicion to interest. Her favourite recording was the uncomfortable winching sound created by a rope bridge in the Daintree settling underneath her feet, the fibres protesting as they rubbed against each other, and she saw how many people recognised the sound from their own childhood, a long-ago time of tree-houses and playgrounds. For the show she left some recordings whole, and spliced others together to create an opulent soundscape, the bridges providing the string, woodwind, and percussion of an orchestra, the melody writing itself, the multiple layers coalescing into a fey-voiced choir.

From the initial interview, Eve recognised that the company creating the show knew exactly what they wanted: gun powder explosions, burning hotels, shouting rabble, and rifle fire. She just had to figure out how to make it on the available budget — a difficult ask when they couldn't afford the copyright fees to access any of the available audio libraries, meaning the sounds would have to be created. The company wanted to tell the story of the rebellion — from the murmurings of dissent regarding the high price of mining licences to the death of two dozen young men on the hastily erected stockade — and they wanted it to be as compelling as any theatrical production, but without any pesky actors that would have to be paid each night. It was to be a fully automated show that could play outdoors every night of the week, no matter the weather, and the sound needed to travel to an audience seated in steep tiers at the side of an arena. Eve wasn't sure it could be done, but as she drove into town — the main street familiar from her visit just two months before, when she had first met Tom — she knew how much she needed this change.

She arrived in town early. The interview wasn't until late morning, so she followed the main street further west until she got to the lake. She had twice walked its perimeter with Tom, both times in the evening, as the light faded and the town settled into evening. The first time they had both reached for easy banter; the back and forth of polite conversation, almost strangers filling too-long silences. The second time, the night before she had left to return to Sydney, their walk had been near mute, their clasped hands the only necessary discussion.

In the interview she shone. Her assured, almost bombastic tone came easily as she channelled Nate and the language of breezy confidence he had taught by way of demonstration. Briefly, she saw confidence for what it was: a performance. Whether it was genuine and deserved, or brandished to hide a deficit, the result was the same and the audience none the wiser. She could see it in their faces: their relief at being told she was the right candidate for the position, her conviction smoothing away any doubts. They gave her the job.

Afterwards, she called Tom from a cafe on the main street. He was surprised to hear from her, and on his way to a meeting; could he call her tonight? Eve felt humiliated — of course that's what she was to him: an evening distraction. He didn't actually want her here, in his town, his life. And yet she had got the job; she would be here for six months. She could hardly avoid him all that time; the town wasn't big enough for that.

I'm here, she said, voice angry rather than plaintive. In Ballarat.

His joy was unmistakable, her fears unwarranted. He was at the cafe twenty minutes later, meeting cancelled; his gently accommodating and sincere presence was just as she remembered, yet impossibly real. He was twenty-one years older than her, but it was more than this that made them hesitate.

Tom was unlike Nate in every way that mattered: he listened to rather than talked at; his enthusiasms were for things other than himself. Mostly, there was an air of uncertainty about him that Eve found endearing: he seemed unconvinced of her interest in him, and continually apologised should he be taking up her time. She had suggested renting her own place while she was in town for the project, professing that they shouldn't rush things, but she never got around to doing it. Within two weeks, she'd packed most of her belongings into the campervan, and arranged a short-term tenant for her flat in Sydney, convincing herself she'd be back for winter. By the end of the year, they were married. And then there was Mina.

•

Eve lies in the tent for hours, but sleep won't come, even when she blocks the afternoon light with a shirt tied across her eyes. There's a splat on the tent's fly, and then another. She tenses herself for the encompassing patter of rain, but it doesn't come; there is just the bellowing of the fabric whipping back and forth. Eventually, she leaves the tent and walks past the rows of built-in caravans and cabins towards the beach. A small boy wearing a wrestling helmet and a Collingwood football jumper draws chalk pictures on the concrete walkway outside the campsite reception. Len stands in the open doorway.

Hiya! How's the tent holding up? Will you be alright if this rain starts?

They both look up at the looming clouds.

It's just rain, says Eve.

Well, that's true enough. Not like it's going to kill you.

I've got to go.

She speeds up and strikes out across the car park and onto the road shoulder. A smooth convoy of cars whooshes past, gaining speed on the flat before pressing uphill. When there's a break in the traffic, Eve surprises herself by darting across the road, her pace quick but stride reluctant — like a person who walks in front of a movie theatre screen, knowing that slouching won't make their interruption any less apparent, but unable to resist the politeness of attempt.

The girls on the beach are sisters. They must be. Same long legs and too-big knees, hair tied back in low ponytails. Their clothes are near copies, the younger girl's reproduced at a slightly smaller size and in different colours. Where the older wears a faded pink jumper, the younger wears yellow. Both have leggings, baggy on their skinny legs and around their non-existent bums. Black, purple. Bought from the same shop at the same time. Been through the same number of washes.

How many mornings had she been Mina's handmaiden? The ceremony of dressing. Waiting patiently as Mina poked one foot into her tights and pulled the leg up to her knees before struggling to lift the second foot high enough to do the same. When she finally managed and pulled them up, the crotch would hang at her knees and Eve would lift her from the floor by the waistband, letting her slide into the tights before setting her down again. T-shirt, her head blindly searching for a way out; skirt on back to front, and Eve would twist it around in a hug, because

Mina hated to be corrected. A call and response of dressing as they chattered about the things she was going to do that day. The people she would see at day care. The possible activities, of which painting was always the most preferable. She would like to paint a picture of a house. With a dog. And a cat. Which is what she wanted most in the whole wide world.

On the beach, the younger girl cartwheels ahead until brought up short by the bark of her big sister, who commands attention before lifting her arms in a prim salute, stretching one leg before the other, the picture of concentration. Presenting to the judges: Eve had seen the school-age girls do it at Mina's Jungle Gym. An athletic version of a curtsy, made before the gymnast commenced each apparatus. The older girl executes a perfect handstand, legs snapped together, toes pointed. The younger watches, then mimics, but her excitement escapes her body in wriggles and bursts; her legs splay and she tumbles to the sand, laughing. Is the younger sister always the clown? Knowing instinctively that she must be able to laugh at herself, that she'll never, no matter how hard she tries, reach the heights of the older one: always two or so years ahead, always more experienced.

Eve would have loved to be a younger sister. To have someone to follow, someone to teach her restraint and confidence. To hold her feet together when she was upside down, as the older girl does now, counting to ten, her arms shaking with exertion and giggles, until they both collapse in the sand. Lotte was the closest she had to a sister, and if things were different now, that's whom she would call.

The sun has dropped behind the low hills; the sky clings to the dunes as a fuzzy static. Tentative raindrops fall, but the weather is not quite ready to commit.

•

Eve had wished for Lotte's arrival in the hospital ward soon after the birth, and in those long days that followed.

It's day three that's the worst, no question, one of the nurses told her. You'll want your mum around, and to have a good cry. But it gets better after. You'll pull yourself up, they always do.

Staring out the window at the brickwork of the hospital wing opposite. Thinking she should count those bricks. That if she knew how many there were in a wall, she'd at least know something. Breasts swollen and aching; nurses telling her everything was going just as it should.

Couldn't ask for a better bub, another nurse said, wheeling the little Perspex cradle and its pink flannelette bundle back to the nursery so Eve could shower in peace and get dressed to go home. In the shower she cleaned a body that still wasn't hers, heavy skin draped about her belly. She had expected to feel empty, a deflated balloon, but she felt heavier than ever, her feet still turned out, her ankles full.

Really though, even if her mum had been alive, Eve couldn't imagine her being much help. She had been a perfunctory mother, and made no apology for it. She cooked — frying sausages, boiling potatoes and peas — and did the laundry, but not much else. She probably only did the latter because it gave her a chance to smoke in peace, stalking past the Hills Hoist to the agapanthus that fireworked against the back fence. Even when clean, the bedsheets smelled like stale smoke. When Eve came home from underage visits to the pub — her parents not even pretending to care where she'd been on a school night — she sank into her saggy single bed, its metal springs reaching for the floor, embraced in the smell of cigarettes: her own, the pub's, her mother's. She often dreamt that she had fallen asleep beside the bar, sticky carpet beneath her cheek. Her rebellion didn't last long. It was an obligatory attempt to raise hell with parents who already resided there. Born a mistake, she remained an afterthought. But her parents loved her in their way. They had to, didn't they? They rarely shouted at her, only at each other. And her father would often tap her lightly on the bum with his foot as she passed between him and the television; she liked to think it was affection.

For the first six weeks, Eve thought the nurse was right: day three was the worst, and everything was better after that. Mina slept often and cried little. Eve wrote long emails to Lotte, telling her of Mina's small changes, careful to accentuate any difficulties in the way that new mothers must to their friends, for fear of appearing smug. She had never worried about second-guessing Lotte's responses before — their friendship had been immune to concerns of hurt feelings or competition — but things were different now. Lotte didn't reply.

In those early weeks, alone in the house but for Mina snuggled in to her chest, Eve pined for Nate's surety and spontaneity. Anything to break the heavy quiet of the house as autumn prowled outside. When Tom returned from work in the late afternoon, kind and solicitous, Eve's longing was interrupted, but in the still mornings, when she would be unreasonably startled by the obnoxious clatter of cutlery tossed in the sink, or find herself scrolling unseeing and urgent through the Facebook feed on her phone, she would recall Nate's eagerness for the small moments. The way each meal was an event, each day an opportunity for a new project or outing.

A few months before Eve met Tom, Nate had turned up at her flat in Sydney. She hadn't seen him for over six years, almost the entire time she had lived there. In a performance that was more despair-driven bravado than reassuring, he'd told Eve his marriage was over, that he and Katie just weren't compatible. His list of complaints was inexhaustible: they barely had conversations any more; she never listened to what he had to say; the children were everything to her, and he was just some kind of bread-winning appendage. Katie didn't pay any attention to him, he decried; they had no connection of the mind.

It's not like the two of us, he implored, head in hands on Eve's couch. We could talk for hours, you and I. You actually cared about my thoughts, my opinions. If I ask Katie what she's thinking, it's always about the kids, usually some way I've failed them. It's never about anything outside of her — it's certainly never about me.

He seemed to have grown younger rather than older: his hair longer and more haphazard, his clothes — faded black jeans, a hooded jumper — those of a teenager. His body still barely contained his energy: knees bouncing up and down, fingernails chewed to stubs. There was the same relentless tumbling of words cutting her off every time she made a comment; what she had once considered endearing enthusiasm now struck her as uncurbed self regard. For the first time she could recall, Eve just wanted him to stop talking. But when eventually he did, sinking back into the couch so that he seemed smaller than he'd ever been, the quiet was near overwhelming, and Eve found herself in his arms, face pressed up against his chest, all of her old feelings for him flooding back. For years she'd imagined him saying those exact words — *I need you* — and, in a rush of comprehension, she knew she could have him back.

Lying in bed, his long limbs wrapped around hers, she knew that if he asked to come and live with her she would say yes. After all, what had she been waiting for? But the thought of him upending her life left her uneasy; the jumper he discarded on her bedroom floor was so out of place after he left as to be almost abhorrent. But he was there, wasn't he? He had finally come to her.

As the year wound to a close he returned every week, telling Katie he had business meetings in Sydney. Eve did not let herself feel anything much about the role in which she had been cast. At the time, she'd thought him sincere in his interest, if somewhat ungrateful for what he had with Katie and the children. But now, as she swung Mina from the crook of one arm to the other, her shoulder twinging with pain, she allowed herself more sympathy for his position and his bid to be free.

For those couple of months, she had been light-headed with his dogged pursuit of her. When Lotte had called, saying she was in Sydney for some Christmas shopping, Eve almost invited her to join them, but she knew even Lotte's friendship wouldn't stretch that far; her friend was unable to forgive Nate for what he had done. And Eve knew, despite his promises and brash, desperate professions of need, that while she would always be able to forgive him, she could never be sure he would stay. She'd ended things with him before Christmas; she told him she would not see him any more, and jumped in her campervan and drove, knowing he would never follow. The following week, she met Tom.

•

When the rain begins to fall properly, dotting the sand in earnest, the girls depart from the beach, the older one leading the way. Eve follows them, turning her back to the endless sea. Headlights pierce the dusk, sweeping around the headland, and she sees the danger with sudden clarity, breaking out into a run, slipping over the still-dry sand, landing on her hands as her feet scuff and flounder. The wind has picked up, and the rain drives almost horizontal; she's throwing herself forward but she's getting nowhere, stumbling from path to car park.

Watch out!

The girls are standing back from the road, the older having taken the hand of the younger, and it takes them a moment to react, so intent are they on watching for cars. They look at her, and look away. They worry she is the danger. She watches their heads swivel back and forth before they break into a run across the road. Their mother stands in the grainy dark at the entrance to the campsite, waiting. As a mother should.

•

It had never occurred to Eve that after the arrival of Mina she might not, in time, get her body back. Different, of course; stretched to its limits and less willing than before, but hers all the same. But with Mina's arrival, Eve found her body seemed to have departed her for good. It was now at her daughter's beck and call: when Mina cried, Eve's breasts ached and leaked, the baby's distress, real or imagined, prodding at her body. Sleep both edged closer and became lesser: a plunge pool to be toppled into and to reluctantly return from, paddling upwards and willing the surface to be further away. Right up until she gave birth, Eve was walking around the lake every day, belly pulling her forward, dragging her toward the ground, to inertia; the only way to stay upright was to keep moving. For months, her body had been telling her it was no longer willing to do her bidding, and she had accommodated its requests with amused indifference. Eating more than she thought possible, hauling herself to the bathroom in the middle of the night, unsteady on her feet. Waking slowly, a hot air balloon lifting into the clouds. While pregnant, Eve found her body didn't want to sit or stand the way it usually did: she was forever deep back in the chair or perched forward on the couch; on her side in bed, rather than face down. In the final few months, she couldn't go running, and for a short time it became impossible to cycle when she couldn't reach the handlebars of her road bike. She bought another bike, a women's step-through frame, the handlebars reaching towards her, so that she sailed through the town like a paddle-steamer, sure and steady. But once Mina was born, Eve's bicycles sat untouched in the garage, and when Ballarat's winter rain set in, notoriously chill and interminable, she was confined indoors, days folding into one another.

Snuffles, hiccups, snorts. Every sound flattened through the tinny speaker of the baby monitor. Drawn as ever to documentation, Eve set up her audio recorder by Mina's crib, the microphone beneath the painted ladybird mobile. She didn't listen back to any of the recordings, though, simply transferring them onto her computer and adding them, unheard, to her library of sounds.

She had thought that with Mina she would escape judgement, at least for a while. Not from herself, ever her own fiercest critic, worrying that she was not doing things as she should: she didn't expect *this* feeling to go away, but rather to intensify. She was ready, too, for the comparisons with other mothers when they gathered at the health centre, prams parked like a circle of prairie wagons. They feigned interest in others' babies as a way to place the development of their own; criticisms were disguised as queries. But she had assumed that Mina would not judge. After all, she had nothing to compare Eve to and no faculty to criticise and assess. She was bonded to Eve, reliant, dependent, and while she did not expect her daughter to be grateful, she did hope for love. From the very first day, however, it seemed Mina was appraising her: noting what she did right and what she did wrong, already knowing the worth of these concepts. Eve had created this person; she had done it well. In the hours after the birth, she was not concerned about how unfamiliar Mina was, and how far away she seemed even when she was latched on to Eve's breast. They were getting to know one another, strangers taking tentative steps. But as the days wound on, Eve could sense she was not getting it right; she was failing again and again.

When Mina was ten months old, she began to cry in a way she had not before. Long bouts of whimpering punctuated with angry squawks, refusing to be settled. She ate so little that Eve was sure she was starving: spears of broccoli sucked on and discarded, avocado smeared across the tray table. Strawberries, bananas — it was all spat out with derision. That purple plastic spoon with its deep bowl and bulbous handle; Eve came to dread the sight of it. Mina opening her mouth wide before sucking the food from the spoon, and then squeezing it out of her mouth, stalactites of carrot drooping from chin to bib. Later, she wouldn't even open her mouth, keeping it clamped shut whenever Eve put her in the highchair.

The ebullient promise of summer held the world together outside, but Eve kept the blinds closed against the glare. The internet offered discussion groups where mothers — some earnest, some joyfully resigned to the mysteries of parenting — listed their offspring in a string of letters and numbers after their username, littering their advice with cheerful emoticons and hopeful animated gifs. Eve trawled the posts, searching for a description of another baby that displayed Mina's infuriating behaviour, but none of the scenarios were quite right. She went so far as to create login details for herself, but could not adequately describe Mina's obstinacy, knowing that even if she could, these other mothers wouldn't properly understand.

Eve listened to Mina and tried to render her sounds in phonetic language, cataloguing the forms as one might birdcalls. She remembered hearing that disease and parasites could affect a bird's song rate and pitch, and so she tried to listen out for any such clues in Mina's cries. She called the maternal health and child nurse to explain, holding the receiver up to Mina's mouth.

She just wants some attention, the nurse told Eve, the exasperation in her voice as clear as the anguish in Mina's.

You've not been giving her enough attention. You don't deserve her, and she knows it.

At least, this was what Eve thought the nurse had said, because this is what she knew was really the matter.

The maternal health centre had no appointments that day, so Eve took Mina to a doctor. In the waiting room, she faced the pram towards herself, so that no one could see Mina's flushed and scratched face, her own hand having angrily marked her cheek. The other people in the waiting room tried not to look at her, but the crying drew them back.

Perhaps you should pick him up, love, said one man. He smiled encouragingly, and Eve obliged, knowing it would make it worse. It did.

Jig him around, said another patient.

Or swoop him a little, like this. A woman cradled her magazine, showing Eve what to do, crooning to its cover of a harried Jennifer Aniston.

Her regular doctor was on holidays, and the replacement was a man she hadn't seen before. His bald head was comfortingly round, as though it had been smoothed by years of use, and he beamed with expectation when she carried Mina into the room.

A baby!

She chose to ignore the way his exclamation suggested novelty, and let him take Mina from her arms, her wailing momentarily stilled. Laying her on the examination table, the doctor gently pushed at Mina's tummy, prodded fingers around her mouth. Eve demonstrated how Mina's upset exacerbated when she was picked up, subsided when she was put down, but never quietened, except for short moments of feeding, her teeth chomping at Eve's nipples and bringing tears to her eyes. She wanted the doctor to tell her she was doing something wrong, to demonstrate the way things should be done, but he only stood back, watching.

There's nothing medically wrong with your daughter, the doctor said. All Eve could hear was that there *was* something wrong, something the doctor refused to take responsibility for.

There is a checklist, though, he said. Hang on, let me find it.

He shuffled the papers on his desk, eventually pulling a laminated sheet from his inbox.

We're supposed to ask all new mothers about this sort of thing, though I suppose it's your daughter who's upset, not you.

He spoke increasingly loudly, throwing his voice above Mina's cries.

We don't need to ask every question, it's a bit dry ... let's see ...

He cast his eye down the page.

Okay, well, what about this one? Are you feeling a bit overwhelmed?

He looked at her hopefully.

A little, she said.

Right. Are you feeling like you have little energy?

She was exhausted, but everyone kept telling her that was normal.

I feel like I've got too much energy sometimes, Eve said. Somewhere deep inside me. I'm not doing enough, I'm not stretching myself; it's like I can't reach anything.

He consulted his list, shaking his head.

No, no, I don't think so. Look, why don't you take this list, have a think about all the things it asks, and get back to me?

He brightened at this idea, ushering her out the door.

She took the baby home and eventually, just before Tom returned, Mina stopped crying. Eve started crying herself then, the minute Tom walked in the door, salty tears that ran to the corner of her mouth as though they didn't want to stray too far. The next day was the same, and the next. The short hours when Mina used to sleep and Eve would do the same, or hang and fold the endless laundry, were memories. She wrote a series of unsent emails to Lotte, headphones clamped in her ears to block Mina's cries, the words unfurling across the screen. *She's an absolute dream most of the time. So interested in the world around her, her big eyes just taking everything in. And she laughs a lot; she does this funny little giggle that's more like a snort.*

She wanted to be angry with her daughter, but she felt nothing. After all, this is what she deserved. She wasn't cut out to be a mother — even Nate had seen that — and she had let herself become pregnant to Tom before he could uncover the same. Mina's screams were stupidly loud, and Eve took to wearing her headphones constantly, the cord dangling at her waist or tucked into her belt, the silicon buds blocking her ears and making her own swallows audible. The cries morphed into long wailing sobs when Mina was held, harried spurts of indignity when left alone in her cot. And all the while, those focused eyes. The slightly furrowed brow as if to say, what was so difficult? What didn't Eve understand?

Everything was noise, and Eve, who used to seek sounds out, became desperate for silence. Not quiet, but silence. She would lie on her bed in the afternoon, in the short periods after feeding when Mina actually did sleep, and listen. The tick of her watch — she would unstrap it and close it in her underwear drawer. Cars passing outside — approaching and then driving away. The whoosh of water running into the washing machine; the click of the air-conditioning turned on in response to the thermostat. The dull hiss of the electricity climbing up the cord to the clock radio. Was it even audible, or was it only a slight vibration of industry as the little unit went about its task of telling the time? Eve switched it off at the wall, and the hiss stopped. For a moment such relief flooded her, until she heard a repetitive tapping. What was it? She haunted the bedroom, listening for the culprit. There — water dripping from the tap in the en suite, no matter how tightly it was turned off.

She took the stack of minidisks she'd been keeping in the garage and burrowed in a plastic tub until she found the player itself. She had listened to those recordings so often that every sound was familiar. The wind beneath the pier at Merimbula. Trains shunting up against each other at Central Station. The call of an oil barge waiting to dock. In this way, she was able to block the endless drone of Mina's crying: walking her around the lake, headphones on, ignoring the disgusted looks of passers-by and the swans haughty with annoyance at the noise.

There, right next to Lotte's image on her computer screen, was a green tick: she was online. Eve pressed the button to connect and waited as the familiar Skype ringtone bubbled away. She had no idea what time it was in Chile.

Hi, Eve.

Lotte appeared on screen. Her eyes darted about as though she was scanning Eve's room, and then she forced a smile.

How are you? Lotte asked. Her hair was pulled back in a ponytail; her face looked thinner than it used to be.

I'm good. Really good, said Eve. How are you? How's work?

You know, same old. It's a really busy place. Lots to do.

Then silence. Neither sure what to say.

How's the baby? asked Lotte eventually. Mina?

She's good; she's asleep at the moment. She doesn't sleep much, she was up every few hours last night ...

That's a shame, that she's asleep. I would have liked to see her.

I could go get her.

No, that's alright.

Again, the silence.

It's so nice to talk to you, Lotte. I'm sorry it's been so long. Things have been pretty crazy with Mina and all, you can't really imagine.

No, I probably can't.

Lotte smiled.

I didn't mean—

That's okay, I understand. Look, I have to go. My shift's about to start.

Okay, well, maybe we can make another time, said Eve, near pleading.

Sure. That would be nice. Okay. Sorry, got to go. Bye.

And with a little whooshing sound, Lotte was gone, and Eve could hear Mina wailing from the bedroom.

Later, she would not remember whether Mina had really cried all this time or whether it just felt that way. Logic suggested one thing, memory another. The days lengthened. Tom seemed to always be there. Checking emails as he piled things in the washing machine, cooking dinner while Eve lay in the bath. She tried to draw from him his memories of his first daughter as a baby. How similar was she to Mina? Had she ever behaved in this way? She tried to disguise her questions as those of a curious mother, hunting for tips that would make life easier. But she worried that Tom wouldn't love Mina in the way he must his first daughter. An adult, a woman of the world, while Mina was such a helpless creature. An encumbrance on them both.

It was Tom who took her back to her own doctor, and then to the psychologist. Tom who never once said, *you're the one who wanted a baby, why are you acting like this?* Tom who delighted in every moment that Mina gave him.

I've never been so happy, and you've never been so unhappy, Tom said.

He had come into the bathroom, where she sat in the bath, and was pouring jugs of water down her back, as though her hair was long and soapy. A lone duck bobbed in front of her, refusing to be upended no matter how many times she tipped it over.

Was your wife ever like this?

He paused in his water pouring.

My *first* wife, he said. You're my wife.

Yes.

A little. Some days. But not so much.

It must have been better with her then. Having a child? Marriage?

Eve counted the seconds until he answered. Three.

No, it wasn't, said Tom. She found it easy, much easier than you. But it wasn't better with her. None of it was.

She leaned her damp hair against his chest, her arm hard up against the cool of the porcelain tub.

Thank you, she said.

It will get better, Tom said, shuffling forward on the bath mat until she could see his face, his body awkward in its manoeuvres, looking for comfort on the tiled floor and not finding it.

You're getting there; it will pass.

Will it? Really? I feel like *I* will pass.

She tried to smile at him and found that she could not.

I feel like I'm a fleeting moment. A leaf in a river, just rushing along, and you're everything else: the river, the banks, the trees. I've come into your life, but you've been here a long time. You've done marriage. You've already had a child.

What about if we moved? asked Tom. We don't have to stay here — we can sell the house, go somewhere else.

It's not that.

She thought of his friends, so welcoming of her, all of them with their unvoiced memories of his first wife, with their grandchildren the same age as Mina.

What makes you think it can't be done again? Differently? Better?

He reached into the tub, flicking the rubber duck on its beak so that it did a nosedive before bobbing up again.

I wasn't a very good father the first time around, you know that. But with Mina, I can be. You've given me another chance.

That's exactly what I mean. We're your second chance.

And I'm thankful for it. This ... — he gestured at the tiled bathroom, the mirror fogged and dripping condensation, taking it all in as though it was his kingdom — This is a good thing, he said. You, me, Mina. It will get better; the psychologist said it would. It's not your fault; it happens to a lot of mothers.

I'm sorry. I feel so ungrateful—

What do you have to be grateful for? Tom cut her off. I should be thanking you, Eve. You've given me so much. Where would I be otherwise? Alone. And turning into an old man, no doubt.

I miss her, Eve said. She doesn't have to tell him who she is talking about.

I know you do, he said.

And he stood up, knees cracking, and pulled a towel from the rails, waiting for her to step into his outstretched arms.

But I miss you.

The following day Mina's eyes were closed, her cries high and thin, as though she was calling for help yet knowing it was not going to come. Eve opened the sliding door and slunk through the heat to the garage. Her three bikes were lined up against the wall; Tom's was hanging from a hook. It was like seeing old friends. She wheeled her road bike into the lounge room, the flat tyres leaving dull marks on the floorboards. She found the bike pump on a garage shelf, beside it the stationery trainer, and took both inside. Eve set Mina in her bouncer so they were facing off against each other, and then she locked the bike into the trainer, breathing heavily as she pumped up the tyres. She was so unfit; sweat was already forming across her neck, and she'd not even gotten on the bike yet.

When she clicked into the pedals she felt light for the first time in months. She found her rhythm quickly, the trainer whirring with the effort of holding her in place. At the noise, Mina's cries stopped. Of course they did. She watched Eve, curious at the way she was all head and arms, soothed by the rhythmic whirr of the back wheel. Sweat soon dripped onto the floor, making it slippery, and the trainer slid forward in short bursts. Eve pedalled, and Mina's eyes began to close. Eve slowed. Mina's eyes opened. Eve pedalled again.

Things improved slowly. Mina began to eat more, and cry

less. Eve graduated from cycling in the lounge room with the trainer to coasting along country roads, the asphalt rough under her wheels, cars swerving out wide around her. Eve let herself forget that this was the second time for Tom.

When Mina was one year old, Eve went back to work. The sound-and-light show had been a success, and, chasing the tourist dollar as factories closed down and abattoirs made way for new suburbs of McMansions, the town wanted to leverage its history as the 'birthplace of democracy'. Eve was commissioned to create a soundscape for a new museum, so that as visitors traversed the room they would be enveloped in the moment of the period being documented, its sound raining down on them from overhead speakers positioned like so many shower roses. The clank of wagons and horses in the streets; rattling tramcars and first-generation motorcars; the schoolyard chants of children engaged in skipping and marbles. Eve spent hours in the library archives, going through old radio programs and annotating background noises, so she could figure out how to recreate them when the recordings were not of good enough quality. By the end of the afternoon she would be eager to get to childcare, restless for Mina's energy, her circular play, her repeated words.

Baby! Baby! She would exclaim from her seat at the front of Eve's bike as they rode through town, her little finger pointing at a far-off pram.

Up! Up! She would cry as they passed the playground. Woof! Woof! For every dog that scampered past.

Apogee! She called at the octopus that was perched above the carwash, each one of its tentacles clutching a sponge.

And Eve allowed her happiness to bloom.

•

The air in the tent is dead. Lifeless. Finished. There is no movement; everything is still, and the damp is trapped in the folds of the sleeping bag, in the piles of clothes. Eve pulled her shoes off at the door, but the sand that had clung to them had also kept hold of her jeans, and it follows her into the tent, scratching at her ankles, elbows; anywhere her body touches another surface, there seems to be sand. She feels but cannot hear her own deep breaths above the rain and the wind that whips at the tent walls, snapping them to dull notes. She tries to shake away the wavering that has taken hold by pretending she has just finished a ride: legs jittery and hands to knees, trying to open her lungs to the possibility of air. Square, uneven breaths — she tells herself they are something other than what they are: the result of exercise, perhaps, of pushing too far. Her bicycle rides have a beginning and an end — there is a particular outfit to be worn, road rules to obey. There is sense.

There had been one aborted ride, sometime after; clipping shoes into the pedals and pushing off down the street, ignoring her shaky breath, arms of jelly, telling herself that once she got into a rhythm everything would return to normal. Got to get back on your bike. Tears had filled her eyes unbidden and skated across her cheeks, as they would on a frosty morning coming down the old volcano road, fingertips numb in her gloves, eyes streaming. She wavered as she came to the intersection, unable to judge the speed of the car trundling ahead. Would it see her? Would it slow down in time? Did she want it to? She released her foot from the pedal, unable to balance, and limped her bike across to the footpath. Unlocking the other foot, she walked home — that place she didn't want to be or to leave, shoes clacking on the ground. For so many years cycling had been the one thing that kept her sane. Long rides on country roads, cars giving her a wide berth, tooting with impatience or encouragement, she could never tell which. Never cared. Legs pumping up and down, a slow burn in her thighs, handlebars loose in her grip.

The last time she went for a proper ride was before everything went wrong. Lying in the tent, Eve's thoughts bang into a rut. Legs shake, arms convulse at her side, hands clench into fists. She thinks of the road, the white line of the shoulder unfurling in front. Tells herself to breathe. The panic subsides.

She wills herself to sleep, but she cannot ignore the gnawing at her stomach so she rummages through the bags: bread, a packet of two-minute noodles. Running through the rain toward the kitchen, she lands deep in a puddle as she leaps to avoid another, water soaking in through shoe and sock, squelching as she makes it inside. She eats the two-minute noodles without tasting them. The fluorescent tubes of the campsite kitchen emit a soft buzz along with their flat light, interrupted only by the clunk of the water pipes from the shower block next door. What is she doing here? She imagines her tent fading from years of sun, its nylon walls drooping to the ground. How long before she started making small adjustments to make herself more comfortable? A chair; a reading lamp; a thicker mattress. Determined to make each day just a little bit easier. The coast would be swarming with families in the school holidays, traffic blocked on weekends for marathons and cycle races and swim meets — it would be like living in Ballarat again, as faces became familiar and social expectations were laid down. If she wants to be alone, she will need to be on the move; it will be the only way to grant Tom the distance he deserves.

She traces the coast in her mind — she could travel past the Apostles and the Shipwreck Coast, head into South Australia and follow the peninsulas, skirting around the gulfs. Lose herself in one of the flailing seaside towns, discover the Australia she'd read about in Tim Winton novels: get a job farming oysters or abalone and live out her days in some deserted shack as a miserable misfit, gossiped about by the locals.

She could kick up north towards the centre, camp on the dry bed of Lake Eyre. She'd been there once before with her campervan; cycling on her mountain bike, she had struck out across the shattered salt pan of the lake's surface until it seemed the world had no edges at all. The sky seemed to melt into the horizon, or perhaps the ground tugged the clouds down. When the sun set, deep bands of colour would swell in the distance, rose pinks bumping into a burnt orange that would leach into pale blue. It was the sort of place that demanded nothing of a person.

Later, Eve lies on her back in the tent, eyes wide open. The rain has begun in earnest now, the tent fly anxiously flapping, the zip sliders tinkling against one another. Mina would have liked it here, in this tent. She had an unusual love for storms; Tom had convinced her that a storm meant all of the fairies and imaginary creatures were having a party, and that something wonderful must have happened to make them celebrate.

*

Like a birthday?

As far as Mina was concerned there was nothing in the world as exciting as her third birthday, which had involved party hats, colourful popcorn, and eleven children dressed in fairy wings. It had been about this time last year that Mina had pushed a chair up against the window during a thunderstorm, almost shaking with excitement as she crowded up against the glass, trying to catch sight of the fairies.

They skate across the glass so quickly that humans can't see them, said Tom. But see the trails they leave behind?

He traced the passage of the raindrops running down the pane. A rumble of thunder crashed above them, and Mina's body tensed, unsure.

Don't be scared — that's the sound of all the giants stamping their feet, said Tom. They're so excited about the party that they're jumping up and down.

Eve watched as he demonstrated, lifting his knees high and dropping his feet to the floor. Mina squirmed off the chair and joined him, jumping two feet together, her brown hair bobbing up and down, working loose from her butterfly clips.

And if you're extra lucky, sometimes you'll see lightning from the party because the fairies set off fireworks that light up the whole sky!

He lifted Mina back onto the chair, standing behind her and leaning his hands against the sill.

And after the party it rains and rains and rains so that everything gets washed away, and the next day, nobody can see any of the fairy or giant footprints in the garden.

The next morning, Mina was at their bed, poking Tom.

Dad, Dad! We have to go in the garden and look for footprints.

Which is exactly what they did. All three of them — gumboots on, raincoats over pyjamas, stomping across the grass and tramping up and down the muddy paths of the vegie garden in the early-morning light.

There's one! Mina bolted for the deck, her yellow gumboots squelching across the lawn. See! She pointed at the fuchsia bush, its flowers in full bloom: the bright popping colours, the stalks and petals bursting from the pod. Planetary nebulas, thought Eve, and brushed the description away.

It looks like a fairy!

Mina was right: the flowers hung from the bush in bunches, the inner blooms their skirts, the outer petals their wings and the stamen like slender legs in pink tights. The wonder on Mina's face was indescribable.

I think I almost saw one, said Mina later, mud still streaking her face and wrapped in her hooded duck towel in front of the heater. A *real* one.

Saw one what? asked Eve.

A fairy. I almost sawed it, but it had to hide, so I didn't.

Do you think at the next storm you might see it again? asked Eve, not knowing that this one would be the last.

•

Hello? Are you in there?

It's Len. He shouts across the sound of the downpour, and Eve tenses, holds still.

Eve? Hello? Are you okay? It's very wet out here. And the wind … look, it's getting pretty gusty. I'm a bit worried about some of the trees, and branches falling.

I'm fine, she calls out, wishing him away.

Look, do you want to come inside? We've got the heater going, it's nice and dry. His voice sounds very close; he is crouching at the door. She can see the light from his torch illuminating the base of the tent.

I'm fine, thank you.

Both listen to the wind moan like a cartoon ghost. It's all make-believe.

Really, I think you should … you'd be more comfortable.

I don't want to be comfortable!

Sitting in the dark in her sleeping bag, holding onto her knees, rocking forwards and back in little bursts.

Okay, okay.

She hears the shuffle of his raincoat, traces the arc of his torch as he stands up.

I'm sorry, she says. She has to make her voice high to be heard above the rain. I don't mean to be rude. I just … I'm perfectly fine here, that's all.

Well, don't come whinging to me when you get swept down the river.

She makes an attempt at laughter that she knows he won't hear. When he's gone, Eve listens for him to come back; almost wishes that he would. Turns to the side and lowers herself onto the sleeping mat. Water seeps into the end of the sleeping bag; she curls up, without noticing the tears soaking into the pillow. She is so used to them appearing there.

5

LOTTE

DECEMBER 2009

Lotte missed the first exit and considered just staying on the highway, letting it take her where it would. She wasn't sure she was ready to see her father yet. One highway would always become another soon enough, the yellow-and-red Shell service stations alternating with the green BP ones. McDonald's. KFC.

She took the second exit from the bypass, the one that led directly into Ballarat, cutting straight through the suburbs to the town centre. Exhausted, she struggled to focus on anything other than the road. The interruption of traffic lights and intersections registered slowly after the smooth continuity of the highway, and, seeing red, Lotte only belatedly realised she was required to act, slamming on the brakes. The sun had set; lights had been switched on in houses that sat well back from the streets. Curtains had not yet been drawn; no one was willing to close away the last of Boxing Day just yet. She was driving too fast to see inside in any detail — the flash of a bookcase, the dancing colour of a television screen. Cars were parked in driveways and on verges; every house she passed seemed occupied, but surely this could not be the case? There must be empty houses, ones that the visitors had come from.

Her father's house was dark, the slam of her car door intrusive. Like most in the street it was a Federation bungalow, the front room presenting with a shallow bay window, the door stepping back beneath a porch. Redbrick walls were offset by creamy white trim, the door and the wrought-iron house number were painted teal: her mother's work. As a child, Lotte had used the front wall of the verandah as a barricade, flinging water bombs at the footpath where friends whizzed gleefully back and forth on their bicycles. A short driveway led to the added-on garage, which was fitted with a downsized gable to both match the house and attempt to disguise its utilitarian ugliness. Inside, the house was dark and cool in summer, warm and cosy in winter, though in the front bedrooms the lamps had to be switched on even during the middle of the day, because the small windows did not let in enough light.

When the doorbell failed to work, Lotte knocked loudly, imagining her dad down the back somewhere, dinner on his lap in front of the television. Maybe he had adopted one of those stable tables. Or a tray with spindly legs, one that could be folded away next to the armchair. She should have bought him one as a gift, but that might embarrass him into thinking he should have a gift for her in return. She tried the doorbell again, pushing harder, and this time it worked. The deep pealing of the bell was so familiar that she found herself inside and outside all at once, and she raised her arm to reach for the door, to answer its call and see who was on the other side.

No footsteps. Someone must have taken pity on him, alone over Christmas, and invited him to dinner. She felt a flush of warmth for the kind people who would do such a thing, though she was sure they'd regret their decision: her father was not exactly a conversationalist. He had always been happy to go along with whatever other people suggested, a trait Lotte once thought was easy-going, and later decided was a sign of weakness. He never seemed to *want* anything.

Lotte backed her car out of the driveway and into the street. She had forgotten about the existence of the town's huge lake until she came upon it, houses forming an immense circle around the shallow body. The last time she had been back, a year after her mother's death, the lake was completely dried up, lake weed rotting in stinking piles in the sun, grass seeds lodging themselves in the fermenting marshy wetlands. When grass grew across the lake bed, it was shockingly green in the midst of the drought. The lake bed then had seemed like a lazy miracle, an oasis thumbing its nose at the dry. But within weeks the grass was drooping, leached of its colour, and the red-billed swans had to be coaxed from their nests amongst the reeds and taken, hissing and spitting, to a sanctuary.

That last visit with her father had felt like it went on forever, and, following an afternoon of long silences, Lotte suggested they walk the perimeter of the shrunken lake. The boathouses were rickety on too-high stilts, their ramps now only able to launch craft to lawn, not water. The park benches appeared lost, with no vista to offer. When they'd reached the marker for the rowing events of the 1956 Olympics, they struck out onto the lake bed, taking tentative steps even though they could see the cracked earth beneath their feet, solid as any other. Other walkers were doing the same, looking back at the shore in wonder, perhaps uneasy that the water might suddenly find its way back. A man walked by, swooping a metal detector ahead of him, headphones clamped to his ears and a supermarket bag tucked into his belt clanking with found objects. Her father told her a story — truth or myth — that a Hungarian Olympian had been so excited to win his race that he was swinging his gold medal around and it flew off the end of his finger, sailing into the lake, never to be recovered.

She would need to look for a hotel, and her best chance was the centre of town. Lotte pulled the Alfa into a U-turn, not wanting to do a full lap of the lake, and headed back the way she had come. Streetlights dropped orange nets to the road, marking out circles of asphalt, and making the night seem darker. She had almost passed by when she noticed an unfamiliar car parked in the drive of her father's house, and a strip of light beneath the blind in the front room: he was home. Lotte parked, and hurried up the path to the door. Just as she was about to ring the bell, she heard laughter: a shriek of it, the kind that bursts out of someone when they're taken by surprise, when they're grabbed from behind and wrestled into a friendly embrace, the laughter muffled into quiet, a mouth covered in kisses. He wasn't alone. Without a second thought, Lotte backed away from the door, high-stepping across the lawn so she didn't loudly stumble, and back up the street, where she unlocked the Alfa and slipped in behind the wheel. She shifted the car into gear, pulling out quickly and taking off too fast.

The next morning he didn't answer the doorbell, but this time Lotte turned the handle and gave the door a push. The car from the driveway was gone.

Hello?

Her footsteps rang out; the carpet had been taken up, the floorboards polished.

Dad?

The doors of the rooms on either side of the hallway were closed, the house dark, but when Lotte walked through to the open living space at the back of the house, morning light flooded the kitchen. A coffee plunger lay upside down in the draining rack. Two mugs. Flowers lolled in a vase on the kitchen table; crumpled wrapping paper poked out from beneath some paperback books on the coffee table. The room looked different — a new lounge suite, a new television. But all the artwork, all the knick-knacks crowding the surfaces, were the same as they'd been for as long as Lotte could remember.

He was in the backyard, leaning over a garden bed that took up much of the lawn. He must have put the vegie patch in since she was here last, but, banked up with railway sleepers, and with tomato plants trailing to the grass, it looked like it had been there forever. At the sound of the sliding door opening, he unbent his frame and turned towards her, and she saw with astonishment that he had gone completely grey. His hair was clipped close to his head and, without the sandy, wispy lengths that used to drift across it, his forehead appeared higher, his face more open. His silver-framed glasses had been replaced with fashionable black-rimmed ones. He was thinner than he used to be, his shoulders no longer office-rounded, and he came toward her in such a purposeful manner that she couldn't even place such a stride with her memories of his reluctant amble. The effect of it all was that he looked young. Younger than Lotte ever remembered him being. He didn't look like her father.

Dad.

Lotte.

He wrapped her in an easy hug, her face pressed against the cotton of his T-shirt, warm from the morning's sun. Pulling away (too soon — she always pulled away from a hug too soon) she saw up close that his face was more lined than before, that he *had* aged. His newly silver hair, though, made his blue eyes brighter than she recalled.

You look good.

The words came out so promptly they sounded insincere, and she wanted to start again, to let him know she really meant it. She felt a sudden, deep affection for her father in this moment, before they became familiar to each other once again, and she wished that she could slow time down, luxuriate in the optimism lent by possibility.

Thanks, he said. This is a nice surprise. No Vin?

He looked over her shoulder towards the house.

He's spending Christmas with his family.

And you thought you should see yours?

His tone was teasing. When she didn't say anything, he went on.

You didn't tell me you were coming, did you?

You know I didn't. The words were sharp, out of her mouth like sprinters from the starting blocks. I never had to check with Mum before I came. I thought you'd be pleased.

He flinched, looked away.

I am. I just meant, had you told me you were coming? I thought I might have missed a message or email or something. You're lucky you caught me at home.

Where else would you be?

Lotte looked around the yard; apart from the vegie garden, everything in the backyard was much the same as it had always been. It was difficult to imagine her father ever leaving this place, ever being anywhere else. *A polestar*, she thought, amused by her own sentimentality.

I'm off to the coast tomorrow.

How long for?

About a week. Until New Year's.

She let the pause stretch out between them, waiting for the invitation. Some beach time wouldn't go astray, and it would mean they could stare out at the ocean, rather than across the table at each other.

Well, I'm glad you're here, he said. Shall we have a coffee?

Sure.

Her father looked at the garden as they turned toward the house, his longing obvious; her arrival an unwelcome disruption to his day.

Back inside the house, Lotte was simultaneously bombarded with the familiarity of her childhood home, and disturbed by the changes her father had made. Where before recipe books had been squashed in the shelf above the microwave, slipping beneath one another, their spines contorted, there now stood canisters for flour, sugar, coffee, and tea, their contents signified by bold letters. Where earrings, rings, and bracelets had once gathered in front of photo frames, on the arms of chairs and on windowsills, there were only sweeps of bare surface. Lotte knew, without opening them, that the drawers were no longer stuffed and hiccupping on their rails, that the pantry would only have one of everything, and each item finished before another was purchased, let alone opened. The new modular couch was decorated with a throw rug folded over one arm. Had her father actually gone out and bought that? But so many other things were the same: the watercolour paintings her mother had done at the adult-education college were still clustered on the wall; the long-necked cats, blue roses climbing up their china necks, still preened by the television. Helen's mark was still apparent; it still felt like home.

So what have you been up to? What did you do for Christmas? I take it you flew down this morning? He lined up the questions as he set down a coffee on the table in front of her, knowing she would only answer the ones she cared to.

I drove, she said. I got here late last night; too late to disturb you. I thought I'd better come and see you before I head off. I'm going to Chile in a couple of weeks; I'll be away twelve months.

Work?

Yes, at the IAO. They've got a direct imager and they've just installed a spectrograph. We're trying to find exoplanets — planets from other solar systems — to see what we might learn from them.

He wouldn't be interested; she knew that. But she kept on, regardless. If we can actually get images of them, not just measurements, it would make an incredible difference, she said. I'll be coordinating one of the teams.

She wished it were her mother she was telling.

That sounds really impressive.

From the way her father shifted forward in his chair, making an effort to pay attention, Lotte knew he wished it were Helen she was telling, too.

Yes, it should be good, she said. Anyway, how are things with you?

With just one comment she fanned his interest away, sure that it was insincere. When was the last time she had spoken to him? Six months ago. If she left this afternoon, she'd be back in Canberra before midnight. Duty would be done, and Vin would be pleased with her efforts.

She'd not been listening. Her dad had told her something important; he was staring at her in anticipation.

Sorry?

Her name's Alison. She was in your mother's book group.

I don't remember her.

She remembers you. I'm sure she'd like to see you again. I'll invite her to dinner. You will stay for dinner, won't you?

He got up from his chair, taking Lotte's empty mug from her hand.

Is it that important?

Her words halted her father on his way to the kitchen.

You don't have to, he said. I thought it might be nice if you met.

So Alison knew Mum?

Yes.

Isn't that weird?

What do you mean?

Well, she knows the woman she's replacing. The one she's competing against.

It's not a competition, Lotte. It's been four years.

He said it as though that was a long time.

Are you going to marry her?

She was ashamed by how quickly she'd turned into the petulant teenager, trying to elicit a boundary from him, to know how far he was going to take this new relationship. But it was absurd. What did he need a wife for?

Of course not, Lotte. It's nothing like that. He loaded the mugs into the dishwasher, and crouched down to turn it on. Look, I've got to get some things done in the garden before I go away, he said when he stood up. You can help me if you want?

He was edging toward the door, even as he said it.

I might go catch up with some friends, Lotte said. It's been a while.

Okay, that's great. Come back for dinner; I'll tell Alison.

And he was out into the backyard, pulling the sliding door hard behind him, taking the steps two at a time, and disappearing around the fuchsia bushes to the garage.

Lotte recalled one wet spring when her school had run a father-daughter games night. Amongst the celebrity heads and charades, the teachers had organised team games like tunnel ball, tag, and tug of war; games that demanded too much from cripplingly self-conscious fourteen-year-old girls, who were no longer able to fling their bodies about with abandon. The fathers were eager to demonstrate their jokey friendships with their daughters, and they clowned about enthusiastically, ribbing each other about their middle-aged bodies, reminiscing about their days on the football field. Standing side-by-side in the gym, Lotte had shared a look of alarm with her dad, and then a furtive smile. She had rolled her eyes and her dad had winked, and then, together, they had slipped out of the gym and run across the oval to where the car was parked on the basketball courts. They'd stopped at the McDonald's drive thru on the way home and they ate their food parked by the lake, the sweet, sticky smell of the burgers filling the car. It was relief she'd felt, more than anything else, as they drove home, her father not complaining when she switched the radio to Triple J. He *does* like me, she'd thought, as they trooped back into the house, ready to tell Helen about the sheep-like behaviour of the other fathers and daughters, and their own daring escape. But the living room was empty, the television silent in its corner: her mother wasn't home. And her dad had gone straight to his study, closing the door behind him, without even saying goodnight. Why did she think things were going to be any different now?

As a family, they brought to Lotte's mind Methuselah, the oldest known planet and part of a bizarre triple system. Deep in the Scorpius constellation, this ancient planet circles a pulsar and a white dwarf, the three bodies keeping discordant harmony. The system is destined to trail into the globular cluster in which it lives and encounter, too closely, another star, which will throw the system off balance. As the lightest of the three, it will be Methuselah that is unceremoniously ejected and left to wander through space alone, a rogue planet with no star to answer to.

As a child, Lotte had always thought it would be her father who would eventually disappear — drifting unnoticed to a place Helen and Lotte's mother-daughter indifference could not reach. She always suspected that he hoped it would be her. Neither of them thought it would be Helen, and could barely believe it when it actually happened — father and daughter left to play at being a family, long after her departure.

Lotte knew she should be heading back to the house. She had spent the afternoon walking around the lake, lingering in cafes and checking her phone for any kind of distraction. She had no friends to visit; she just didn't want to be making conversation with her father while he looked longingly at the garden or his watch. She ordered another drink. The bar was massive, a converted pub on the main street; voices bounced off the floorboards, while table numbers sprouted from amongst bowls of chips and plates of lurid-orange tandoori chicken pizza. Having bought one glass of wine and finished it too soon, she'd ordered another within minutes of sitting down. Couldn't she just stay here for the evening? The night's crowds were trickling in; posters on the wall proclaimed Christmas drink specials. *Two-for-one Vodka Cruisers and Coronas!* Six boys arrived in their new check shirts, hair swept across their foreheads.

What do you order in a bar where the average age is eighteen? No, make that seventeen.

With her phone pushed to her ear, Lotte watched the girls teeter in, clutching at purses and phones, lifting their stacked shoes high, stiletto spikes causing them to waver and bump up against each other like seahorses.

A dry martini, laughed Eve. Without a doubt. Where are you? At Mooseheads?

God, that place was awful.

Just the name of the dive all the uni students used to drink at was enough to bring back the smell of old beer in carpet and the feel of soggy cardboard coasters.

No, I'm in Ballarat, said Lotte. I'm visiting Dad.

At a dodgy bar? Eve sounded sceptical.

No — but I had to escape, said Lotte. I've been avoiding going back to the house all day, and now here I am in some kind of school holiday hellhole. Where are you?

Down the coast. I found a really nice campsite not far from Merimbula. Beach views, bike tracks — what more could a girl need?

Sounds alright, even to me.

One day I'll get you on a bike, laughed Eve. So what's up with your Dad? How come you're there?

Vin guilted me into it after Christmas at his parents. Said I should see Dad before I go to Chile.

So you told him?

Yes.

And?

He was pretty peeved. But he's okay now. He knows I have to go, Lotte said. This kind of career opportunity doesn't come twice.

Ah Vin — he's always been such a sweetie.

Lotte took a sip of her wine and didn't answer. She watched as three girls leaned into one another at the bar, peering at a cocktail list. Behind them, a group of boys stood self-consciously, each with one hand wrapped around the reassurance of a beer, the other thumb-swiping at a phone, and all of them talking past one another, not making eye contact for more than a moment, instead keeping an eye on the girls at the bar, or on the door for new arrivals.

Did *your* dad ever see other women? asked Lotte. After your mum?

No, said Eve slowly. I don't think he even considered it. But he barely left the house. Why?

Dad has a girlfriend. Alison. She actually knew Mum — can you believe it? They were in a book club together.

Lotte tried to imagine her dad taking Alison on a date. Where would they go in a town like this, a place of cafes and nightclubs and not much in-between? And what on earth would he talk about? His boring job at the council, drawing up maps? His garden?

I guess it's a small town, said Eve. There's probably not a huge dating pool. It must be weird though, to see him with someone else.

I haven't met her yet, said Lotte. We're having dinner tonight; it's going to be awful.

She might not be that bad.

I just don't know how he could be ready to see someone already. It's only been a couple of years. It still feels like Mum is around, you know?

She'll always be around; Alison won't change that.

I know, said Lotte, her voice small.

Eve had been like this throughout her mother's illness. Solicitous and reassuring. Vin's sympathy was unwavering, but it was Eve who offered the hours of conversation Lotte needed to come to terms with what was happening. When she complained about her mother reading excerpts from a prayer book, or confessed how repulsed she was by her mother's disappearing body, Eve didn't shy away. Instead, she asked questions, pushed and pulled the conversation well into the night, letting Lotte dissect it from every angle before finally putting it aside.

Summer-evening shadows sidled up the main street, a landscape so familiar it almost felt as though her mother might turn up, and Lotte realised she would never be privy to what her mother would have made of Alison. Inexplicably, even years after her mother's death, Lotte could still be shocked by the absoluteness of it. Her mother was never coming back; she did not exist any more. Lotte could conjure up Helen's face effortlessly: the expressive mouth, the fine lines around her eyes. She remembered the way her mother had laughed, hooting almost, eyes dancing, and the way she'd run her fingers along strands of her hair, from the base to the tip, when she was concentrating. She used to eat yoghurt for breakfast, with a sliced banana on top of it, though in winter it was porridge instead. And she'd often left cups of tea, half drunk, all around the house, never satisfied they were hot enough. Lotte knew all of these things, but she would never know what her mother thought of Alison. This didn't seem possible.

The voices paused in their conversation as she came down the hallway, then picked up again as she ducked into the bathroom. She ran the tap, splashing her face with water, drinking some of it greedily from her hand. She shouldn't have had that last glass of wine, but the walk home had done her good. She could do this; she could find out what her mother might make of it all by asking the very same questions that Helen would have asked.

You must be Alison.

Lotte rushed in to the living room, where her father and a woman were seated on the couch, a platter of cheese and biscuits in front of them on the coffee table. Too late, Lotte realised she hadn't dried her hands, grabbing at Alison's arms and feeling the skin slip as she bent in to kiss her on both cheeks. And because it seemed strange not to, she bent and kissed her father, too, the smell of his aftershave the same as she remembered.

It's nice to see you again, Lotte.

Alison smiled at her, nervously tucking her blonde hair behind her ear, anxious lines dipping in the middle of her forehead. She was wearing a white T-shirt striped with navy beneath an emerald cardigan with cropped sleeves. Lotte did remember her. She used to wear pearls, all the time. Dropping her children off at school, doing the supermarket shopping, playing tennis. Helen had thought her pretentious.

It was all Lotte could manage to carry on the conversation, so caught up was she in watching the way her father and Alison treated each other. He was attentive — filling up her wine glass, going to get more biscuits, including her in his answers — and in return, she was gracious. Is this how her parents had been together? But her mind kept coming up blank. Memories of each of them abounded, but always separate from one another. When the conversation flagged, Lotte encouraged Alison with questions about her job as a speech therapist at the local hospital; she asked where Alison got her hair cut, and admired the gold bracelet that encircled her wrist. A gift from Lotte's father, as she had suspected.

How did the two of you meet?

She'd waited until they'd moved out to the deck before she asked, her dad firing up the barbecue, Lotte and Alison sitting in the light-fall from the lounge room, looking out at the shadows of the yard, the vegetable garden a smudge across the lawn.

We knew each other through your mother, of course, said Alison. *But we were reacquainted through a social night at the gallery. A speed-dating night.*

She giggled at this, apologetically. Everything about this woman was muted and polite. Answers calibrated to not offend, giving just enough response to move the conversation along, but not so much she might actually direct it anywhere. Her voice went up at the end of every sentence, as though she wasn't sure of anything she was saying, and her hands fluttered about her face, smoothing down her hair, checking her necklace was sitting right, dusting her chest for dropped crumbs. It surprised Lotte that her father had gone looking for this after someone like Helen. Lotte pictured him sitting at a long table, a name badge stuck to his chest, hoping against hope that there was a woman in this town who might be right for him.

And you hit it off?

She barely bothered hiding the disbelief in her voice.

Yes, we seemed to.

Alison looked fondly over at Lotte's father, as he went back into the kitchen to get something.

He's a nice man, your dad.

What do you remember about my mother?

Alison smoothed back her hair, took a sip of wine.

Helen was a lovely woman. I didn't know her that well, just from the book club, and school. But she was fun to be around, wasn't she? Vivacious, I suppose you'd call her. It's terribly unfair, what happened. I mean, we were all shocked. She was always someone who was so very much alive.

And now she's not. Which is quite convenient for you, isn't it?

Alison giggled nervously then pursed her lips, lines appearing again across her forehead. She didn't say anything more; she wouldn't bite. Lotte watched her dad come back to the deck balancing a plate of uncooked meat, wondering what Alison saw in him. As the meat hit the barbecue in a sizzle, she continued.

You're divorced, I'm guessing?

Alison nodded.

There wouldn't be very many eligible men of your age in a

town like this, would there? I mean, you've really hit the jackpot, haven't you?

That's not very fair.

Alison spoke softly but firmly, enunciating every word. A speech therapist trait?

I remember my mother coming home from meetings of that book club, said Lotte. And she'd have us in hysterics with her stories of all you women, dressed up and with your best baked goods on show as though you'd just rustled them up in five minutes. Trying so hard to be literary, searching out themes in the novels as if they might actually *mean* something.

What are you two talking about?

Her dad came over from the barbecue, tongs in hand, and gave Alison's shoulder a squeeze.

Should only be a few more minutes, he said.

We were just discussing our favourite novels, said Alison.

Books?

He laughed at this, heading back to the barbecue.

Lotte must be pulling your leg, Al, she doesn't read; she doesn't have time for what she thinks is a load of rubbish. Do you?

Reading make-believe stories? No, I don't.

It was an old argument, and Lotte slipped easily into the role her mother had also played. Helen was forever reading books and lambasting them for trying so hard to be realistic when they were so obviously a construct — why couldn't they just admit to being an art, a plaything?

Why read fictional stories when you could be discovering useful facts? Ways to make the world a better place?

She means space, her father called out from the barbecue. That's the only thing Helen thought worthy of consideration, and Lotte's just as bad. They take it *very* seriously.

Even with his back to her, she could hear the amusement in his voice.

Think about a novel, said Lotte. It's about made-up people going about their made-up lives. What does it really teach you about anything you don't already know? People can be nice, they can be awful, bad things can happen. End of story. But think about space, about the cosmos. You start looking there, and you really have to think about things. About where we come from and where we're going. Useful things, things that can actually change our understanding of the world, not just how we *feel* about it.

So art and personal experience are of no use, is that it? Her father flipped the steaks onto a plate and delivered them to the table. Despite all the meaning they give us, the sustenance and language to express our emotions and share our human experience. Pointless, all of it?

Not pointless, replied Lotte. Just not important.

Her dad winked at Alison, passing her the salad.

And I suppose you think what you do is *very* important? Looking for planets too far away for us to even reach. Planets we can't get to, we can't live on, we can barely see … *That* may as well be make-believe for all the difference it makes to this.

He included both of them in his gesture. *The good life*, his open arms were saying.

You know it's worthwhile. Take Alison's job as a speech therapist, said Lotte, including Alison with a generous smile, but directing her comments to her father. She teaches people to communicate after a stroke, and she knows what's effective because of science. And your job, Dad — drawing maps. It's practical and useful. That makes it worthwhile. At least, it was before Google took over.

Lotte remembered going to visit her father at work when she

was young. A day home sick from school, perhaps? The office he shared with four others was cluttered with poster tubes and stacks of paper. There were filing cabinets with skinny drawers where a lot of the maps were kept, and whiteboards with lists of projects. Most intriguing had been her father's desk, set at a slant and with a chair so high he'd had to lift her off the ground to put her on it. There were rulers attached to the edges of the desk; they could be moved up and down, meeting at right angles across the paper. He had showed her the project he was working on at the time, something to do with a new gold mine that was going to be tunnelled under the town. The different maps were drawn on sheets of plastic — water pipes, electricity, roads, telephone cables, gas pipes — and when they were all layered on top of each other, they looked like a pile of pick-up sticks.

His desk now would be completely different. She doubted he even drew by hand any more; it would all be done on computers. New suburb divisions, communications cabling, stormwater drains. He probably even used Google Maps as his starting point, his job slowly devoured, like so many others, by the rise of the internet.

Just like your mother, hey?

Her father took a mouthful of steak, raising his eyebrows in a warning she could read clearly, despite it never having been aimed her way before. A look that she'd only ever seen him give her mother. *Be nice.*

Well, I guess we'd all know, wouldn't we? After all, we all knew Mum. Lotte took a sip of wine, relishing the antagonism even as she told herself to tone it down. And here we all are without her. Isn't life strange?

I'm not exactly sure what you're getting at, Lotte, said her Dad, giving Alison a reassuring smile. And it was that, more than anything, that made Lotte snap.

She's not even been gone four years, and here you are, ready to replace her. It's insulting. To her, to me. And to Alison.

The words came so easily; she slammed them down on the table.

This isn't about me, said Alison. She had put down her cutlery, wiped her mouth with a napkin.

It is, though, said Lotte. She felt a reckless surge of protection toward Alison, while simultaneously wanting to hurt her.

You've walked in here a stranger to all of this. It's only fair you know how things really are. My mother is still very much a part of our lives, and you should be aware of that.

Lotte turned to her dad.

I mean, how is Alison supposed to feel when the house is still full of Mum's things? Doesn't that say something? There are things here she had before she even met you.

Or you. His reply was sharp.

I grew up in this house; it's my childhood home. This house is full of my memories.

But it's not full of you, is it, Lotte? You've come back here, what, twice in four years? You couldn't care less.

He held her gaze, a challenge. I think you should leave.

You're kicking me out of my own house?

You don't live here.

Lotte could see him reach out for Alison's leg, but she was sitting too far away and he had to retreat.

But Alison will be living here, won't she? When you get married? You might have to get rid of some of Mum's things then. Or will you just sell, move somewhere else? Have you even considered how I might feel about that?

That's none of your business.

He stood up, the chair clattering behind him on the deck.

I think you've said enough, Lotte.

I might go home, said Alison. She stood as well, not looking at either of them, her hands smoothing her hair.

No, you don't have to leave.

Even as he stretched out for her hand, Alison pulled away.

I'd rather go.

No, Lotte's leaving.

But with a little shake of her head, Alison was through the sliding door in seconds, a terrorised rabbit fleeing for safety, father and daughter watching as she scooped her handbag off the bench and disappeared down the hallway.

Look what you've done.

Lotte stared at the salad on her plate, the lettuce slick and brilliant green, a single white disc of radish like a full moon. Everything from her father's garden; she hadn't even known he liked gardening.

You can do better than Alison. You deserve better. You can't go from someone like Mum to … to someone like that.

You barely knew your mother, he said, sitting back down. You've got this idea of her that's not real. You were her child, so she treated you like a child. You don't know what she was really like.

We were close. Closer than …

Than we were? Perhaps. He shrugged his shoulders. But that hardly matters now, does it?

So that's it. You just forget Mum and move on to an entirely new life?

It's not about forgetting.

He picked up his cutlery as though the conversation was finished. But then he put down his knife and fork, his hands in his lap.

Do you remember the way she could switch on and off? Her

134

interest, her intensity? Don't you remember the times she used to ignore you?

The silences in the car after being picked up from school; her mother leaving the house, not mentioning where she was going or when she'd be back, even when Lotte was really too young to be left alone. The fact that her mother could never remember a single one of Lotte's friends' names, asking them to introduce themselves again and again over the years, much to Lotte's embarrassment.

It wasn't personal, she said. She was scatty like that.

She was selective.

He began scraping the unfinished meals onto a single plate.

She knew herself, said Lotte. She knew what she wanted.

He laughed at this, shaking his head in open astonishment. You really didn't know her at all. She had no idea what she wanted. No idea at all. Yet we all had to sit back and watch her figure it out.

Lotte felt something shift inside of her at his words.

She wanted a career, she said. You know she wanted to be a scientist, not a science teacher. Why do you think she did all of that volunteering with the astronomy club, all those nights at the observatory giving talks to tourists?

He didn't answer for a moment, stacking the plates.

Is that where you think she was?

Of course that's where she was. What would you know? You'd just be in your study every night, doing whatever it was you do with your time. Drawing your stupid maps. She wanted a career, a proper one. She wanted to be an astronomer. But you went and got her pregnant, and that's what held her back.

And now you're living out her dreams, is that it?

He stood up, picking up the dishes.

There's nothing wrong with wanting more. You always wanted to punish her for that. Why couldn't you support her instead of holding her back?

Well, I guess it's too late for that, he said, and went inside.

She needed him to be contrite, defeated. But all she could see was how alive he was, how real. The muscles flexing across his calves, the weight of his step sounding out on the floorboards. It wasn't fair, that he was the one to survive.

She dreamt she was on a space shuttle, cramped and folded into the tiny space of a hull. The shuttle seemed to stretch to accommodate her each time she moved, then contracted slowly, forcing her to tuck her arms tightly beneath her until her hands went numb and she woke feeling she was tethered to the bed, heavier than a body had any right to be. On Jupiter, her body would weigh two and a half times its usual weight — her muscles wouldn't know how to move her limbs, her heart would quickly tire. Not for the first time, she noted that a hangover is simply the assertion of gravity. The blood draining from your brain, because your heart finds it too difficult to pump. Your vision narrowing; your ribcage too hard to lift.

The sun was blocked by the blinds, but still light squeezed in around the edges and flaunted itself about the room. She felt her stomach rise up to meet her rib cage and swallowed rapidly. She didn't want to face her father, not just yet. Memories of last night circled her consciousness, and she batted them away. She needed a glass of water.

The benches of the kitchen were clean; the outdoor table had been completely cleared. A pineapple sat near the stove. It hadn't been there yesterday. She took a knife from the second drawer, a chopping board from behind the stove top, instinctively knowing her way around the kitchen. Saliva pooled in her mouth as she cut the base off the pineapple, the sweet smell of it making her gag, so that she had to grab for a glass, drink down a mouthful of water. She sliced a round, cutting off its skin and notching out the eyes. He must have bought the pineapple this morning. For her? Or had he simply forgotten to put it in the fridge? Vin said it was a tradition, to have a pineapple in the house if you were expecting guests. He'd bought one the time her parents had stayed with them in Canberra, planting it in the middle of the table like a portly overseer and slicing it up at dinner, not caring that it didn't go with the chocolate mousse.

Her father and Alison had gone to the beach. That's what the note said. Port Fairy, a long way down the coast, and they'd be there the rest of the week until New Year's Day. *You're welcome to stay at the house, or to join us, but I didn't want to wake you.* It was polite necessity that had him including the invitation, she was sure: she wasn't going to turn up on his holiday, nor would he want her there. Lotte even felt a rush of relief to see Alison's name there, to know that she hadn't been run off completely.

She thought about going back to bed. She'd slept in her old bedroom, but it could have been anyone's, her teenage belongings long gone. There was an exercise bike in the corner, and a vacuum cleaner. An old couch was pushed up against the wardrobe, piled with boxes. Lotte lifted the flap of one and skeins of wool sprang free. Purple and white, the strands twisted like wildberry ice-cream. She recognised the jumper her mother had been knitting back then, and idly thought about finishing it off before realising that she couldn't. She had no idea how to read a pattern, and she dropped so many stitches that her mum had always fixed the holey mess for her when she reached the end of a row.

Sipping her coffee, she wandered through the house. All

the decorations — the wall hangings, the vases, the bookends — were her mother's. Four years on, and you still couldn't tell he lived there, or anything about him except that he was tidy. She realised then that there were no photographs in the house. It was this, not the tidiness of the house, that really marked its difference. Her mother had been a great one for memories: the fridge covered with photographs, more of them framed and crowded onto dressers and bookshelves. Lotte walked through each room of the house, looking. Not a single photograph anywhere. Of anyone. He must have put them all away.

She hesitated before entering her father's bedroom. The wardrobe was empty on what had been her mother's side, the white shelves bare. Lotte was just about to let the wardrobe door close when she saw, on her father's side, a huddle of perfume bottles on one of the shelves, behind his folded jumpers. She picked one up, sniffed, and was immediately taken back to her mother's embrace. It was a childhood smell, triggering the recollection of one moment when Lotte had so completely captured her mother's attention that she was almost breathless with the anticipated disappointment of losing it. She could understand why he kept these.

It had been the school holidays: grey rain drizzling, the whole sky made of cloud, and no shadow to tell the time of day. Lotte had created a cubby house beneath the dining table — blankets for walls; chairs and the clotheshorse put into service as awnings. At nine years old she was too old for this kind of play, she knew, and she had left her dolls on the shelf of her room (though she was still worried they might resent her for it). She had a set of cards, each one decorated with a different type of dog and their defining characteristics and personality traits, and she was categorising them in an attempt to find the one she wanted most, and then make a case for her parents to buy it for her. Her mother had delivered Lotte's lunchtime sandwiches to her, sliding them in under one of the blankets without comment. *Thank you, Mum*, Lotte had written on the note she delivered back, and beneath it a grid listing her five favourite types of dogs, with ticks that showed they met all the necessary requirements. *Friendly; quiet; short hair; can be trained; cute.* Something in this note must have amused her mother, because her face appeared, light flooding the hideaway.

I see you've been busy. Can I come in?

Yes.

But even as she wriggled over into a corner, making space for her mother, Lotte had been unsure how to proceed. Delighted by Helen's unexpected presence, she was already dreading the moment she would leave.

So you've been doing your research on dogs?

I want to make sure I pick the best one.

And then what?

And then we can get one. Maybe.

Maybe we can, her mother said. What else do you do in here? It's pretty dark.

I have a torch. Lotte handed it over to her mother, who flipped it on, holding it beneath her own face.

Do I look scary? Do you tell ghost stories?

Sometimes.

Her mother lay down on her back, and Lotte did the same. She could smell her mum's perfume, and thought it strange. It was her going-out smell; she rarely wore it around the house. The torchlight danced across the underside of the dining table.

If this was the sun, it would rise over here and set over there, her mum said.

The light obediently traversed the wood.

Then where does it go?

Around the other side of the world, so they can have day time. And we have night time.

So it keeps going round and round every day?

No, the Earth goes round the Sun.

Lotte kept quiet, not wanting to get it wrong.

Remember I taught you the planets? They all go around the Sun. It stays still.

Why don't they crash?

They have orbits. Like a track to follow. They can't move off the track; they can only go forwards. Hold this. Her mother handed Lotte the torch. Point it up, she said.

Lotte shone it at the underside of the table and watched as her mother took a yellow crayon and drew a circle, scribbling to fill it in with colour.

Using a different colour each time, she drew in all of the planets — purple Venus, red Mars, blue Saturn with orange rings.

Each one goes around the Sun, all in the same direction but at different speeds. Mercury's really fast, and it's closest to the Sun, so it has the quickest years. Jupiter is really big and it moves slowly, but spins super fast. So fast that it bulges in the middle. A year there takes twelve of our years, but a day is only ten hours long.

She drew the planets' orbits in white, looping in egg shapes about the sun. It reminded Lotte of the relay teams on sports days.

Do they pass each other?

Well, yes. But they're too far apart. It would take maybe twenty years for us to fly to Pluto. That's why we don't really know what it's like yet.

Do they line up?

They must, her mum said. Though I don't know how often.

She thought for a while. Maybe every thousand years?

For the first time, Lotte had suspected that there were things in the universe that even her mother didn't know.

All these years later, Lotte knew the answer herself. Putting the perfume bottle back in the wardrobe, she went into the living room. She pulled out one of the dining chairs from the table, and then another. It was probably no longer there; it looked like the table had been varnished since then. But she crouched, knees cracking with the effort and tried to see. There *was* colour, smudges of it at least, and she lay herself down on the floor, shuffled in beneath the table like a mechanic under a car, the blood rushing at her temples and momentarily blacking out her vision. There they were — the crayon planets as vivid as the day her mother had drawn them. And then she laughed out loud: she had forgotten her own contribution to the diagram, added only when her mother had tired of instruction and left Lotte once again to her own devices. In the centre of the drawing, the sun was sporting black sunglasses and a devilish grin, and the entire universe had been hemmed in by a border of pink and orange petalled flowers, every one of them wearing sunnies.

It wasn't every thousand years, she wanted to tell her mum now. There was less chance than one in a billion of the planets lining up. The inner six planets align in the same quadrant once or twice a century, but, because of each planet's differing right ascension, they will never be all in a row like a school project diorama. It was near impossible, but nothing was ever completely impossible. One chance in a trillion billion million, perhaps?

6

EVE

Unzipping the door of her tent, Eve's eyes seek out the feathered treetops reaching for the lightening sky. The moon has long since dipped below the horizon, while Venus has stepped into her role as morning star. The rain has stopped hours before; by now, Len is no doubt snoring in his bed, his concern for her safety forgotten. In the pre-dawn everything holds still, letting the water sink and settle. Time to look for fairies.

Eve walks through the campsite and crosses the highway. The dunes are banked high, waves calmly sloshing forth and retreating as she slides and slips her way past where the sand has been pockmarked by rain. The sea has followed the moon, pulling back from its morning high — a house-proud matron sweeping the sand clean in her wake. No street lamps or houselights are visible from here. It is only a small beach, a cove really, where summer holidaymakers are discouraged from swimming by the absence of a surf club or even a patrolled stretch of sand: families trudge around the headland for that, or drive back into Lorne. Back when Eve was still part of a family, that's what they had done. Tom watching from the beach as Eve floated beyond the breakers, her pregnancy seemingly put on hold as the weight of

142

Mina was dismissed by the gentle swell of the sea. It was Tom who'd first brought her here to this beach. The summer before Mina was born: a year after Lotte had left.

*

Stretching her leg into the sun, Eve stood, body stiff, and picked up her bike. She'd come a cropper on a corner towards the end of a track that snaked its way through the hills and gullies of the national park: she banked too tightly, and the bike slid out from underneath so that she scraped her leg on a rocky outcrop. It hurt like hell, and while she'd rummaged in her backpack for water to clean up, her phone had rung. Lotte. A haphazard story of how she'd disgraced herself with her father's new girlfriend, and how, despite the fact she had come all that way, he had now disappeared on holiday. Eve had let her talk, offering the right encouragements, flexing her calf and watching the blood trickle toward her ankle, and then dry and flake in the heat. It was only as they were about to say goodbye that Lotte had mentioned something more serious.

Hang on, said Eve. So you had the tests done, but you didn't get the results?

She was incredulous. It was so unlike Lotte, who always needed to search out an answer for everything.

There's no point, Lotte had replied. I either have the mutation of the gene or I don't. Knowing about it won't make any difference. It's not as though there's a solution.

But if you knew, you could try to prevent getting cancer, said Eve. She didn't understand Lotte's flippancy.

The only prevention is major surgery; it would mean early menopause — can you even imagine what that might be like? I'm only thirty, Eve. Would you put your hand up for that? It's not even about having kids, but think of what that would do to my body — hormones all over the place, hot flushes — it would be horrible.

But you must, whispered Eve into the quiet.

Look, I don't want to live in fear; I don't want to be making all my decisions based on the possibility of this one thing. I just want to get on with living. That's what Mum always wanted — she hated how she became this sick person, how everything became about the cancer.

Lotte talked on, and Eve stared out over the bush, her gaze running up the drip-bark trunks of the shedding gums to their canopy, green against a rude blue sky. She must make Lotte change her mind. After almost fourteen years of friendship, she could not imagine a world without Lotte in it.

How long are you in Ballarat for? asked Eve. Maybe I'll come down? I'm on the coast; I don't have to be back in Sydney until mid January.

All the way here? Only another day or so, said Lotte. Dad's gone down to the coast anyway, but part of me just wants to hide out here; try not to antagonise Vin.

It's only about eight hours, maybe less, said Eve. I'll leave early tomorrow; I'll be there by mid-afternoon. She tried to hide the urgency in her voice, knew how flighty Lotte could be if she detected sympathy. But it wasn't just that. In the back of Eve's mind, she realised a trip down to Ballarat was the perfect excuse to stay away from Sydney and any surprise visits from Nate. She had let his calls go unanswered, but she wasn't confident of her resolve should she see him in person. The further away she was, the better.

Really? Lotte's voice brightened as she thought about it. Only if you're sure.

Eve had bought the campervan years ago while still a student, finding it justified her desire to leave town at the end of every week and drive as far as she could, looking for anywhere to bike or to record new sounds. Sometimes Stu came with her, bringing his own bike; sometimes Lotte, with a stack of data that she would work through while Eve cycled, meeting up in the evening to eat and talk long into the dark, as moths and mozzies ducked and weaved in the lamp light.

After she had explored the mountain-bike trails near Canberra, Eve took to taking a second bike with her, a road one, for all the times she couldn't find any suitable mountain paths. Despite her initial hesitation, she came to like road cycling almost as much — it didn't offer the thrill or adrenalin of mountain biking, but the exhaustion at the end of the day was the same, and it was only with that that she would be ready to face another week.

One summer, she drove north into Queensland, zigzagging between the coast and inland rainforests. She strapped wooden planks to the roof racks and laid them down each night to drive onto, so she wouldn't get bogged on the muddy verge. Sometimes, when she got to a part of the road that was too rough for the van, she'd pull onto the shoulder and unstrap her bike from the rack, fill a drink bottle and set off into the hills. The rain scored the road with turbid rivers that seemed to summon her tyres, the bike impervious to the application of brakes as she slid her way forward. She'd return to the van covered in mud and scratches, before driving back the way she had come and taking the smooth tourist highway to the next town.

When she moved to Sydney, she thought about getting rid of the van. Each time she passed it on the way to work, she was reminded of how urban-bound her world had become. But it still gave her the means she needed to get out of the city, giving her the opportunity to mountain bike, to record new elements for her soundtracks, to keep busy with her projects so that she had no time to be lonely. No time to think about what Nate might have been doing, and who he was doing it with.

Driving into Ballarat in the late afternoon, Eve felt the engine shuddering, the seat beneath her too warm. The van was due for a service, but it had always been reliable. She found Lotte's street easily, trying not to think too much about the strange clunk as she switched off the engine; she would have to look into it tomorrow. Now that she was in Victoria she might head along the coast; take any road that would keep her far from Sydney, and from Nate's push for answers.

She remembered the house from Helen's funeral a few years before; an old-style bungalow with a deep porch and bright-blue front door. The funeral must have been held about the same time of year as now: the trees dropping their leaves in the heat, for all the world looking as if it was autumn; the front lawn faded and yellow. Despite having known Lotte for over a decade at a time, she'd only met Helen a couple of times: once when she visited Lotte in Canberra, and then at Lotte and Vin's wedding, which had taken place a few months before she died. A fraught affair, the wedding joy had threatened to dissipate under all the undeclared emotion, each of the few guests knowing why it was taking place so hurriedly, none of them able to wish the couple happiness for the future without stealing a look at Helen, slouched in a chair, a too-bright scarf wrapped around her head, washing out her features.

Eve brushed those memories away and rang the doorbell. And there was Lotte, dark hair dripping wet, wearing a pink dress patterned with bright orange lobsters, their claws snapping at the air. As a piece of clothing it made no sense — the colours clashed, the print was nonsensical and almost childish — but on Lotte it looked just right, hitched to her curves and flaring from her waist.

I'm so glad you're here, I was starting to get bored! Lotte embraced Eve on the doorstep, talking the entire time. I've just made iced tea. Dad has all this mint in his garden, I've been adding it to everything.

Within moments they slipped right into their comfort zone, interrupting each other's sentences with gentle jibes, miming disbelief at stories retold for maximum laughter. Lotte mocked Alison, and her own immature jibes from the night before, seeking Eve's reassurance that she hadn't behaved as badly as she knew she had.

She was just so ... prim! Lotte searched about for an excuse, laughing at her own childishness.

Your poor father. All he wants is a lady friend, one that he probably knows doesn't live up to Helen, and he gets you on his doorstep, making fun of him. Eve knew exactly what Lotte was like when she had opinions. She could barely remember what the father looked like — could recall only a tall, quiet man, politely accepting the multitudes of condolences after the funeral.

I just know Mum would have found Alison ridiculous. And he knows that! Surely he could do much better.

It's a small town, said Eve, raising an eyebrow. Perhaps it's slim pickings.

The afternoon slipped into evening, the iced tea was replaced with mojitos, and eventually, as she knew she would, Eve told Lotte about the re-emergence of Nate.

No. Lotte pursed her lips, suddenly serious, shaking her head with certainty. No, Eve, you can't go back there. He was a total cad to you! How long were you in Sydney before he went and found someone else? A month?

It was five months.

No way, you deserve better than that.

He's not that bad, said Eve. You just never liked him. Anyway, I've told him I'm not interested. That it's been too long.

As if that's the only reason. I liked him well enough, Eve, I just think he treated you like dirt. Did you ever find out whether he was seeing Katie while you were still living in Canberra?

No.

Well, you don't want to know. Don't go and get involved with him now.

I won't! I've already told him it's over.

So you were seeing him?

It was nothing; it was just a few times.

Lotte rolled her eyes, and then smiled. Well, thank God you're here, because I know exactly what you're like. I can just see him turning up at your door again with two kids in tow and you taking pity on him.

Eve knew Lotte was right. But Lotte didn't know what Nate was like. What it felt like to have that impetuous energy turned on you. The way it was impossible not to go along with everything he said. She remembered so clearly the phone call that had ended their relationship years before. He'd helped her find a flat and move to Sydney; he travelled up from Canberra every weekend, the harbour-side city a new playground for his enthusiasms. He made friends there — friends that she could call on in the long weeks of loneliness, although she rarely did. And then, after four months, he called to say he couldn't come that weekend, or the next. He didn't return her calls for weeks; he wasn't at home when she drove down to confront him. And then he phoned.

Eve! I'm so glad to have caught you.

For a moment she was convinced she had been the one who

had caused the absence, that she'd been too busy and unavailable. But every word of the following conversation was etched on her mind, as clear as any recording.

I wanted to let you know, I have news. I know it will come as a shock — it certainly did to me!

Nate? Where the hell have you been?

Eve's tone, angry despite her apprehension, reminded her of her parents.

That's what I'm trying to tell you, Eve. It all happened so fast. I'm getting married — we're having a baby!

He spoke the words as though they were things that had happened to him, a passive receptor. For a tiny moment, she thought she was included in the 'we'. All she could hear was his breathing; in the background, the squeaky rumble as a window sash was lifted.

Eve? Say something. I know it's a surprise, believe me; I didn't plan any of it.

She did believe him. Nate was a man who never needed to plan, whose untroubled future rolled ahead of him, yellow-bricked and gentle.

You're not joking, are you?

Hoping against hope, her stomach dropping away.

I wouldn't joke about something like this, not to you Eve, he said with admonishment in his voice, so that she was forced to take on the role of the antagonist rather than the slighted. How easily it came to him: the righteousness that he knew she wouldn't question.

You can't be too surprised, Eve. I mean, you left me, moved away — I was right here and willing. But you always wanted something more: Sydney, a career. It's not as though settling down and having a family was what you wanted, we both know that.

She would always regret that she didn't hang up on him then. Her wants were something they had never talked about. Dumbfounded, she let him continue for almost twenty minutes, listing his reasons and excuses. All the while small, fluting sounds nudged involuntarily from her throat, encouraging him on.

It's been really nice to talk to you, Eve.

A big breath then, as though he'd been holding it all this time.

I told Katie you would understand — I have to admit, I was a bit nervous about making this call, but you've made me feel alright.

In the eight years they'd known each other, it was exactly what she'd always done for him. Eve was devastated, even as she felt she should have seen it coming. She was almost too embarrassed to tell anyone, but when she called Lotte, her words nearly incomprehensible amongst the tears, Lotte had driven up to Sydney immediately and stayed a week on Eve's couch. Letting Eve cry, then pushing her to rage, and finally to laugh.

Sitting in the blush of summer dusk as Lotte refilled her glass, Eve knew she couldn't go through that again.

Just let him go, Eve. There's nothing for you there.

I know, I know. Eve stirred at her drink, trying to dissolve the sugar. But when I saw him, Lotte, he was just so *real*. You know? He was so familiar, he was right there and everything was easy. I mean, I've seen loads of guys in the last five years and not one of them has made me feel like that. What if he's the one? What if he really does need me?

That doesn't mean he gets to have you. Lotte snapped her glass down on the table, a judge's gavel. Don't do it, Evie. You just can't.

While Lotte cooked, Eve watered the garden, methodically stepping up and down the rows, marvelling at the vegetables and their simple optimism: ready to take on the next day, to grow a little larger, a little firmer. She pulled leaves off each of the herbs: pungent basil, tart lemon mint, dusty thyme. Was it possible to just move out of Sydney to the country? Some place Nate had never been, and would never go? Somewhere she could build a life that he had never touched? How could she still not know what she wanted? The one life she possessed already had him in it; for better or worse, all future men would be comparison studies. So why not return to the original, the one she knew best? That's the thought she had kept returning to over the last few weeks as Nate had kept returning to her bed.

After dinner they sat on the back deck. The full moon kept the night at bay; they could hear the neighbour's dog snuffling along the fence line.

So you got the tests done, but you haven't found out the results. Eve returned suddenly to yesterday's conversation, knowing it was best to catch Lotte off-guard. Lotte sighed, her annoyance clear, but Eve wouldn't let it go.

It's not like you, Lotte, to leave it up to chance.

It *is* still chance — knowing doesn't change the result, it just changes what I do about it.

Isn't it best to do something?

That's what Vin says. Lotte reached over to the fuchsia bush and popped open the bulb of a flower, its scarlet petals spreading to reveal a purple interior. Look, she said. It's like a planetary nebula, all colour and fireworks.

Eve watched her pop one bloom after another.

What does Vin think about you going to Chile?

He doesn't want me to go.

Really? Eve was surprised at this: Vin had always been so supportive of Lotte's career. Of Lotte.

Lotte shrugged, carrying on popping bulbs.

He thinks I'm putting things off, she said, eventually. Life things. Buying a house, having kids. But it's such a good opportunity — I can't turn it down. We never know if there's going to be funding for these kinds of projects; we have to jump on it when we can.

She spoke at length then of planets near and far. Of the way the solar system had been searched for clues of life: inaccessible oceans discovered on the moons of Jupiter beneath kilometres of packed ice; ancient river beds on Mars; geysers of water vapour and ice on Saturn's Enceladus moon. She told Eve about the missing planet: how the rock and debris of the asteroid belt followed an orbit as definite as any planet's but was never allowed to become one, because the gravity of the sun pulled at the broken pieces from one side while the mass of Jupiter tugged from the other. Like divorced parents whispering in a child's ear: *Come this way. No, come this way*, until undecided became unformed, a planetary dream unrealised.

She told Eve how astronomers now had to look further afield for life, counting exoplanets in other systems and considering their chemical makeup to see what could be learnt. Another planet that could support life, if it came to that. It seemed ridiculous to Eve, too far away and unlikely to bother with. Concerns of the future, not the reality of the present. The world couldn't even recognise the Earth was dying, let alone coordinate a shift to a planet light years away.

Is Vin right though? Eve interrupted Lotte's talk, turning to face her. Are you putting things off?

She let Lotte see her smile; they'd always been good at pulling each other up in conversation, holding their answers up to interrogation.

The house, kids? Eve continued. All those things that people do. The things Vin wants to do?

She waited for Lotte's laugh, her recognition at being caught out, but her friend took a long time to answer, and when she did she spoke slowly, rising awareness in her voice.

No. No, I'm not putting things off. The words dropped out of her, heavy with reticence. The thing is, Evie, I don't actually want any of that ... I don't think I'll ever want it.

Kids?

Lotte shook her head. I don't. Definitely not now, and I don't think I ever will. A smile grew from her bemusement. You know, I'd never properly thought about it. I guess I just thought I would want them one day. That my biological clock would kick in.

It might, said Eve.

She had been surprised by her own yearning, which only grew over the years. Her envy for Nate, and everything he had with Katie. Was he really willing to throw that away? That's what it would amount to, if he chose Eve. The children relegated to weekend visits and sleepovers; Eve cast in the role of stepmother.

Lotte shrugged.

I guess, she said. But no. I don't think it will.

She stretched her arms up to the sky, lacing her fingers and pushing into the emptiness, as though a weight had literally been lifted from her shoulders.

I know it's what Vin wants, said Lotte. I keep telling myself that should be reason enough. But what if it isn't?

You have to talk about it with him.

Lotte slowly nodded. I know, I know.

She twirled one of the fuchsia blooms in her fingers. Tomorrow. I'll go back to Canberra tomorrow. Lotte stood, and began gathering glasses from the table. I feel bad that you came all the way down here, just for one night.

Eve recognised the closure in Lotte's tone. Already the discussion had been packed neatly away into the past, her mind switched to the next task.

That's okay, said Eve. I'll take the camper down the coast. I've got my bike with me, and it won't be as hot down there.

You can stay a couple of days, said Lotte. Dad won't be back until the end of the week. You could check out the mountain-biking trails out Sebastopol way. I think there's all these hills that are actually mullock heaps from the gold mines. Or come up and stay with us — anything to keep you away from Sydney and Nate. Lotte waggled her finger at Eve as she headed to the kitchen door.

And following her inside, Eve did her own bit of friendly mothering. And you get your results, she said. She waited until Lotte put down the glasses on the kitchen bench before grabbing her arm and pulling her into a hug. I mean it, she whispered, not letting go until she felt Lotte's nod.

You're not Lotte.

His voice jerked her out of drowsy complacency. Late morning. When the window's blind billowed in the breeze, light charged forward in strong lines, touching a water glass on the bedside table before landing as a rainbow across the wall. When the open window inhaled, the light dimmed.

It's Eve, isn't it? Lotte's Eve. There was amusement in his voice, and Eve turned toward the sound. A man leant against the doorframe, arms crossed.

Eve edged away from sleep, wondering where she was, letting the room fall into place. Lotte's house. Lotte's childhood house.

Yes.

I'm Tom. Lotte's father. I don't think we've met, not properly.

They *had* met, at Helen's funeral. The memories surfaced, one by one, like a jury sidling into the dock. Outside the church, Eve had shaken his hand, but then, feeling she had been too formal, she had leaned in to kiss his cheek, immediately becoming embarrassed that she had been too forward. During the service he had been ashen and composed. His thumb had stroked the head of the wooden pew continually, as if it were a reminder there were still things that were real and could be touched.

I don't suppose you know where Lotte is?

Tom took a step back, into the hallway, looking left then right as though his daughter might come around the corner.

She's gone back to Canberra, said Eve. She left at about six this morning. She said I could sleep here, that you wouldn't be back for a few more days.

Eve's embarrassment, lethargic with sleep, caught up with her. She was in this man's house. His bed. She clutched at the sheet, pulling it up to cover her chest even though she was clothed.

It's okay. I don't mind that you're here. And I don't bite.

A friendliness in his voice; a want to put her at ease.

I came back early, Tom said. Things weren't exactly working out down the coast. So I thought I might as well spend some time with my daughter. Who doesn't seem to be here.

As her eyes adjusted to the dark, Eve could make out Tom's features. A high forehead; slightly beaked nose; black-framed glasses.

She went back home, since you weren't here.

Well, sorry to disturb you. I'll let you get back to sleep. Tom pushed himself away from the doorframe, made as if to walk away and then paused. Though I'm about to make some coffee, if you'd like some?

Yes, sure. I'll join you. I … Her voice trailed off even as it sounded like she was going to say something more; the hesitation, the intake of breath at the end of her sentence. Tom waited; Eve waited.

Right, well, he said. I'll just be in the kitchen.

When he closed the door it slammed heavily, plunging the room back into dark. In response, the blind tapped gently at the windowsill, and Eve got out of bed, pulling on shorts and fastening a bra under her singlet. What must he think of her, sleeping in his bed like some kind of Goldilocks? She wished she had slept on the couch, but Lotte had insisted. She stuffed her clothes in her bag, looking around to make sure she was leaving nothing behind. Running her tongue over her teeth, she contemplated a shower, toothpaste. But she couldn't stand there in his en suite while he was waiting.

Opening the bedroom door, she thought about just slipping down the hallway and escaping. The front door was open, only a flyscreen door between her and the bright morning. Her camper van was parked just out the front, and she could simply disappear; she didn't want to be a nuisance. Nevertheless, she carried her bag into the living area: there would be too many explanations to make later if she just left. Lotte would think her ridiculous.

How do you have it? White? Black? Sugar? He had his back to her, his shirt stretched across broad shoulders; he was a man at ease in his own space, and she could only feel she was intruding.

Black, please.

Eve went red: she usually took her coffee with milk, but, already feeling like she was imposing, she didn't want to be demanding.

Tom passed her a mug.

At least she ate the pineapple, he said, seeming pleased.

The what?

I left her a pineapple. It's something Vin does, for guests. I thought it might make her feel at home.

Eve nodded, not sure what this conversation required from her.

I guess you won't see her again before she goes? said Eve.

To Chile? I guess not. I don't see her all that much anyway.

I suppose she lives quite far away. It must be hard to make the time.

When Tom didn't say anything, Eve kept talking into the silence: For both of you, I mean. You must both be busy, very busy and both live far away — from one another — it would take time … She tumbled from one word to another, making little sense.

The relationship between time and distance? said Tom, amused. I'm sure Lotte has a very complicated equation for that, and I can tell you now it doesn't involve speed. Certainly she's never in any hurry to see me. She was always closer to her mother. As you know.

Tom's eyes seemed to take her in then, measuring her against something known.

Eve laughed. Well, she's about to ditch her husband for a year, so I wouldn't take it too personally.

She felt a stab of shame, making fun of Lotte in her absence, but something told her that Tom understood.

Anyway, I really should get going. Eve stood, gulping her coffee, and the legs of the stool scraped rudely on the floorboards, leaving a long mark.

Shit, sorry.

Don't worry about it. I keep meaning to replace the little rubber stoppers on the feet, but I never get around to it. Too busy, I guess.

Eve heard the tease in his voice. They both contemplated the scratch on the floor.

Is that your van out front? The camper?

She nodded, seeing immediately the familiar powder-blue paint, seats of navy-and-cream vinyl plaid, the gear stick that poked out from the wheel column. A sticky reverse that you had to push up into. And then she remembered the clunk of the engine as she'd pulled in last night. Without some serious mechanical attention, it wasn't going to get her far today.

So that's your bike in the back? asked Tom.

Yeah?

You know a bit about them then, do you? Bikes? I've got this frame, see, an old bike I haven't ridden in years. Not since I was your age, probably.

They both blushed into the pause.

Anyway, I was thinking of doing it up, said Tom. New gear set, new seat, wheels, that kind of thing. The guys down at the shop told me it wasn't worth it, but I don't know if they're just trying to make a sale, make me buy something new. Or maybe they're right. Maybe it isn't worth it.

Show me.

Eve followed him out the sliding door, the house casting long morning shadows across the back garden and the vegetable patch. She almost ran up against him when he paused to unlock the garage's back door, and she had to jump back hurriedly, almost tripping on the hose she'd left lying across the path when she'd watered the night before.

Bloody Lotte. Never putting anything away. Just like her mother.

He bent to wind the hose back onto its bracket.

Sorry, that was me. I watered the garden last night, and I

guess I just left it lying there.

He paused, grinning. Bloody Eve, then?

She followed him into the garage. And it was there, crouched on the oil-stained floor of the garage, dust motes lingering in the angular light that wedged the door open, that she felt it. Familiarity. It wasn't déjà vu; there was no feeling that she had been there before, enclosed within that small moment. It was more that she would be there again: the two of them intent on something, on each other. It was the beginning of what seemed to have always been.

When Eve started her camper van, the clunking sound of something wrong was impossible to ignore. She and Tom lifted the bench seat to look at the engine, but the problem was not apparent. Eve drove the van slowly into town, Tom giving directions, Eve noticing how hot the engine was running beneath the seat, and trying not to panic.

I'll take a look this arvo, said the mechanic. Or maybe tomorrow. Sorry, got a lot on.

Eve looked around the almost empty garage.

You're lucky I'm even open, said the mechanic. Being holidays.

Tom and Eve walked back toward the house, Eve pushing her bike, Tom carrying a bag of her clothes, some books.

I can stay in a hotel, Eve offered. It could be a while — he doesn't seem to be in any hurry.

It's really no problem, said Tom. The house is near empty with just me rattling around in it. Don't waste your money. He smiled at her. Though I will want my bed back.

Back at the house, Tom made sandwiches. After lunch, he planned to spend some time in the garden. Unless there was something she wanted to do? They could go to a movie, perhaps? He offered the suggestion like an apology.

I'll take a walk, said Eve. I haven't seen much of the town before.

Make the most of it, said Tom, laughing. I can't imagine you having reason to come back any time soon.

As the sun retreated, they sat on the back deck drinking white wine, the condensation making rings on the table. Tom told Eve about his job as a cartographer, the way maps were both exacting and imprecise.

To map something is to simplify it, he said. You can only include what is necessary. You know the London tube map?

Eve nodded.

It's become the model for all metro maps. It doesn't show you where any of the stations are; it only shows you where to begin and end your journey, and the scale is irrelevant. The man who drew it was an electrical draftsman. He mapped the tube as though it was the passage of electricity through a circuit: it can go only forward, or be stopped and redirected. So he mapped the stations in relation to one another and the lines they were on, rather than in regard to the city above.

I once tried to map Canberra using only sound, said Eve. But I couldn't think outside of the geographic — where the sounds were located on an actual map. I didn't know how to let the sounds create their own landscape.

They talked long into the night, both of them conscious of time passing, neither of them making a move to bring the day to a close.

The next afternoon they walked around the lake, hands in

pockets, conversation easy. After forty minutes, when they had completed one lap, they set out again. And then again.

Tom was nothing like Lotte, and yet he was strangely known, as if all their conversation had already happened long ago and was simply being revisited. That night, Tom opened a second bottle of wine. He said later it was because he wanted to have an excuse: something to take the decision out of his hands. But in the end, it was Eve who decided.

They were sitting on the steps of the deck, the cement of the path beneath their bare feet still warm from the day.

I'm getting bitten, said Eve. She could hear the mosquitos hovering near the fuchsia bushes, the occasional one dive-bombing her with a whine, but always lifting too quickly to be slapped.

Time to call it a night, said Tom.

Eve pushed herself up off the steps, but before she got to standing, she paused. Sat back down. Their arms were touching now, their thighs, their knees.

Or we could stay up a little longer, said Eve. She kissed him, and then kissed him again, noting his lack of hesitation, as though he had been expecting this all along. She did not want to think about what she was doing. For as soon as she did, she pulled away.

I'm sorry; we shouldn't do this.

Foreheads touching, hands clasped.

Because of Lotte, said Tom. It was not quite a question.

Yes.

But she's not here.

This wouldn't happen if she was.

No.

Eve watched Tom's thumb stroke hers. She didn't want to let go.

How would we explain? said Eve.

She's not here, said Tom. She's never here, but we are.

And he took her hand, pulling her to her feet and into his arms.

Four months later she was back in Ballarat for the interview for the sound-and-light show. By the end of the year, a small wedding, at which they were each other's only family, Lotte's presence promised but not delivered. And Mina. Then there was Mina for them both to be intent upon, with her captivating and naive guile, her endless noise, laughter and demands, buoying them through the monotonous storms of daily life.

•

Eve stands alone on the beach. At this hour, and in this near night, it's uninhabited. Like one of those planets that Lotte spoke of: an Earth double, with a sci-fi sounding name and hope for the future. Do they know, these planets? As they're happily spinning about in outer space, are they aware of the peering intensity of Earth's inhabitants, all so willing to run away from past mistakes?

Eve remembers Lotte popping the unopened blooms of the fuchsia bush, an action Mina would make her own years later. A sisterly trait? She pushes the thought away and trudges through the soft sand, her calves complaining at the effort. Five years had passed before Eve saw Lotte again, their friendship a direct casualty of Eve's happiness with Tom and Mina. Five years she has always promised she wouldn't regret, and yet here she is without a thing to show for it.

7

LOTTE

The fox lets out a short squeal, its yellow eyes narrowing as it advances towards her, and Lotte takes another step backwards. She's reluctant to break eye contact in case the creature takes it as some kind of affront. Darting forward, the fox lunges, and then Lotte is slipping, her feet fleeing beneath her, her knee screaming pain as loose rocks cascade down the ridge. She lands on her back, wheezing, the wind knocked out of her, her lungs seizing up, and as she gapes at the air, mouth opening and closing, she thinks she might never breathe again.

It is probably less than a minute, but it seems like much longer before her lungs manage to draw in air. She is eight years old and flat on her back beneath the playground monkey bars, Mr Wilson running across the chip bark and kneeling by her side: *just breathe, just breathe, it will come back*. She draws in small coughs of air and then greedy longer drags. No one knows she is out here: as far as the observatory is concerned she is no longer an employee; she might have left the base already. Her breath dodges just out of reach, heart hammering. What time would it be back home? Early evening: Vin will be heading home from his office — she can picture him locking his door, crossing the campus as the streetlights come on. Dusk hanging high above the city, the kind unwillingness of summer to cede the day to night; a trail of red tail-lights as he drives out of the city. And that is it; she cannot picture any more. She had visited his new house once, back when he still referred to it as 'theirs'. *Sorting things out*, they had called it, newly awkward with each other.

Her breaths are coming slower now, each one longer than the last. Her knee is still pounding, jerking its pain along her leg, and the realisation lifts slowly into her conscious. She has dislocated her kneecap. *Shit*. She must have twisted too fast as she tried to back away from the fox, the ligaments giving way as easily as they had once done on the high school netball court, another time on a dance floor late at night. Both times a trip in an ambulance, painkillers as a doctor pulled her leg straight, popping the kneecap back into place and then holding it fast with a splint. Lotte tries to wriggle her toes, and groans at the shooting pain. She lifts herself onto her elbows and looks down at her leg. In the moonlight she sees her foot pointing left where it should go straight up. Already her body is giving up on her, setting out on its own course.

Trying not to panic, she concentrates on taking long, slow breaths, rolling her shoulders, twisting at the waist. Every other part of her is fine, and if she holds still her knee settles into a dull, bearable pain. Maybe this isn't too bad. Maybe if she just waits a while, lets her body relax, she will find the audacity to override the pain, straighten her leg, and pop the kneecap back into place herself. She lies down slowly, cursing herself for coming so far alone; she'd been unable to sleep earlier that night, playing out the next few days in her head. The checking in of her luggage; the long flight. And then what? Where will she go?

Ever since the diagnosis, she had thought about calling

Eve. But no matter how often the thought reoccurred over the following weeks, she dismissed it. They each had their own lives now; they had chosen different paths. Or rather, Eve had chosen a path too close to Lotte's own; Lotte had come to a standstill and watched Eve walk ahead, not once looking back.

Only a few months after arriving in Chile, Lotte had phoned the genetic-testing counselling office in Sydney. She bulldozed into the conversation and convinced the counsellor to give her the results over the phone, feeling like she was lying as she explained she was out of the country and couldn't attend the clinic, no matter their policy. *Positive*. For months she had trained herself to hear that word, playing out the moment in her mind again and again, in the hope that when she finally did hear it she would be immune to its meaning. Its promise of preventative surgery, of reconstruction, of removing parts of her that she tried to convince herself she would not miss.

But at the same time a smaller Lotte, one who lived deep inside, striding about empty rooms, heels striking floorboards with purpose: that small Lotte told her that the test would not come back positive. That if she imagined receiving the bad news often enough, it would not happen. She shied away from the logic that disputed this thinking, from the laws of probability that dictated her fate, and when the counsellor finally relented and gave her the results, she first felt a burst of satisfaction that she had gotten her way, and then shock at what had been said. *Positive*. She possessed the same defective gene that killed her mother. Brushing off the condolences, Lotte had thanked the counsellor and hung up, not wanting to hear about the following steps, the decisions to be made.

She'd done it — she'd heeded Vin and Eve's nagging and found out the results. But she was determined that nothing should change. The facts remained the same; only her knowledge of them had altered. Even so, Lotte discovered how it was that a heart could be heavy. At the centre of every galaxy is a hot, supermassive black hole of incredible heft, its existence so fraught that it effortlessly twists space-time, skewing everything within its vicinity. And so it was. The possibility of the future shut down when she heard the counsellor say those words; Lotte instinctively understood that she would share her mother's fate, her life shorter than it should be. The preventative surgery was experimental at best; she knew that, she'd done her research. She knew how often the cancer found its way through anyway, popping up in the slightest bit of tissue that had been left, determined as only a mindless organism can be. She couldn't stop it, but she could stop anybody else from having to witness it. And so for the next few years she had put the knowledge to the back of her mind.

Calling Eve now would be a mistake. She might refuse to answer. Or worse, she would pick up the conversation exactly where it had been left off, as if time had wrinkled, collapsing the intervening five years to an unnoticed moment. Besides, that was how it all began — a phone call to Eve — and look how things turned out. One small action, and the world shifted on its axis.

Lotte had phoned Eve just after she crawled out from under the dining table five years ago, leaving her mother's crayoned solar system in its infinite stasis. She'd lain on the couch, her hangover fading into the day, the phone pressed against her head, talking until her ear was warm. Eve understood: Lotte's want to accept this job; her initial hesitance to tell Vin, and the implications of what it might mean. The haste of her father and Alison's relationship, the absence of her mother right when she was needed most.

In the desert, Lotte can feel the bite of sharp rocks against her back and shoulders. Shifting her weight she releases her muscles, realises she has been holding them tight to stop from shivering. She closes her eyes briefly, then opens them as though the scene might change of its own accord. The stars above are about all she can see from here; they flood the sky, barely a dark patch left untouched. She makes out the Coal Sack in the Milky Way, the Magellanic Cloud wispy and unconvincing. She shifts her head to try and catch a glimpse of the Southern Cross — the closest thing she knows to a pole star — but when she tries to sit up her leg seizes in protest and she howls, the fox lifting its head before returning to snuffling at the ground, pursuing the scorpions wherever they scurried. That's all it was after. The stars are dimming now. Lotte still cannot seem to pull enough air into her lungs; all she can see is those airport doors sliding open, a sea of people behind the barrier, and not one of them waiting for her.

She hadn't returned to Australia for Tom and Eve's wedding, which had been held in Ballarat just after Christmas, a year to the day after it all started. She hoped the distance and the cost of the flights would be enough of an excuse, and she'd followed that up with hints dropped about securing leave at such a busy time of year. But her father's emails were unusually insistent. *We'd really love you to be there,* Tom wrote. *It would mean so much to have you with us.* In a fit of sentimentality, she'd booked the leave; her father was in love, he had found someone to spend his life with. She should be pleased. *But why did it have to be Eve?*

The emails kept coming. Chirpy updates on the wedding plans, changes he was thinking of making to the house. *Please let us know when you'll be here,* he wrote. They wanted something from her that she wasn't able to give. When her mother had been dying, only occasionally conscious, her eyelids fluttering, a priest had come to perform the last rites. An ordinary-looking man:

beige trousers over leather slip-on shoes, a blue shirt unbuttoned at the neck. His hands were warm and clean, like a doctor's, and he greeted Lotte and her father by name as though they'd met before, shaking with one hand, clasping with the other. From a bag, he'd taken a prayer book and an embroidered scarf, which he'd draped across his shoulders, the ends trailing down his chest. It had been a relief to have him there: he had authority; he'd been in this kind of situation before and was equipped with a whole book of things to say. He was the person to bestow a blessing, not Lotte.

On the day of the wedding, Lotte visited the floating islands of Lake Titicaca. She had sent an email of apology, but hadn't waited for a reply. Instead, she decided to travel up through Bolivia by bus, day fading into night, the roads falling away in mudslides, the salt pans endless, lifting to the sky. Every time she checked the time, she converted it to the hour back home, and then shook the thought away. Australia was no longer her home. Upon arriving at Copacabana, she took a tour boat to the floating islands berthed nearby — islands that were formed by masses of lake reed tied together.

The damp smell of rot was pervasive: as the islands sank into the water, the families cut more reed, laying the swathes down on the surface, and braiding them together. A pre-Incan people, the Uros built the islands as large boats that could be moved if under threat. Speeding toward the township, two-stroke engine bleating blue smoke into the atmosphere, Lotte wondered what could be more threatening to a way of life than an endless stream of curious onlookers like herself. They clambered off the boat and onto the soggy ground. In silence, men demonstrated the process of creating the islands to the huddled tourists: Argentinians sipping mate from a thermos, Italians cupping their hands to light cigarettes. A choir of woman wearing bright pink-and-yellow pompoms on strings around their necks sang a folk song of their own, and then a lacklustre version of 'Row, row, row, your boat' in hesitant English, their faces blank. Lotte was humiliated on their behalf and on her own. How many of them preferred the days the tourists were directed to one of the other islands and they were left in peace to carry on their regular life instead of playing roles in this living museum? They sang for tips only because the tour-ticket profits were pocketed by the boatmen, who lived in the comfort of town. The women laid out their wares on bales of reeds: tablecloths, cushion covers, wall hangings, all embroidered with machinery-like perfection and of much better quality than any of the tourist tat found in markets in town. Afterwards, they waved forlornly from the doors of their reed huts. Went inside to await the next boatload.

She returned to the IAO early, and was relieved to be back at the telescope, spending her nights gazing deep into space. There was a barrage of emails from Eve, from her father. It frightened her, how needy people were. Her father for her blessing; Vin wanting her at home — wanting a family, a future. Eve wanting forgiveness for marrying Tom; for falling in love with Lotte's father.

It was her own fault. Lotte had called Eve from the couch that day, and Eve had patiently listened. When Lotte had no more to say, Eve offered to visit. She was staying in her camper van on the Sapphire Coast; she had holidays until mid-January. She would drive down the Hume and keep Lotte company, while her father and Alison enjoyed their week at the beach. But Eve arrived, and Lotte left, and Tom came home early, and nothing was the same again.

A couple of years ago, Voyager 1 had reached the heliopause

— the edge of the sun's reach, where its solar wind can no longer push back the competing wind of the surrounding stars. When the probe traversed this field of giant magnetic bubbles, it became the first spacecraft to leave the solar system and enter interstellar space. Upon reading the news report, Lotte had reached for her phone to call her mother; it was only when she found herself pointlessly scrolling through her contacts that she sharply remembered that her mother had been dead for almost six years. While she knew Eve had not taken her mother's place, Lotte could not forgive her friend for doing so.

Seventy-eight, seventy-nine, eighty …

Lotte counts the stars, her eyes alighting on the next before the number of the last is out of her mouth. How many of them were suns with their own planets? How many planets had been counted?

And what can these planets tell her, lying here in a desert, her knee dangling to one side and screaming accusations when she tries to move it? She is shivering now, her shoulders aching with the effort of holding themselves still, her hands bunched in her pockets. She must get up and find help, but every time she shifts her weight, the pain seizes her body, forcing it still.

Help, she calls, unsure. She feels ridiculous as she cries out, knowing there is no one close enough to hear. Help! She turns her call into a yell and listens into its empty wake. All she can hear is the slip of sand and small rocks beneath her own boots; the scuffing of her sleeves against her waist. She would pity herself if she thought it would help.

Bending at the waist, she sits up, jaw clenched. If she can pull her leg straight, the kneecap will slip back into position, and the pain will disperse. She knows this from experience, but she has always had someone else to do it for her. Someone to grab her ankle and quickly twist her foot so it points at the sky. Reaching down to her shin she wraps both hands around her calf. And twists.

The pain seizes her entire being; her hands are thrown up, and she's screaming.

Owwwww!

She's let go too early — her kneecap hasn't shifted, and sweat breaks out over her entire body, chased by fear. She can't do this by herself; it's impossible. Yet there is no other choice.

Lotte waits for the pain to subside to a throb and begins shuffling backwards, extending her arms behind her then levering her body up and back, propelled by her good foot. Tears run down her cheeks and into her collar; her leg is a dragging deadweight, her own groan animal-like in its despair. She reminds herself that it is not possible to die of pain alone; she heaves her weight back again as her water bottle, attached to her belt with a carabiner, clanks and scrapes on the ground. She remembers the litany of her colleague's more gruesome facts, each one more outlandish than the last, as he'd entertained her in the long hours one morning with different ways to die in space. They'd begun with the most obvious — that if it were possible to get close enough, you could drop yourself into the sun and burn up in 5700 Kelvin heat. They had laughed about it at the time — that you wouldn't even burn, that your body would simply evaporate. That even if it could withstand the heat, the gravity force of the sun would siphon the blood from your body through your feet.

Lotte jerks back another pace, squawking as her boot catches on a small ridge. There were other ways — what else had they listed? You could find yourself caught in Saturn's winds, which race five times faster than any hurricane on Earth; they would tear you to pieces, flinging you further than you could ever return from. Or you could dive from a two-kilometre-high cliff on Mercury, smashing into one of the planet's many craters, each one named for an artist, of sorts: Tolstoy, Matisse, Twain — you could take your pick. If you wanted to go up before you came down, you could stand on an icy geyser on Neptune, which would spurt you eight kilometres into the blue hydrogen-and-helium atmosphere. Which sounded a hell of a lot more attractive than taking a walk in the sulphuric rain of Venus, or falling into a black hole, stretching like spaghetti as you went — your legs becoming longer before your body tore in two at its weakest point, probably somewhere around your waist, stretching and snapping until oblivion.

She is drenched in sweat now, her palms pierced by rock and coated in sand. There is no way she can make it back to the residence like this, not once the sun's up; she'd walked at least forty minutes to get here, so it must be a few kilometres back. Breathing heavily, she stops to catch her breath. Remembers her mother drawing lines on a piece of paper, where they ran off the edge and shot across the next page. Lotte was young, early primary school it must have been, and Helen was trying to explain what 'parallel' meant. She took Lotte out to the backyard and got her to walk along beside her, arm outstretched.

See, if we stay on the paths we're on, we will never touch, no matter how far we walk.

Her father must have been watching from the kitchen because at dinner that night he put down his fork and coughed. You know, that's not quite true, he said. About walking in parallel.

Lotte watched her mother roll her eyes and laugh.

I knew you wouldn't be able to let it go, she said, teasing.

The world is round, Tom continued. So even if you walk in

parallel, if you keep going straight, not going around any fences or buildings, or taking a step to the left or the right, you will still get closer; eventually, you will come together. And he had nodded, satisfied.

Light is appearing in the sky, the sun making itself known. Lotte heaves her leg back once more, and then again. She needs something to brace herself against, something immovable so that she can use her whole body to twist and not just her hands. There are two large boulders to her right, further up the incline. She shuffles towards them, three quick pulls, whimpers bursting from behind her clenched teeth. It must be only another fifteen metres, but as she tries to lift her body again she finds she cannot, her body convulsing as she bawls out her pain.

That's here. That's home. That's us. Where was it Carl Sagan placed the pale blue dot of the Earth, minuscule in the universe's cosmic vastness? *A mote of dust suspended in a sunbeam. The only home we've ever known. On it everyone you love, everyone you know, everyone you ever heard of, every human being who ever was, lived out their lives.* She has never felt more alone.

She needs to get her foot hard up against the boulders, snug in the crevice between them. Lotte drags herself the final stretch, her boot catching on the uneven ground and extending her pain beyond what can be comprehended. Finally, she reaches the boulders and shuffles around until her foot is aimed toward them. She has to somehow get her foot in-between the boulders, where it won't be able to move as she pulls her kneecap into place. She gently grasps her leg, but, as she lifts, her fingers touch her kneecap, loose and swimming at the side of her leg, and the nausea comes upon her without warning, the vomit bursting out into her lap, spattering across her clothes. The contents of her stomach burn at the back of her throat, and she sobs with self-pity. She is not supposed to be here. She is supposed to be tucked up in bed, her bags packed and her alarm set. *Check in*, she thinks, sobbing and bracing her knee with a hand on either side. *Take-off. Landing.* She laces her fingers under her knee toward the top of her calf and lifts, shrieking as her foot flops up then lands hard between the boulders, pain engulfing her knee to her hip. Her face a wet mess, she throws herself onto her back, as though to distance herself from the hurt, and she screams.

Her chest is heaving, and the stars are indifferent, observing her plight and offering her nothing. It is a cruel role reversal, a pointed disregard. She needs to get home; she needs to be away from here. *Passport control.* She pictures it. *Luggage carousel. Customs.* She slows her breathing, sits up again and flicks at the traces of vomit on her jacket. When she gets home, she will call Eve; Eve will make everything alright. With her good sense, forward planning, and acceptance. She will come to the hospital, she will listen as the doctors talk through her various treatment options. The chemotherapy, the double mastectomy. For, just as the presence of the gene predicted five years ago, Lotte's body has taken its cues from her mother. Three weeks ago, she found a lump in her breast, and the biopsy report from the hospital in Antofagasta said it was not benign. Not this time. She doesn't yet know whether it's found its way into her bloodstream, her lymph nodes, but she knows it is time to go home. That she cannot do it alone in Chile — the endless hours of treatment and slow recovery. She had seen it all before; as well as giving her the gene, her mother gave her the insight. Lotte knew what was ahead. She would go home, to her father and Eve, if they would have her.

She readies herself with her hands by her hips, palms down against the ground. Counts aloud, trying to take command. One, two, and on three Lotte lifts her body and wrenches herself to the right, twisting her leg as she throws herself to the ground, falling onto her shoulder. The relief is instant. Her kneecap locks back where it should and all the other muscles release their terrified grasp. The acute pain appeases, slipping away into memory, replaced by something so much less insistent that it is a comfort.

With shaky breaths, Lotte pulls herself to her feet, greedily reining in the adrenalin; she must not lie there and let her muscles seize again. As long as she keeps her leg bent, doesn't straighten it enough to give the kneecap a chance to slip away, she knows she can weight-bear on it. She will be able to hobble back toward the residence; she will be able to go home. The light has lifted colour into the world as she slowly straightens herself up, her leg tentative beneath her, the ache of the stretched and torn ligaments wrapping itself around her knee like a pressure bandage. Blues and yellows tease a faint line of cloud; the sun hasn't made its way over the horizon just yet, but it will, in time, as surely as it does every other morning.

8

EVE

At this moment, it is unfathomable to Eve that the sun will ever haul itself over the horizon. She can see the grey lift of it, a band of dirty cloud fumbling at the edge of the sea, but she cannot believe that it will become day. Cannot bear it. How is it possible that time moves forward when everything of hers has halted? What is time but a measure, a creator of distance between what was and what is? An impassable border between states of existence, a border marked only by tense. They are a family; they *were* a family.

She concentrates on the horizon, arms wrapped around herself, rocking back and forth, feet making flat pat-pat sounds on the damp sand. Two waves, maybe three? That's all it will take before her dull impressions will be washed away. It is not getting any lighter. It cannot.

She walks towards the sea, tries to suppress the tensing of her body as the first wave rolls across her feet. The sharp numb of cold is immediate, but within a few moments her feet will be warmer than her shins; as she goes deeper, her shins warmer than her knees. Her jeans hold the water — she feels the weight of them dragging at her hips. It won't be a surprise to anyone; it

176

will be a relief. Her knees clench, and the next wave throws itself at her waist, soaking her clothes. *Mina came up to my waist*, thinks Eve. *She was half the size of me.* And it is this unthinking use of the past tense that undoes her.

She lets go of herself, her hands trailing in the water. The next wave that comes causes her to jump, throwing her hands up to protect herself from the splash, hopping on one foot as her body instinctively tries to keep itself dry. The water grabs at her wrists, soaking the sleeves of her hooded jumper, the cuffs becoming heavy bracelets encircling her arms. A seagull screeches, another yells back, and she wonders whether the water will fill her ears so completely that no sound will evermore be carried to her.

•

Eve remembers. She was the one who'd heard the doorbell, the one who walked down the hallway calling over her shoulder.

I'll get it!

Not expecting anyone, and not even wondering who it could be. A postcard summer day in early January, still laughing at Tom's lame joke about the cows that had Mina in stitches (*Knock knock. Who's there? Cows. Cows who? Cows go moo, not who!*), and blissfully unaware that any interruption could herald all that this one would. *Ding-dong.* If they had not been home; if they had all been in the garden too far away to hear. If. If. If.

She opened the door to a small moment of disbelief, and then climbing joy.

Lotte!

Eve.

A bottle of duty-free gin in one hand, a soft toy in the other, luggage by her feet, and no explanation for her five-year absence.

Eve flung open the screen door, hugging Lotte and drawing her close. Trying not to heed the warning in the stiffness of Lotte's body.

You're back!

Speaking the words into Lotte's hair, her neck. So glad to see her. Five years in Chile, and there she was.

Come in.

Eve stepped aside, holding the door open to let Lotte pass. Lotte didn't pause, just strode down the hallway toward the living room as if she owned the place.

Eve struggled behind with Lotte's suitcase. In the kitchen, Eve watched Lotte and Tom briefly hug. She saw that Lotte's knee was strapped: a recent injury, flesh-coloured tape stretching down her calf. Mina circled, a wary lamb, butting in at Tom's legs.

And this must be Mina.

All three adults looked down on the little girl, her dark hair curling at her neck, a necklace of purple and orange beads clutched in her hands.

Say hello, Min, said Eve, encouraging, holding the pride in the back of her throat.

Mina considered each of them in turn, aware of the way they were all so much taller than her, but that they would wait, enthralled, for her words. She said nothing.

Go on. Say hello. This is Lotte. Your ... sister. Eve blushed, sure that the hesitation would be noticed, commented on. She had almost said 'aunt'; it seemed more natural.

You're not my sister. Sisters are babies.

Mina held the string of beads up as though she might bestow them on someone, then slipped them over her own head.

Yes she is. This is Lotte. Remember we told you how a long time ago Dad had another little girl, just like you, and now she's all grown up?

Eve turned to Lotte. We *have* told her about you, she said. We talk about you all the time.

She immediately regretted the insecurity in her voice.

That's okay, said Lotte. She held out the toy to Mina. A llama wearing a knitted poncho, its eyes closed beneath improbably long lashes.

I got you this, Mina. It's a llama.

Mina stepped forward, flashing a look at Eve, just to be sure, before reaching out to accept the toy.

Say thank you, said Tom. He crouched down to Mina to inspect the toy, and Eve saw how uncomfortable he was with all of this; it wasn't just her.

Thank you, said Mina, parroting the words, eyes only on the toy.

Eve scooped up the laundry Tom had been sorting, and offered Lotte a seat. Every gesture felt loaded with meaning, so anxious was she that Lotte might think she was asserting herself. Her home, her family.

When did you get back?

Eve saw the hesitation, the way Lotte pretended to be absorbed in Mina's inspection of the llama while gathering her thoughts.

A few days ago. It's been so busy at the IAO, it was difficult to get away; we had so much to finish up.

So you're going back? This is just a holiday?

No, I'm not going back. The job's finished.

Lotte wasn't giving the full story, but Eve knew she had given up every right to ask.

I thought I'd just come by and see you all, before I head up to Sydney. There'll be jobs there, something like before.

And Vin? Eve wanted to ask, but didn't, already knowing the

answer. Every question would lead to a dead end; they had lost the shape of one another's lives.

What happened to your knee? Have you hurt it? asked Tom.

It's fine; it's an old injury. It stiffened up on the plane.

The conversation stop-started its way through the morning, only really gaining momentum when Lotte described her work at length, all of them relieved to have a topic that was so far from themselves, out of reach of consequence.

We've discovered hundreds of planets since the program began, said Lotte. We've been using radial velocity tracking where the weak gravity of the planet pulls the star in a small circular orbit, making it wobble — and that's the bit we can detect. But we've started using direct imaging now. They're actually working on the site for a new telescope, just nearby, which will be able to image the planets in a much more sophisticated way than we can at the moment.

Lotte had changed, decided Eve. She was thinner, her hair longer. None of her clothes were familiar: the blue cotton dress, the cream scarf with bright orange polka dots that had been wrapped loosely around her shoulders and was now balled in her lap. She watched Lotte's fingers twirl the fronds of the scarf; saw that she wore no rings.

Don't you think? Lotte was staring at Eve, expecting a response.

Imaging, said Eve, scrabbling about for a word to hang on to. That sounds interesting.

Woefully inadequate; the disappointment was clear on Lotte's face. They had never been like this; it had always been so easy to fall into step with one another, picking up the conversation where it had been put aside the last time.

It is, actually, said Lotte. At the moment we can find the

planets because we can figure out they're there. It's like how Neptune was found by mathematical prediction rather than observation: Uranus's orbit didn't make sense, so they knew something was tugging it off course, and then they figured out the location and size of a planet that would be able to do so. Once they knew what they were looking for, it was easy to find.

Trying to pay attention, Eve shuffled her body on the couch. She drew her knees together, jammed her hands in-between her thighs. Putting her body in lockdown, so she wouldn't get up and start doing something else: the laundry that needed to be folded, the groceries that had not been put away. *They can wait*, she told herself. She thought through picking up the socks, pairing them and tucking one inside the other. Dividing the clothes into three piles — hers, Tom's, and Mina's — like a croupier dealing cards.

How's Vin? The words were out of Eve's mouth before she could stop them. Have you seen him?

He had gone to South America twice, Eve knew, sometime in the first year: once not long after Eve had moved to Ballarat, and the second time not long before Eve and Tom married. He'd met up with Lotte, and spent a week with her in Buenos Aires before they took a bus together up to Iguazu Falls. There was a mission town on the way, Vin had told her, built by Jesuit priests in the fifteenth century, and now in crumbled redbrick ruins, its grandeur destroyed by the Indigenous people who were glad to see the missionaries flee. Lotte and Vin had walked around the ruins for two hours, then sat at plastic tables on the town's main street, eating ice-cream that had melted and been refrozen so many times it was only crystals, no cream. *I couldn't think of anything to say to her*, Vin had told Eve later. *In Buenos Aires, it was fine — we were surrounded with people, we had to decide where to eat, how to get back to the hotel, which bar to stop and have a drink at. But that town, its endless ruins. Everything was so still, and covered in red dust. It felt like Mars. Rutted roads, baked in the sun. The temple walls pushing into the sky. I said that to her — it could be Mars — just for something to say. And she just smiled at me and nodded. She was humouring me. Her mind was elsewhere, I could see that. She was thinking about the work that I had dragged her away from. She never said it outright, not until later, but I realised then that the trip wasn't a reunion for the two of us, it was a goodbye tour. She wasn't coming home, not to me.*

At the time, Eve had tried to reassure him, convince him that he was mistaken, but Vin had been adamant. And in the end he was right: she had left them both behind.

He's well, replied Lotte, voice cool.

How long are you in Ballarat for? asked Tom.

I'm not sure. I thought I would stay a couple of days here, if that's okay? Get to know my little sister.

They could hardly say no. But Lotte talked her way into the silence nonetheless. Handing them back their hesitations as if they had refused.

It is my home, you know. It still feels that way to me, no matter how much you've changed it.

And it always will be, Tom said. He smiled, reaching for Eve's hand. She didn't want to take his, but she watched her hand lift and accept, slotting into his.

Even when things change, Eve said.

They certainly do, replied Lotte. And she waited just a moment before laughing. Long enough for Eve to know she hadn't been forgiven.

●

Eve feels incredibly strong, standing there as the waves come forward, beating into her chest and crashing behind her on the shore. The waves pull her up gently, and then heavily drop her to the sand, her toes instinctively curling in the effort of finding purchase. It's the weight of her waterlogged clothes that gives her the strength to keep going: they won't allow her to float away, no matter how much she wants to. A step forward, and then another, closing her eyes to face the breaking waves, diving under one of them, hair streaming back from her head, face free and exposed. She tries to rise to the surface, lifts away from the sandy floor, but her clothes, so reassuring when standing, are too heavy, too tangled, the hood of the sweatshirt wrapping around her neck.

She cannot breathe: the air is water, it fills her throat, her lungs, and there is no sound, just a pounding in her ears. The morning sky is the same colour as the water; no way is up, everything points down. This is how Mina would have felt, in her last few minutes, and Eve feels this understanding still her, pressing down on her chest, closing her throat, her eyes, her mind.

It is only a few seconds. She is not so deep, the waves not so powerful. Her feet kick with dedication, and her arms windmill as they should. Her instinct is still to survive, though she could find no such thoughts in her waking mind. Breaking through to the surface, hair plastered across her face, in her mouth and eyes. When she tries to tug the hair away, she sinks again — one beating arm, those kicking legs, unable to keep her afloat — managing only the smallest breath as she goes down, mouth full of seawater. Coughing instead of breathing, out not in. She comes up to the surface again, more annoyed than afraid, flicking back her head to tame her hair, egg-beating her legs and treading water as she turns back to the beach. The streetlights of the next town are still on, but the sky is blushing. She takes another lungful of water as she sinks under, and the panic pushes her forward into a breaststroke. She revels in the pull of her muscles, noting their annoyance at being called into service after such a long hibernation, their resistance at having to drag the weight of winter clothing as well as herself.

Her teeth are chattering as she lets the swell of another wave drop her to the sand, and she's walking slowly, pushing through the waist-high water, leaning forward, jeans chafing at her legs as the waves recede, when she recalls that this is exactly what it was like, immediately after. The realisation of what she had done causing a buffering delay between her mind and body. In the hospital, unable at first to stand up from the row of chairs in the waiting room, and then finding herself not only standing but also walking down the corridor.

They say that it is normal to keep replaying moments from just before. That it's healthy to search out what went wrong, to consider what might have been done differently, and realise the infinite nature of possibilities. To know that this accident just 'happened' in the same manner as any number of other accidents could. But it's not the accident itself that her mind keeps returning to. She has no memory of that; there are no triggers to her understanding.

The smack of the flyscreen door, that's the last thing she remembers. She hauled up the roller door, the dust coming alive in the sunlight.

Standing in the shallows, teeth clenched and jaw aching, clothes leaden and reaching for the ground, she can only remember what went before.

•

It was a period of colour: neon pink and blue trim on Lotte's clothing, apple-green nail polish on Mina's tiny nails, Lotte's booming laugh, which always sounded warm and orange, the pale yellow of the pineapple that Tom bought in Lotte's honour. Eve had been happy to see Lotte — there was no confusion about that — but the days that followed tumbled into one another, gathering speed as they careened towards the inevitable.

I want to talk to you about what happened, said Eve.

They were both sitting at the kitchen table. As soon as the words were spoken, Eve realised how little she had thought about how Lotte might respond. All of her daydreams were about the apologies she herself would make — the reassurances that she had never meant for any of it to happen, and the saving grace, she hoped, that what had resulted was the best part of her life, the crux everything else was built on. Surely Lotte could not begrudge Eve the love of Tom and Mina. But Lotte's attention was on her iPad, which she tapped at furiously, and when she looked up, her gaze was caught not by Eve, but by Mina and Tom in the backyard: Mina's tentative jumps on the trampoline, ostentatious in its safety features, surrounded as it was by netting walls and padded cushions over the springs.

I never had a trampoline, said Lotte. I wanted one, but Dad said it wasn't the kind of toy an only child had. He thought I wouldn't use it enough.

Eve twisted in her chair to properly look out the window. Tom was on his hands and knees, pounding at the mat, and Mina was laughing hysterically, falling over every time she stood up. Eve smiled; Tom would be complaining tonight about how he was too old for that business, but then he'd be back out there again tomorrow. It had been his idea to buy Mina the trampoline for Christmas; Eve wouldn't tell Lotte that.

We haven't talked about all of this, Lotte. Did you get my emails?

Lotte kept staring into the garden, the iPad discarded.

Yes.

But you never answered.

What was I going to say? She shrugged, smiling at Eve. What's done is done. And I'm not angry about it.

You're not?

Of course not. Lotte laughed. It's your life. Not to mention it's a relief to know you finally got over Nate. I thought that might never happen. He was never good enough for you.

Eve chose her words carefully.

He wasn't as bad as you think.

He married somebody else, someone you had no idea he was seeing.

It was more complicated than that.

How could she ever expect to explain it to Lotte, for whom everything was always black and white?

It was Lotte's turn to study Eve, which she did at length.

Well, it hardly matters now, does it? Now that you've moved on. You've got your new family now.

She was speaking in platitudes, and Eve tried to cut through.

But if that's how you felt, why didn't you answer my emails? You were the only person I wanted to talk to, and you weren't here. It was hard for me, Lotte. I felt so bad about it all. When I met Tom, I wasn't expecting any of this. And I wouldn't have gone there, I really wouldn't, except I knew it was going to be something special. I knew it would work. And when you didn't answer me ... I wanted to know you were okay. You said you would come to the wedding.

Lotte stood up from the table and made her way to the door.

They weren't really for me, those emails, Lotte said. They were for you — you wanted to make yourself feel better. And it worked, didn't it? I mean look at you guys now, you've got it all going on.

Eve followed Lotte to the door. She tried to see with Lotte's eyes: her own father playing with a small child, one that could have been his granddaughter. She remembered their conversation years before, Lotte's dawning certainty that she would never have children. If Eve was thirty-seven, Lotte must be thirty-five: there was still time. There was no reason that Lotte couldn't have any of this, if this is what she wanted.

I missed you, Lotte. I wished that you had replied, there were so many things I wanted to tell you. And it was hard for me, with Mina. She wasn't the easiest … I didn't find it easy.

Lotte took a moment to answer.

It's not that I didn't care, she said. It's just that I don't think I had anything to offer. I don't know anything about children; I wouldn't have been the right person to help anyway.

It's not about that, said Eve. I just needed you.

Well, it seems you're happy now.

I am, she said. We all are.

Eve tried to let Lotte's words take away the cloud of misgiving that had been haunting her ever since their friendship had faltered.

I just wish it was with somebody other than my father.

And Lotte was out the door and walking towards the trampoline before Eve could reply.

Lotte stayed almost a week, her presence exciting Mina to the point of irritability.

Why isn't Lotte awake? whined Mina on the fourth morning of Lotte's stay.

Mina kept climbing down from the chair and heading to the

hallway to look at the closed bedroom door. It was close to eleven.

I don't know; she must be tired, said Eve.

But I'm not tired.

Well, Lotte went to bed late. See what happens when you don't go to sleep at bedtime? You get too tired to wake up in the morning.

But why didn't she go to bed?

I don't know, Mina. You'll have to ask her.

She took this as permission, running to the hallway.

Mina! No, let her sleep. You can ask her when she wakes up.

A face of thunder. Eve knew what was coming next.

I'm bored.

How do children learn this word, this concept? Mina used it as a way to stop whatever it was she had been doing — when she was ready to get out of the bath, when she had finished eating: I'm bored.

How about some play dough?

No.

Drawing?

No.

Lego?

No.

She knew what it was Mina wanted to do: finger-painting. Lotte had sat with her on the deck yesterday, newspaper spread all around, paint pots upended on paper plates. Eve had had to hose down the deck when they were done, splatters of paint everywhere.

It surprised Eve that Lotte was good with Mina. But who was she to judge? How many times had Eve rued, if not Mina's existence, then the hours of attention her existence demanded? The time spent in idle chitchat with other parents at the childcare pick-up, or poolside during swimming lessons. The endless, cyclical chatter and pleading that accompanied every mealtime. That it was all wrapped in unprecedented joy only made the feelings of guilt more apparent.

Perhaps because it was new to her, and temporary, Lotte showed none of Eve's own resignation to Mina's needs. In the hours that Lotte bothered to emerge from the spare room, she gave Mina her full attention, and while at first Eve had hovered nearby, not wanting Mina to overwhelm, increasingly she had been glad to be able to slip away and concentrate on her own work. Lotte devised plans that she and Mina could do together, while Eve sat at the dining table cobbling together a new museum soundtrack: listening to recordings of children's playground chants, the thwack of a tennis ball on a plastic cricket bat, the ding-ding of a school bell.

Baking biscuits one afternoon, Lotte encouraged Mina to throw choc-chips at her from the other side of the kitchen, catching some of them in a mixing bowl: the rest had to be swept up later. By Eve. Pasting pictures onto cardboard so Mina could make her own puzzles. Cutting finger puppets out of felt. All tasks that Eve would surely do if she had the time. Which Lotte had in spades, it seemed. She remained vague about how long she was staying; hadn't made any mention of further plans. Eve, not wanting to make her feel unwelcome, was reluctant to ask when she might be leaving, and happy to take advantage of her goodwill until the childcare centre reopened from its end-of-year break.

Each evening, Eve hoped they might have an opportunity to rekindle their friendship. But apart from the first night, Lotte would become impatient at around six o'clock, leaving her game with Mina unfinished, and rushing about getting her things together before leaving the house without even a goodbye. Four nights in a row she had gone out, returning late and sleeping through the morning. Eve knew it shouldn't have annoyed her — what did she care if that was how Lotte wanted to waste her days? But every time Lotte went out, Eve wondered where she was. Whatever she was doing was obviously much more interesting than this: Eve snatching moments with her work, trying to get things done around the house. Tom in his vegie garden, or taking Mina to the park. The presence of Lotte made Eve see everything they did with a critical eye. Shouldn't she be out and about, too, rushing off to things and coming home late? Had she and Tom become a cocooned couple, inward looking and self-protecting? Somehow she had cultivated this quiet sensible life. A life: safe, meaningful, worthy in its own small way. But with Lotte observing, passing her wordless judgement, it suddenly seemed inconsequential. Lotte with her talk of exoplanets and outer-space discovery; the dedication of people working on something bigger than themselves toward ends that wouldn't even be achieved in their own lifetimes. Talk of travel and astronomer friends from all over the world. *I'm bored*, thought Eve. *I'm boring*.

Your toes aren't pretty, Mum.

Mina held her foot up for Eve to inspect her painted nails. Red and pink this time.

Lotte has pretty toes; I have pretty toes.

Eve looked down at her feet, toes unadorned. Mina was right. Her whole outfit was drab: brown sandals, grey skirt, navy singlet. There was nothing wrong with her clothes; she liked her clothes. Until last week, that is: now they were making her feel old. Lotte seemed to have a thing for fluorescent colours. The strap of a handbag, a geometric T-shirt in eye-popping blues and yellows. Chunky necklaces of plaited vinyl or lacquered wood. Colourful, all of it. Mina was in love. She mooned about after Lotte asking endless streams of questions, treasuring a gifted bangle or hair clip. Sisterly love, Eve recognised with trepidation.

When Lotte appeared from her room, she was gorgeously tousled in sleep.

Do you want something to eat? Breakfast or lunch? Eve tried to keep the resentment from her voice.

I don't mind. What do you think, Miss Mina? Lotte made a confused face at Mina, who was delighted to be included.

Lunch! No, breakfast!

So keen to get it right.

Breakfast it is, said Lotte. It's not even twelve. Are you having breakfast, Mina?

She had her breakfast hours ago, Eve interjected.

But I want breakfast again, whined Mina.

I'm sure we can arrange that, said Lotte. She gave Eve a theatrical wink, as though they were in this together, and lifted Mina up onto a stool.

I was wondering if you'll be around tonight, Lotte? For dinner?

Sure, said Lotte, shrugging. I can be. Why?

I just thought it might be nice to have dinner together. I don't feel like we've spent much time with you. It's been so long, and you'll be leaving soon enough, so it would be such a shame not to.

Eve's words were so formal that she cringed.

Sounds good, said Lotte, turning her attention back to Mina. Maybe we can dress up for dinner, Mina? Put on our best dresses!

Yes!

Unabashed joy on Mina's face, as though she'd never been allowed to wear a dress before.

I can wear my red dress!

Me too! exclaimed Lotte. High five?

She held her hand out for Mina to slap.

Now, Rice Bubbles or Corn Flakes, Miss?

•

Seaweed is splayed over the beach, its roots exposed, the tendrils of foliage flung carelessly wide. In summer, it will dry into steaming, leathery heaps, later becoming razor-sharp ribbons to cut unsuspecting feet. For the moment, though, freshly deposited and with no sun to parch it, the seaweed lies soft. Hugging her knees, trying to stop the shivering that rattles away at her, Eve reaches for some seaweed and begins untangling its mess of fronds, just as she used to comb Mina's hair with her fingers. It is a kind memory, that one.

They'd been staying in a cottage much further down the coast than she is now, close to Port Fairy, and Eve was teasing Tom, asking him if he had brought her there to break up with her, like he had done to Alison just a few years before.

Come on, you know it wasn't like that!

He was standing at the kitchen bench, whisking eggs and cream together, turning the B&B's breakfast supplies into a bread and butter pudding. Eve was sitting with Mina in front of the fireplace, combing and drying her hair while Mina did the same to her doll. Perhaps it was the dozy warmth of the fireplace, or being exhausted from an afternoon collecting seashells in the rock pools, but Mina had been still for more than five minutes; it was almost too good to be true.

Lotte told me you were ready to propose to Alison. That's what she said when I turned up to keep her company: Dad's down the coast with his lady-friend, I think he's planning on making her my stepmother.

And instead I got stuck with you, laughed Tom.

It was the kind of gentle, teasing conversation they had often had before Mina was born, before Eve sank into the melancholy that had accompanied her first year of motherhood. There were still glimpses, moments when she knew she wasn't doing it right, that she was doing Mina a cruel disservice through her ineptitude, but for the most part, things had returned to an even keel. Even so, it had been Eve who'd had to lead Tom back into these lighter conversations — he was loath to offend or confuse her about his feelings, even in jest.

You poor old man, you, said Eve. I bet Alison didn't even know what was coming. She was expecting a proposal on New Year's Eve, but you went and dumped her instead. I mean, that was harsh, Tom. I never would have picked you for such a stone heart.

That's not fair, said Tom, playing up his innocence. I wasn't even thinking of marriage until Lotte mentioned it. She was just causing trouble, stirring me up — you know what she's like. She started saying these things in front of Alison, and I had to make it up to her, and suddenly things became more serious. Once it was out there, and I could see that Alison wasn't opposed to the idea, I decided it wasn't fair on her: that's why we separated. I couldn't keep on seeing her if she was after something more serious than I could offer.

And then you drove home and found me lying in your bed.

The best decision I ever made was to come back early.

He brought a piece of bread over to Mina.

Here you go, sweetie.

Ta! Dad, why do giraffes have long necks?

Why do you think?

Annoyance flitted across Mina's face. But I want the answer, she said.

But if I tell you the answer, then you won't figure anything out for yourself.

Just tell me why!

Because I said so. Tom laughed.

That's not an answer!

Why not?

Because it's not.

Mina crossed her arms, fed up. Eve fought the urge not to laugh.

Why do you think giraffes have long necks and horses don't? said Eve.

Mina shook her head, not willing to join in.

What do giraffes eat? asked Eve. Do they eat leaves?

Yes. Her response tentative and drawn out.

And where do the leaves come from?

Trees!

So do you think they have long necks to reach the leaves in the trees?

Mina smiled despite herself, her mood able to change completely at speed.

Yes!

Eve watched the thoughts ticking over, pieces fitting together.

Horses don't eat leaves, do they? asked Mina.

They eat hay, said Eve.

So they don't have long necks.

And Eve watched this bit of information sink into Mina's mind, to lodge there as something forever known.

Lotte hated horses as a child, Tom said. She would refuse to read any book that they were in.

He rarely brought up his previous life as a father. Eve was always aware of it: that he had already experienced everything that was so new to her; that he wasn't stumbling around in the dark trying to figure it out. But he tended to keep his experience muted, rarely speaking of Helen, or of Lotte's childhood, so that Eve had a strange kaleidoscope vision of the time: stories collected years before from Lotte, and incidental comments by Tom or friends of his, all mixed up with the photograph albums in the living room bookcase. Eight volumes, the first holding a ragged collection of faded photographs from Tom and Helen's university days, the next dedicated to their wedding and those of unfamiliar couples. The fashions of the era were seen in the high-necked and long-sleeved dresses of the women; the men resplendent in pale suits with velvet trim and ruffled shirts, ballooning sideburns and oversized glasses masking their faces. Eve tried to match the couples with Tom's current friends — the ones whose jests with Tom alternated between sly congratulations on scoring such a young wife, and scornful bemusement at going through the rigmarole of young children once again — but she was unable to make any connection: the social circle of the photographs must have been primarily Helen's.

Helen, who was a young dewy-eyed girl in her bridal photographs, holding a bouquet of red roses, scarlet ribbon trailing to the ground. Unlike other photographs of Helen from that time, which captured her clowning for the camera — a glass of wine or cigarette in one hand, her head thrown back in laughter (sometimes her face was just a blur, the shutter not quick enough to still her constant motion) — the wedding photographs captured her unmistakeable beauty. Her deep-lidded eyes and delicately shaped eyebrows; her full lips and high cheekbones. Eve had spent hours looking through these photographs, nudging them back into place where the glue had dried and they had slid to the bottom of the page. She tried to detect any early signs of discontent in Tom's face, his hair wild and long, his eyes a startlingly bright blue. But she sees only what anyone would expect: a bride embracing the moment, revelling in the attention, and a groom who cannot believe his luck at capturing such a creature. Rarely do Tom's eyes seek out the camera — more often, they are trained on Helen. Looking at these photographs does not make Eve happy, but look at them she does, jealous and mildly repulsed by her own uncharitable feelings.

The other six albums were filled with Lotte, beginning with the baby photographs, one taken in hospital, her tiny body swaddled just as Mina's had been. The wristband with her name neatly typed is pressed in alongside the photograph, and the birth notice clipped from the local paper. *Tom Wren and Helen Jansone are delighted to announce the safe arrival of Charlotte Marie Wren.* There was no birth notice for Mina; instead, a post on Facebook, a tally of 'likes' and comments of congratulations. A completely different era, but sisters nonetheless. It was impossible not to see a hint of Mina in the photographs of Lotte as a toddler. They shared the shape of their faces with Tom, and a surly look of concentration. As Mina grew, Eve found herself flipping through the photo albums hungrily, wanting to get hints of the life that would play out for Mina: Lotte pushing a trolley of building bricks, painting at an easel, dressed for her first day of school. All of these photographs Eve had absorbed into her own memories as she tried to see Mina through Tom's eyes.

Lotte still hates horses, said Eve. She thinks their teeth are creepy.

Tom laughed. She got that from Helen. She thought they looked too similar to human teeth. She did like to have opinions on everything.

I only met her a couple of times; Lotte adored her. Eve spoke carefully. Having spent so much time looking at the photographs of Helen, she felt as though she were in possession of knowledge she was not supposed to have.

She was the kind of person everyone loved, said Tom. Or if they didn't, they'd think it was somehow their own fault.

He was about to say something more, but then closed his mouth, kissing Mina on the forehead. Eve felt the distance between them expand.

Anyway, I better go finish this pudding.

True to form, the topic was closed. Later, the bowls emptied of pudding and Mina tucked away in bed, it was Tom who stepped back into the conversation they had left.

She wasn't perfect though. Helen, I mean, Tom said.

Nobody is, said Eve, unsure of where the conversation was going.

No.

Tom took a sip of wine, stretching out his toes to the fire.

No, what I meant to say is that *we* weren't perfect. Helen and me. We almost split up, a couple of times, actually.

Really?

Eve couldn't keep the surprise out of her voice.

Helen left me, said Tom, shrugging at the simplicity of the confession. She was having an affair.

As he went on, he avoided Eve's gaze. He got up from the armchair and moved to the fireplace, where he shifted the ember guard aside and shoved one of the logs further back into the grate with his foot.

When was this?

He gave the log another shove, sparks flying up the flue.

It went on for a long time, actually. Years. I suppose it was more than an affair. A relationship, perhaps. Around the time

Lotte went to uni. Empty nest syndrome, I suppose the magazines would call it. Though to be fair, it had felt empty for a long time before that.

He picked up a poker from where it hung, weighing it in his hand before leaning over the fire and giving the logs a shove.

Helen was enthusiastic. She was intoxicating, for want of a better word. Though maybe that is the right word, because there was a hangover, eventually. When her focus was on you, it was incredible: it was like you were at the centre of the universe. But as soon as her attention was caught by someone else ...

Tom leaned the poker against the fireplace and came back across to where Eve sat on the floor, sitting down behind her on the couch.

That's what it was like, actually, he laughed. When you stand in front of the fire and it's beautiful and warm, but then it gets too hot, so you step away. And then you're cold, far colder than you were before.

Just like Nate, thought Eve, staring into the flames, wondering if he wanted her to speak, not knowing at all what to say. Lotte had never mentioned the affair; she had always given the impression that her parents were made for each other. Doting and devoted, even.

I doubt it was the only affair she had, said Tom. I remember when I realised that's what was happening. I'd come home early with Lotte — one of the few times we actually did anything together, just the two of us — but when we got home, Helen wasn't there. And I just knew that she was seeing someone. She told me as much, towards the end, but I didn't want to know the details. It was a man she volunteered with, at the observatory. The strangest thing was, he was a nice bloke. Not that he wouldn't be.

Tom seemed to stumble around in his words, frustrated when

they weren't quite right.

He was ordinary. Like me. He was no one special. Which made it all the worse. I always thought that Helen would leave me one day; I knew I could never match her, be what she was. But I always thought it would be for some ... charmer. I don't know, an artist, a musician or someone. A performer. That's what she was; always on. But he was just this regular bloke, quiet almost, and they both had this thing about astronomy. They were obsessed with it.

Like Lotte.

Like Lotte. She always wanted to be just like Helen, even when she was little. Two peas in a pod. She was never much interested in me; I couldn't compete with Helen. No one could.

Every time he paused, Eve wondered if he would go on. Wondered if she wanted him to.

Anyway, this man. She was seeing him for months. I knew for a long time before I said anything to her, because I knew that would be it: once it was out there, she'd leave me, and I wasn't ready for that. Looking back, I wish I hadn't been such a coward. That I'd said something earlier, saved us all the trouble. But back then, I just couldn't imagine life without her. We met when we were so young — we were nineteen.

Eventually, it just became ridiculous, a pantomime being acted out. Me pretending I didn't know where she was going every night; her pretending to still be interested in me. And one night, after Lotte had moved away for uni, we sat down and talked about it, and we decided we would go our separate ways. It was a relief, really. I knew she had stopped feeling anything for me years before. And while I still loved her, I knew that wasn't going to be returned. God, it sounds so sad.

Tom laughed, the sound hovering above her head like a

cloud, and Eve turned to look up at him.

But it didn't feel that way, he said. We'd had a good run, and I didn't regret that. And I knew it would be better for both of us if she left. So she did. And then she found out about the cancer.

That must have been awful.

Eve went to lift herself off the floor and sit beside him, but Tom's hands lay heavy on her shoulders.

She was only with him for a few weeks, said Tom. I mean, actually living with him. But it was me she called when it happened. To go with her to the appointments, talk about treatment, that sort of thing. And she asked if she could come back. If I would help her get through it. I didn't even think twice about it: of course I said yes. And she never saw him again, not properly. He came to visit a few times, over the years, but it was obvious he was uncomfortable.

Was it his choice or hers? That she go back to you?

I never asked, said Tom, laughing. I'm making myself sound so pathetic. But it just didn't seem to matter at the time. I think it was her decision, though. I think she just thought it would be too hard, that they didn't know each other well enough. Maybe he just didn't deal well with illness, I don't know. Maybe she didn't want him to see her like that: twenty-five years of marriage takes away any sense of pride you might have. Perhaps she should have given him a chance and she didn't.

But she went into remission, didn't she? Did she think about leaving then? Once she was better?

I don't think she ever did, said Tom. We knew that the remission probably wouldn't last for long, and we were right. It was a strange period, but it was nice, really. It was just a friendship by then, not really a relationship, but I suppose most long marriages are similar. The thing was, we were both happy enough with what it was. Rattling around in the house, just the two of us — each doing our own thing and enjoying each other's company.

Does Lotte know about the affair? She never mentioned it.

No, Tom said, pulling Eve in close to him. I don't think Helen would have told her. Helen would have hated Lotte to think she had failed at something. She would have waited until the last possible moment to tell her about it. And then she didn't need to.

They sat in silence for a while, the wood popping and spluttering in the grate.

Do you think Lotte will forgive us eventually? asked Eve, her head on Tom's shoulder.

Do you think we need her to? replied Tom.

•

Her hands are too numb to keep combing at the seaweed. They ache, they won't bend as they should. Eve stares at them, at the colour drained away so that her nails are moons of pale violet at the ends of her fingers. She's not sure what part of her is shaking. Her jaw is clenched tight, and she hugs her legs, but still she shakes. Where clothes cling to her, they are cold and then burning hot; her heart is beating too fast, too loudly. She knows that she must unfold, let go, stand up. Knows that she must breathe. A panic attack, but it can't be: there is nothing left for her to panic over. *Just breathe* — that's what the psychologist used to tell her when Mina was a baby, when she felt the anxiety building, when her body would freeze, the edges of her vision blurring and darkening as though saving her from seeing too much.

Back then she'd wanted to breathe. When the panic would take hold, she wanted to regain her calm as soon as possible, to rid herself of the heaviness that tagged along behind. Wanted to be light and deft for Mina; wanted to be herself. But now? Now she doesn't want any of it. Not to breathe, not to regain her calm, not to survive this heaviness. Because to do even one of those things would be to forgive.

9

LOTTE

The first night Lotte spends at her father and Eve's feels like she has landed in an alternate universe. Why did she think it was a good idea to come back here? But where else could she go?

Evening falls, and the light from the kitchen picks out a child's bicycle on the backyard lawn. Moths dip and sway in the beam. The ordinariness of it all. Lotte tries to imagine herself out of the room; what would they be doing if she weren't here? Sitting in front of the television? Laughing? Instead, the dining table serves as a life raft they can all hold onto, a barrier to stop them from accidentally touching one another, or jumping ship.

Sorry, it's not very exciting. Eve apologises again for the steak and salad, and in every comment Lotte hears reproach: *If we knew you were coming ...*

Eve's hand on Lotte's dad's back as she passes him in the kitchen; him grabbing her about the waist. The conversation bucks and twists between polite questions of work and circumstance, but every innocent sentence points at the oddness of the situation; how little they now know of one another. There is refuge in talk of movies and travel, Lotte blindly reaching for amusing anecdotes from the endless hours of her flight, which had been spent muffled by painkillers to dull her aching knee. All three dote on Mina rather than talk to one another. A gorgeous child, this sister of hers. How carefully she speaks her words, looking people in the eye to check they understand. Whenever Mina says Lotte's name, she stretches it out, calling for attention, unexpectedly tripping up her heart. When Mina goes off to bed, the conversation keeps falling into silence.

Excuse me.

In the bathroom, Lotte unclasps her bag and checks her phone. No messages. But who would contact her? Not a single person has her number; she'd only picked up the SIM card at the airport. Her email inbox has only newsletters and recruitment emails. She slowly washes her hands, inspecting the unfamiliar moisturiser and soaps that line the bathroom bench. Plastic toys laze in the tub, cartoonish eyes watching her.

I'm sorry, I'm quite tired. I think I'm probably jet-lagged. Do you mind …? Pausing in the kitchen, Lotte shrugs her shoulders at Eve and Tom, miming apology. Eve jumps to her feet.

Of course. I'll set up the bed in the study.

She hurries past Lotte into the spare room.

Sorry it's been so long, Dad.

I understand, he replies. It can't have been easy, these last few years. For you.

She thinks about telling him then, about her illness and everything that lies ahead. It's not the sympathy she fears, but the apprehension he might feel at having to watch, for a second time, someone go through all it entails.

You seem happy, she says instead, offering an olive branch.

Her father nods. And you?

Eve appears from the hallway. Do you want to bring your suitcase in? she asks. You can unpack while I make up the bed.

Night, Dad. Lotte steps forward, about to cross the room and kiss him on the cheek like she so often had. But things were different now, somehow.

Night, Lotte.

In the spare room, Lotte and Eve move carefully around one another. Eve apologises for nothing being quite right: the house not tidy enough; the room set up as a study rather than a guest room; the sofa bed being uncomfortable. While she fusses, Lotte looks at the photos crowding the pin board above the desk. Mina as a baby, a toddler, a little girl. On the floor; in a highchair; dragging a tiny suitcase through an airport. But the one that she cannot look away from is slightly blurred, taken too close. A selfie of her father, Eve, and Mina. Tom kissing Eve's cheek, Mina looking up at her parents, desperate to be included.

I'm sorry, says Eve, sitting down on the bed she has just made and looking directly at Lotte. It must all seem very strange to you. Me living here, Mina ...

It's fine, says Lotte. Really. She stands by her suitcase, holding Eve's gaze but saying nothing more.

I've really missed you, says Eve. There're so many times I've wished you were here to talk to.

Well, I've had a lot going on; it's been a really busy time. Lotte goes to crouch down at her suitcase but her knee twinges. Shall we talk in the morning?

Okay.

Eve stops next to her on the way to the door, but Lotte doesn't look up, and Eve closes the door behind her without another word.

Lotte contemplates her suitcase, but cannot bear to open it and be reminded of how little she has. There are some things in storage in Canberra, but this suitcase is the sum total of her life of the last few years. They must think her pathetic.

Lotte quietly opens the door of the study, listening out for the clank and scrape of Eve and Tom clearing up in the kitchen. She closes the door behind her and is down the hallway, through the front door and onto the street, walking towards the town centre. The urge to sob drops upon her from above, suffocating any other sense. Teeth clenched, she fights back, but the tears come anyway — deep, shuddering breaths as she refuses to slow her pace.

She turns into the next street, then doubles back in the direction she had come. Walking, stumbling, the roads quietly empty as though no cars have ever driven here. Her knee twinges again when she catches a foot on the uneven ground; it is as though the desert fox is stalking her even here.

The gates of the cemetery are locked. A brick fence surrounds the perimeter, too high. Following the fence line, she comes to the original allotment, fenced by a row of wrought-iron fleur-de-lis spikes. She cannot climb that, not with her knee still stiff and swollen. But she cannot leave without trying.

She hasn't scaled a fence like this since she was a child. She steps onto the bluestone foundation, boosting herself up, ready to swing her leg over the top. But her legs refuse to lift and pull, her feet too wide to get a footing, her knee wincing with apprehension. She can't do it. And she sits on the grass, leaning against the bluestone, more alone in her hometown than she has ever been in the desert.

Two days later, and she feels jittery in this fast-moving family who all seem to have things to do: Mina corralling her dolls, Tom in the garden, Eve moving things about the house, a bee to pollen. There is no in, no opening for Lotte. A dwarf planet, that's what Pluto was in the end. Orbiting the sun with enough mass to form a sphere, but lacking the gravitational field to pull objects into orbit; instead, lumpen rocks and astral debris cloud the air around it like regrets. The loneliest planet of them all, her mother used to call it, with no purpose of its own.

Watching Mina, arms and legs seemingly interchangeable as she flops onto the furniture and sprawls herself upon the floor, Lotte cannot tear her eyes away. Rhyming songs mixed with Christmas carols are sung to dolls and teddy bears, deep breaths and long pauses at the commencement, and a rushing at the end, all the words tripping over each other without regard for tune. She rushes from one activity to another, toys abandoned in her wake and then reclaimed without reason. She is the most observant and rude of conversationalists, listening intently as she pursues a pointed line of inquiry then breaking into giggling laughter, blatant surprise at the stupidity of adults.

Seahorses don't have feet, she tells Tom as he noses his way through the living room, eyes bulging and arms tucked in by his sides.

He jumps a little, feet together.

Now you're a kangaroo! She cackles at his ridiculousness, kicking her feet up in the air.

This is what Lotte is missing out on. She thinks of calling Vin to let him know she is back, but then she would have to decide what to tell him next.

Instead, she excuses herself from the animal antics and calls the hospital in Sydney. She books in to see a specialist the following week. The appointment sits there in the future, a small point of control and certainty, after which there is only confusion. Lotte finds herself reaching for her breasts every time she is alone, feeling for the lump and being oddly reassured by its presence. Like a mathematical proof, it confirms that she had no choice but to be back in Australia: she needs to get her health taken care of. And yet.

Conversation with her father and Eve is not easy; she is unpractised at its ease and flow, her instinct for direct question and answers not allowing room for comfort let alone intimacy. In the afternoons it becomes worse: the feeling of being an encumbrance, someone to be looked after and entertained. Twice, Lotte walks into town in the early evening and installs herself at one of the bars that has popped up in the last few years. The music is too loud for anyone to try and talk to her, and most of the clientele is too young to bother. She is left with her own thoughts, chasing each other about her mind.

•

Vin came to visit her twice in the first year she was working at the IAO. As autumn fell, they spent their holiday hiking in Patagonia, Lotte's enthusiasm for the expedition faultless and unusual. Towards the end of the year, Vin visited again, and Lotte took leave, flying down to Buenos Aires for the first time. Waiting at the airport to greet him, she was strangely nervous, as if on a first date rather than seeing her husband after months of absence (the hiccupping and dwindling of their Skype calls notwithstanding).

That afternoon, Lotte disentangled herself from Vin's arms and left him sleeping. She strolled the streets of Buenos Aires with no endpoint in mind, crossing to walk in the sun where it filtered between the tall buildings, surprised to find herself in a place so European. The same slate-grey mansard roofs of Parisian apartment buildings; small balconies overlooking wide boulevards. After twenty minutes of walking through streets littered with the imprudent purple of jacaranda trees in full bloom, the streets opened up into a square, and the palm trees bobbing above the geometric flowerbeds were the only reminder she was in the southern hemisphere. At one end of the plaza was a rose-pink building, like a child's drawing of a princess's castle, with the Argentinian flag flying from its roof. Lotte dodged the heaving buses to walk towards it, only to find it was undergoing renovation, surrounded by placards and scaffolding. In the forecourt was a maze of display boards, an outdoor exhibition of world press photographs from the year before, current affairs moved swiftly to history. Barack Obama, eyes closed and standing like a pillar in his black wool coat and leather gloves moments before his inauguration; a giraffe collapsed in a Kenyan ditch, felled by drought; women shouting dissent from a Tehran rooftop. Should she know more about each of these things? Murderous drought in Africa, vote rigging in Iran — yet what use was it to know?

A coffee in hand, she took a seat on a park bench, watching people go about their day. A group of women began to gather by the pale obelisk in the square's centre. Each pulled from her bag a white scarf and tied it over her hair and beneath her chin. Lotte had heard about these women: grandmothers and mothers of the disappeared. She had not realised they still marched, that there still must be reason to: their revolutionary children long ago disappeared by the government, their grandchildren adopted out to families of government officials to be brought up with no knowledge of their parents' fates.

She had already made her decision, and knew it was the right one. How many times had she and Vin had a discussion about their future? Searching questions about what each of them wanted, but never directly asking. Only once had it been an argument, just before she left for Chile, both of them trying too hard to prove her relocation was purely to do with work, and that their relationship was not under threat. He showed her a house he thought they should put a bid on. Three bedrooms, a double garage, and already a cubby house in the backyard.

It's perfect for kids, he said, tapping through the images.

We don't have any, she had replied, and tried too late to make it sound like a joke.

But we will, he said. When you come back. Maybe we can get started when I come to visit? He smiled at her, almost a wink, but her face froze; it wouldn't smile back.

Vin, I don't want children.

Even as she said the words she was surprised by how unfamiliar they sounded, as if even the thought had not yet been properly articulated. But repeating them to herself she knew they were correct. From the look on his face she could see it wasn't a sentiment he shared.

What do you mean?

She shrugged, apologetic. I don't want children. I just don't feel the need for them in my life.

Her voice drifted as she watched him shaking his head, his face crumpled. *Our life*, she could almost hear him thinking. *You're saying you don't want children in* our *life.* But of course he said nothing so blatantly emotive, proceeding with caution as though she might get spooked and flee from any sudden accusations.

But we've talked about this before, said Vin. A lot. You always said it's something we would do. Later—

I think I meant never.

She urged an apology into her voice, but the words fell flat. He was right.

It's not something I want to do. I have no desire for it, Vin, I don't think I'd be good at it. I'm happy with what we have; I don't want to give that up.

What makes you think you'd have to?

And they'd argued then, long into the night. Lotte trying to justify her decision and resenting having to. Searching for new ways of explaining, but falling back on the only thing that made sense. The truth: she didn't want them. Would it have been so hard for either of them to believe if their roles were reversed? Why did she feel like she was failing him in so many ways? She stacked her reasons up one by one: her job; her lack of want. And the trump card: her genetics. If she had the gene mutation like her mother, she might pass it on to her daughters — not to mention guaranteeing them the same grief as she had gone through, that of losing a parent so early. Vin valiantly attacked each argument, labelling them strawmen and burning them down, and Lotte saw she had failed to make herself understood. Selective IVF, advanced technology, prevention, he said. He would take leave; she could go back to work. In the tired hours of the night — the lights in their lounge room too bright, but neither making a move to switch them off — Vin made Lotte feel that her decision was flawed in some way, that she was missing important evidence, and drawing illogical conclusions from what she had. She almost capitulated, hinted that with time she could reconsider. Yet deep inside she nursed a tiny feeling of relief, of something released under pressure and gently spreading. She didn't want children, that was all. A small thing, but a little truth she could hold, something that belonged just to her. Her mother would have understood.

The position in Chile became an unspoken reprieve for them both. It was work not choice that took her away from him. She missed him fiercely, particularly in those first few weeks, which were tainted by his resentment at her bombshell. Time and distance returned their equilibrium. The same delicate balance that each moon had to find: the safety of a planet, or the freedom of going it alone? Asimov called it the 'tug-of-war' value — the measure of how much a moon is pulled between its planet and the sun. How much anyone is torn between two things they want in equal measure.

Following his observation to its logical conclusion, Asimov reasoned that Earth's moon is actually a planet in its own right — after all, its tug of war is technically being won by the Sun. Asimov saw the moon and Earth as a double-planet system rather than a parent and its satellite: the two planets circling the sun in step together, Fred and Ginger. The moon is always 'falling' towards the Sun, he said, an unfaithful mistress, while all other satellites fall faithfully for their dedicated planets. If the Sun pulled a little harder, the moon might just break away.

Watching the grandmothers and mothers link arms and step out, Lotte felt definitively alone. She was relieved she would never know the particular loss they were forced to reckon with. Parenting was not for her, she was certain of that. In coming to her decision, she had freed herself from a future she had never been ready for. And now she had to do the same for Vin.

The week in Buenos Aires was like the honeymoon they never had. Long mornings in bed, late nights in restaurants, bars, busy plazas bundled up against the cold. Each time they went to bed Lotte said a silent goodbye, straining into his embrace, searching deep for the memories to hold onto. In Puerto Iguazu, they stayed in a hotel with a bath shaped like a water lily, green mats on the floor like lily pads, and towels rolled to look like swans parked on the bed. At Iguazu Falls, standing on a metal walkway as the water thundered into the Devil's Throat below, sending up rainbows in the spray, Lotte resolved to tell him that evening. And then the next. But it wasn't until they returned to the Buenos Aires airport, her flight to Chile called before his to Sydney, that she told him.

I think we should separate, she said. End this. Divorce.

She stumbled over the words, swapping one for another, struggling to make her meaning clear.

I'm not in love with you, Vin. Any more.

Tacking the last phrase on as though it would make any difference. To convince them both that things had changed, that they were no longer what they had been. But the words were clumsy, matching the decor of the Starbucks-inspired cafe in the departures lounge. She was sure he would recognise the lie, but what other reason could she give?

I think you should find someone else, she said. Someone who wants the things you want.

What she wanted was for him to refute her in that moment. To declare that he could only ever want her, whatever that entailed. But he didn't answer for a time, his eyes searching out an alternative reality over her shoulder, somewhere back by the check-in desk.

Have you? Found someone else? At the IAO?

She tossed up the merits of taking this option. One lie begets another.

No, it's not that, she said. I just don't feel there's anything left between us.

She wished she hadn't used the word 'just'. It made it seem as though she was being offhand or flippant. A decision she'd come to lightly. She wished she could explain properly, but she knew the more words she uttered, the more options she risked offering.

You've already decided, he said, not bothering to frame it as a question.

I'm sure.

Vin pushed back his chair and stood. His T-shirt was hitched at his belt, a triangle of exposed skin underneath. His hands held the back of the chair, his close-trimmed nails so familiar.

It's not about love, is it?

She felt his eyes bore into her, willing her to look up.

Does it matter? she asked. I want you to be happy, and you won't be happy with me.

That's for me to decide, he said.

I've already decided. Lotte spoke only to his hands on the chair. Yet she made herself look up; she owed him that. His face was white, jaw clenched. Eyebrows collapsing toward his nose, the whole facade about to crumble.

Goodbye, Vin.

You know I'd do anything for you, Lotte. Give up every single thing I ever wanted if it meant keeping you.

She nodded, her throat closing, heart pounding in her ears, swallowing as though it might keep the emotion in check.

I know, she said.

When he walked away, he didn't look back. She will always admire him for that.

•

As Lotte tries to fill her days at Eve and Tom's, she finds herself drawn to Mina, enraptured by the little girl's certainty at her place in the world. She is surprised by how much she enjoys the childish art projects, the conversations running in circles. But one afternoon when Eve, Tom, and Mina planned to go to a friend's barbecue, Lotte pleads a headache: she doesn't want to tag along.

She finds her mother's old address book in one of the kitchen drawers while looking for some sticky tape to fix Mina's torn finger-painting. Its spine is cracked, some of the pages loose and feathered at their edges. The handwriting is familiar, the rounded 'o's and loopy 't's happily balanced on the blue lines. Some of the addresses have been crossed out, a few of those amended with a new entry just below. Green ticks parade down the edge of each page, marking off some of the entries, all of them landline numbers. Lotte is taken back to a moment years ago, watching her father in profile, Adam's apple dipping as he swallowed repeatedly, brow furrowed. Lotte would read out a name from the address book, and he nodded or shook his head. When he nodded, she dialled the number, passing the receiver to him where he sat slouched on one of the kitchen stools. Sometimes the phone rang out, or an answering machine picked up. He would shake his head, and Lotte would press the catch into the base of the phone, cutting the call.

When somebody answered, Tom waited for their greeting before giving his own, and Lotte would put a tick next to their name in the address book, concentrating on the mark on the page, not wanting to listen to the conversation.

Usually his gathering silence would be enough — they would understand before he even began to say. But sometimes he automatically answered their greetings: *Good thanks, and you?*, his reply inviting the telling of some small anecdote to which he would listen in near silence, offering only the most hesitant of encouragements as the person at the other end of the line talked on. It only took forty-five minutes to call every one of Helen's friends and let them know. When they finished the calls, Lotte and Tom sat at the dining table and wrote the death notice for the newspaper. The language staid, reluctant to admit too much pain. How much was there by then? Only numbness. Relief. The pain wasn't theirs, not yet.

Having found sticky tape and mended Mina's artwork (a lion or butterfly — she was convinced it was both things), Lotte turns the pages of the address book back to the beginning. Not recognising the name next to the first green tick, she runs her finger down the page. *Diane Allan*. She'd taught with Helen, and she'd lived on a property out of town. Lotte recalled a brunette bob, the fringe blunt and unforgiving above brightly coloured glasses. Diane sometimes gave Helen a lift home from work when it was raining; on those nights, Lotte would arrive home, dripping, from the bus stop on the corner to find the two of them sitting in Diane's car parked in the driveway, the rain sparkling in the beams of the headlights.

Hello?

Can I speak to Diane, please?

Just a minute.

The tap of the receiver on a hard surface, footsteps going and coming.

Diane speaking.

My name's Lotte. Lotte Wren. I'm ringing about my mother, Helen.

A pause.

Lotte, yes, how lovely to hear from you. I think of your mother all the time, she was such a wonderful woman.

There was a longer pause and then Diane's voice brightened. What was it you were calling about, Lotte?

From where she stands in the kitchen, Lotte can see a trio of linocut prints — cherry blossoms and temples — that her parents had brought back from their trip to Japan the year Lotte went to uni. She wonders if Tom and Eve and Mina go on holidays together. That's what families do.

It's just … I've been thinking lately, about how I never … I thought it would be nice to know what other people remember of my mum.

The words rush out of Lotte, thoughts coming together as she speaks them.

Well, says Diane after a moment. She was a beautiful woman, just beautiful. It's awful what happened to her, we all thought that. But surely you knew her better than me?

Lotte can hear the raised eyebrows in Diane's voice, as if gesturing to someone about the strange nature of the call but determined not to be ruffled.

I guess I've just been thinking about how other people saw her, and how they remember her. I don't want to feel like she's been forgotten.

Diane takes a moment to reply.

Your father remarried, didn't he? It was fairly quick, wasn't it? It was four years.

She's very young, I heard. Much younger than your father. What's she like? Is she a bit, well, you know?

She's fine. She's nice, says Lotte, her defences rushing to Eve.

Must be different to your mother, though? I mean, Helen was the life of the party; she was always in the thick of things. She had a lot of friends, I don't know how she did it, really — I've barely got the time to keep up with my own family. But Helen was a great one for social events, not like your father at all. Everyone loved Helen.

Diane warms to the subject as she speaks, interrupting

herself when another memory strikes her, telling Lotte about her mother's sense of humour, her determination to get even the most uninterested children involved in science by assigning them messy projects such as papier-mâché exploding volcanoes, or aircraft that could save an egg from smashing when dropped from the classroom's second-storey window. They are stories Lotte has heard her mother tell, nothing new, but there is something reassuring about hearing them from Diane.

She talked about you often, Lotte. She was so proud of you going off to uni, studying physics, wasn't it? Astronomy? Just like her?

Yes. I work for an observatory now.

She would have been happy about that. Look, Lotte, I have to go, I've got my grandchildren coming soon. I hope I've been helpful, it really was lovely to hear from you.

Lotte hangs up. Nothing Diane had told her is new, but even with a twenty-minute conversation, she feels closer to her mother than she has in a long time. Lotte turns the pages of the address book, looking for the next entry that is accompanied by a green tick, and picks up the phone.

Lit by a single spotlight that tickled at their manes, three retired Clydesdale horses munch hay in the bare paddock of the open-air museum. They don't flinch at the orange and red lights that flash beyond the trees, or the rifle fire cracking across the horizon. The sound-and-light show plays out seven nights a week, fighting once again (and twice on Saturdays) the battle between gold miners and police for which Ballarat is known. The miners had brazenly pilfered the Crux constellation for their cause, emblazoning a blue flag with the bright white stars of the Southern Cross. Eve had worked on it, Lotte recalls, using the job as an excuse to move to town, to get closer to Tom. Such a calculated manoeuvre; Lotte can almost admire its audacity.

At the top of the hill, night has lifted itself into the clouds. The streetlights of the city criss-cross the landscape like tartan, fogging the sky with insolent spill. The observatory, built by a passionate amateur and gifted to the town back in a time when people still did such things, is too close beneath the umbrella of light pollution to be of much scientific use any more, but it is popular with tourists, families, and school groups. She hasn't been back here since her mother stopped volunteering.

Lotte sits in the back of the small theatre wearing 3-D glasses and watching a cartoonish film that compels the planets to swoop and hurtle past one another like brazen roller-derby competitors on the chase. She'd spent the afternoon in a cinema, too, watching two new-release films — anything to avoid the awkwardness of being at the house. After the film, a man comes to the front of the stage: Simon. He had called her that afternoon, replying to a message she left on his phone; his was one of the numbers in Helen's address book, but Lotte can barely remember him. He was eager to talk, insistent that she come and meet him at the observatory that night — he lived out of town, he didn't want to have to drive in twice, didn't want to talk on the phone. Lotte was wary — over the last two days, the conversations with her mother's friends had been wearily similar. All of them remember a bright, vivacious woman who worked hard and died too young. A woman who is sounding less and less familiar with every phone call; time never moves backwards.

Simon's beard juts forward, and when he uses his arms to gesture he does not look at his hands, staring past their waving and demonstrating to the audience, giving the impression that his hands are nothing to do with him. He throws in a few well-practiced jokes; the audience laughs. He is not as engaging as Helen was: he has none of that infectious joy that demands enthusiasm. When he asks the children in the audience if they can name the rover currently exploring Mars, a small child in the front row goes one better, explaining in her confident, piping voice the significance of Curiosity's most recent findings. After a PowerPoint presentation, the families follow in a crocodile line to a telescope set up in one of the large domes, where they will be able to view Orion up close, and perhaps even Jupiter — though considering the size of the telescope, Lotte suspects it will appear little more than a russet-coloured Christmas bauble.

When all the children have had their turn at the telescope, Lotte steps up. Jupiter is tiger-striped in red and beige, and in a straight line, three to the top and one to the bottom, are the bright spots of the Jovian moons. Everything in its place: Jupiter's four lovers, trapped in an eternal orbit. It was their discovery by Galileo that hinted the Earth was not the centre of the universe: here were four moons orbiting a planet, begging the question, what might the Earth be orbiting? She recalls her mother's descriptions: Io, her surface potted with lava-spurting volcanoes, was the most protective and jealous of the four. Europa, much more composed, a smooth layer of ice trapping forever an enormous sea and the possibility of life. Ganymede, larger but lighter than Mercury, the biggest of all the moons in the solar system. And Callisto, that crotchety old aunt, a face of craters and a heart of rock and ice; she is out of step with the three other moons, who all orbit their king with a neat resonance, a family devoted, one being unable to move without the others following. Lotte cannot tell which is which from the telescope, each one just a pinprick of light.

If you look to the outer part of the eyepiece, not the middle, the image will be clearer. Simon's voice taps her on the shoulder.

You need to use your peripheral vision, he continues, because the rod cells towards the edge of the retina are better suited to night viewing, though they're not so good on colour—

I know, she cuts him off, taking one last look before relinquishing the telescope to a child who wants another go.

Lotte?

Simon sticks out his hand, and she shakes it.

I didn't recognise you — you've grown up. He stares at her face as though trying to place her. Or trying to place somebody else. I'll just finish up things here, and then we can talk.

He gives a final speech to the group and passes around a baseball cap for tips, patiently answering all of the children's questions. The families trail down the hill toward the carpark, children quiet with tiredness, parents buzzing with the satisfaction of an outing complete.

So.

He tips the coins into his hand and folds the cap in half, stuffing it in the back pocket of his jeans.

Would you like a cup of tea?

Despite the warm night he wears a navy-blue polar-fleece vest, the Southern Cross embroidered on the breast, a single silver thread linking each of the stars. Simon leads Lotte to one of the old brick buildings ringed in footlights, its dome disappearing into the night so that it looks oddly stumped. Inside is a boardroom, a large polished wooden table ringed by chairs. He stops at a panel of light switches, turning them on one by one, a quiet buzzing emanating from each wall.

You should take a look; we've had them restored. He disappears into a side room to make tea. Black or white?

White.

The room's windows flicker brilliantly into view, lit by fluorescent tubes fixed in the window frames. One of the windows is fringed with gum leaves, a stained glass kookaburra and a magpie against a setting sun, while in the sky above, Saturn frolics with two other planets. In another window, an owl reposes to one side of a globe, blue birds perching on the other, as opposite as night and day. A third window features duelling telescopes, each one pointing across the view of the other. The pictures are like a child's colouring book, thick guiding lines and strong blocks of colour.

It's been almost nine years, hasn't it? Since Helen …

He hesitates, glancing at her to see if he is required to say the dreaded word.

Died, says Lotte. She remembers now, seeing him at the funeral. Hunched shoulders as if he could hide his height, a brand new shirt that still bore the creases from being folded in its plastic sleeve. She'd been surprised he was there; she hadn't seen him for so many years, she thought he must have moved away.

Simon sets the tea on the table. I was surprised to get your message, he says. I didn't suppose you'd want to talk to me.

Why not?

He pauses, takes a sip of his tea.

No reason. I guess I just meant it was a surprise to hear from you. Kind of out of the blue.

I was just curious, says Lotte. About my mother. In my memories, she was always busy, running around and trying to get things done.

Simon nods. She was the driving force for a lot of the stuff we did here, he says. Most of the committee were more interested in the telescopes themselves, you know, men who just wanted to get them restored, wanted the place recognised as something special. For them, the observatory was a monument. But Helen wanted to invite people in — kids, families, school groups. The committee thought she was being too inclusive, that she was at risk of dumbing down the importance of the place. But she'd give as good as she got, asking them what good a monument was if there was no one to see it.

Did she seem impatient to you? Lotte asks.

Impatient? I don't know if that's the word I'd use. Adamant, perhaps. Once she made a decision, she stuck to it.

Lotte looks around at the stained glass windows, the museum atmosphere of the room. She can hear the bitterness in Simon's voice, and attributes it to workplace politics. He wouldn't have been the first person her mother butted heads with.

But did she ever seem like she wanted more than this? Lotte asks. Did she ever want to really study astronomy, to be a scientist?

If she didn't have a child, she wants to add. What might her life have been if it weren't for the arrival of a daughter? An alternate reality where Helen excelled at her passions, where Lotte never was. She wouldn't hold it against her mother.

Helen? No. Simon says with certainty. No, this was her hobby. She never wanted it to be a job. Astronomers — the ones at research facilities, universities, that sort of thing — it's a job to them. It's all about the physics, the science. They're so busy writing papers and chasing grant money that they don't have the time to actually look up there and see what's going on ...

He trails off, taking in Lotte's amusement.

You studied astronomy, didn't you? I remember now.

Lotte nods. I just came back from five years at the IAO.

Well, you'd know what I mean then, says Simon laughing.

They talk then, about the planet-hunting projects Lotte has

worked on and some of the more recent discoveries.

Do you still hold those stargazing parties? Lotte asks. I remember Mum taking me to your place out of town.

She recalls the unfettered enthusiasm of the astronomy club members, their friendly competitiveness as they set up their telescopes, comparing specs and prices.

Sometimes, says Simon, smiling. Helen loved it out there. She would have been happy—

He stops himself, gulping down his tea.

What were you going to say? Lotte's curiosity is piqued. You don't think she was happy?

I'm sure she was. But I didn't see her after she got sick.

He gets up, holding his hand out for Lotte's mug, signalling the talk is over. I better get going, says Simon. Got the dogs at home.

He heads into the kitchen.

I don't think there's anything else I can tell you, he calls out. You know, it's been about fifteen years since I last saw her. She stopped volunteering here a long time ago. She didn't come back after she was sick; she stayed at home with your father.

Simon appears in the doorway of the kitchen, tea towel in his hands.

He was never interested in astronomy, says Lotte. And I suppose Mum no longer had the energy.

Something like that, says Simon. I better lock up here. But you go ahead. It was nice to see you, Lotte.

They shake hands for a little longer than necessary, before Simon turns back to the kitchen. Lotte wants to step up behind him and give him a hug; his misery is palpable. *Tell me*, she wants to say. But she doesn't want to know.

She walks through the car park and along the shoulder of the road. Just before she comes to the main road a ute passes her, slows, then pulls ahead into the roundabout, taking the exit that leads out beyond the suburbs.

Walking back to her father and Eve's, she thinks about those stargazing parties. The astronomy group members with their layers of rain jackets, and woollen jumpers covered in dog hair; their plastic containers of homemade food, which they offered round incessantly; thermoses of tea and bottles of cordial. At sixteen, Lotte had found it completely uncool, and she'd expected her mother to be the same. Yet there was Helen, in the thick of it all, listening with rapt attention as two men compared filters, later helping a uni student set up his tripod on the rocky ground. As the night wound on, Lotte had found herself enjoying the easy camaraderie of the group, their commitment clouding out the knowledge that others might not find it all as fascinating as they did. It was this freedom that Lotte saw reflected in her mother: something had been released in her; she was no longer striving. It was only in its absence that she could identify the nervous energy she always associated with her mother, energy that kept Helen just ahead and out of reach.

The only other time Lotte has seen that same calm descend on Helen was when she had accompanied her to church. Only a handful of times, and only then to be of use — carrying a pillow for Helen to sit on, driving when she felt too tired — never thinking of it as something they might be doing together. Once, they'd gone to the cathedral in the centre of town, and Lotte sat beside her mother in the pew, considering the burnished-gold eagle that adorned the pulpit, the hanging lanterns and elaborate tiled floors. Too much in the aid of so little. A polished golden tabernacle, a silver chalice of wine: gratuitous riches for a god who'd apparently invented the very metals they were formed from.

She preferred it when her mother wanted to go to the small church where the funeral was eventually held, because, after the first few visits, Lotte would leave her mother at her prayer and go walking along the lake foreshore. Lotte felt an entirely different reluctance at that small church than the grand cathedral: it felt immoral to accompany Helen into that simple, honest space, unadorned and encouraging of the kind of self-reflection that Lotte did not want to engage in. In the end, it made the funeral all the worse: back in that same space again, reminded of all the times she had left her mother there, so eager to get away and have some time to herself. After each visit Helen seemed content, as though she had lost her manic efforts at living: the crossed conversations with multiple friends; the ransacking of the house for keepsakes from the past. Instead, she was happy to sit quietly with Lotte in the car, paper cups of hot chocolate in their hands, watching the black swans glide about on the lake's surface, looking for the one bird whose red beak had somehow faded to a dull pink.

She hopes the house will be in darkness by the time she returns, but the lights are on. She quietly walks down the hallway and slips into the study. There on the bed lie two dresses — one of her own, and a much smaller one. Two red dresses, just like she had promised Mina they would wear. She forgot all about her promise to be home for dinner. She should go out and apologise for being late, but she feels so suddenly tired. Surely Eve was just being polite, trying to involve Lotte in a family she is no longer a part of.

She will leave tomorrow, and find a place to stay in Sydney for when the surgery is over, and before the chemo starts. A bolthole to hide out in until she is ready for all of this again. She remembers her mother once describing the complications of family as a solar system: each person like a planet, keeping their moons spinning close and influencing the paths of their companions. They grab at anything that comes near: a free-spirited satellite, a comet, a space shuttle. Drift too close to another and you risk falling down a planet's gravity well, being destroyed on its surface; stay too far away and you risk being cut loose, discarded into the ever growing reaches of outer space. Helen had been cut loose long ago; maybe it was Lotte's turn. After the treatment she will get a job at one of the observatories over in Western Australia, or South Africa. Somewhere new and just far enough away.

10

EVE

AUGUST 2015

Are you alright?

Her body has no edges. She cannot feel the hands on her shoulder, the sand beneath her head. Len's face appears in front of hers, eyes brown, flecked with hazel. No, Mina's eyes were a steely blue, just like Tom's. The paramedic had opened one of her eyes, shone a torch in it, the pupil flooded with black. Mina had not flinched at the intrusion. She had been loaded in to the ambulance, Tom scrambling behind. Tom not looking back to see if Eve was following him.

It's Eve, isn't it? You're cold, you're shaking, we've got to get you inside. What were you …?

But he doesn't finish the question, because he's not sure he wants to hear the answer.

There is sand in her mouth. Her tongue recoils, she spits, again and again. Teeth pass against each other, and the crunch of the sand between them roars in her ears.

Come on, let me help you up. We'll get you inside.

Dad, what about the stuff?

There is a young boy standing nearby his head encased in a helmet, a puffy jacket ballooning around his chest. He's holding a fishing rod, and the fly dangles, catching the sun.

Leave it, Jordie. We'll come back for it later.

They stumble up the beach, past an esky and bucket. Rather, Eve stumbles, and Len stoops so his weight is under her arm, pushing her up. Wet jeans rub at her legs, and her feet seem to take steps.

You'll be right in a minute. It's a bit cold for swimming, isn't that right, Jordie?

She should have a wetsuit, Dad. He speaks with confidence, his small feet lifting high above the sand and stamping down. It's winter. The surfers have wetsuits in winter, I've seen them.

When they get to the road, Eve doesn't feel the asphalt beneath her soles: her feet bump across the road, heavy with numbness. Wind slips its clammy fingers beneath her shirt; her jeans sag at the waist, so she has to clutch hold to stop them from falling down.

There is a house behind the camping ground office. Inside, it's warm and dim, and Len directs her to sit on the couch. How wrong her wet jeans and her sandy feet are; how inappropriate. The pamphlets had mentioned 'inappropriate' behaviour; how to spot if someone is too sad, or if they have grieved for too long. She wants to sleep. They had told her — reinforcing the point with a pamphlet decorated with photographs of dew-dropped flowers — that denial is a stage of grief. That acceptance is one, too. But every time she thinks about these stages, she pictures the Tour de France, the dense peloton like rainbow parakeets flocking up the mountain, thinning through hairpin bends, and dripping over the finish line, one at a time. Each stage mapped out with an elevation profile, the steep gradients like a heart-rate monitor soaring skyward, then plummeting to the level. But each of those riders gets to finish the stage. Yellow jersey or not, they complete, rest, and move on to the next, until they scoot across the finish line, bumping over the cobblestones and past the Arc de Triomphe. They choose to race.

I'm sorry. My tent. I'll be okay. I'm just cold.

That's alright, there's no rush, we'll get you sorted. Len disappears through a doorway. The boy is watching, his hair sticking up between the ribs of his helmet.

Were you going fishing? She feels an adult's need to fill the silence.

He nods, then looks towards the doorway, visibly relieved when Len comes back bearing a towel, a blanket, and a dressing gown.

Here you go. You get those wet things off, and wrap this about you. We'll just be in the kitchen. He puts the pile next to Eve on the couch. His caterpillar eyebrows scurry towards one another.

Will you be okay?

Yes, thank you. I'm sorry.

Come on, mate, Len says as he shepherds his son out of the room. Let's get some breakfast.

But what about the fishing?

In a minute — we'll go back in a bit.

She rubs the towel against her face, her tongue, gagging on the sand that refuses to leave. Manages to unzip the hoodie, but her fingers are too thick to undo the jeans. She pulls at them but they snag on her hips, which don't lift when she tries to move, so she gives up, folding herself down over the towel.

This is what it would have felt like. Mina: still alive, but her body refusing to be told what to do. When Mina was a baby, Eve had expected her to lie so still and quiet that she might worry about whether she was still breathing. But like all babies, Mina was rarely still, woken by her own snuffles and sighs, her arms and legs flying about, involuntarily waving, accidentally whacking herself in the face before she learnt to control her limbs. As Mina grew, Eve was consistently surprised by her strength: her ability to hold up her head; to crawl at speed; to pump the pedals of a tricycle. Perfectly normal milestones for any child, but ones that Eve observed with fascination, still able to see the tiny newborn shadowing the girl. When Mina first pulled herself to her feet, and, soon after, lurched from the coffee table to the couch, Eve was astounded. But Mina herself had seemed accepting, satisfied with the way of things.

How often had Eve begged her to sit down or sit still, or wrestled her squirming and resisting body into the pram or car seat? And then, so suddenly and without complaint, she had become still. Too still.

•

The key was on the stand in the hallway — she remembered that clearly. But before that? And afterwards? All of it had disappeared. It was there, she knew it was, but recalling those moments was like looking through frosted glass: colour, movement, muffled sound. She had picked up the key. Even now she can see, very clearly, her hand reaching out and closing around the pineapple keyring. How many times had she wished she never picked it up, that it was still lying there, ignored amongst the other keys and loose coins? The feel of it was familiar in her hand, the plastic brush of the spiky foliage, the rubber softness of the fruit. It was Lotte who had bought that keyring for her: a memento from one of their camping trips to the Sunshine Coast. Eve doubted Lotte remembered buying it, so why did she?

Before she picked up the key, there was the argument. She knows this because Lotte had apologised for it profusely. But before that? It was an ordinary day. Which it wasn't, of course. The only days to ever be described as 'ordinary' are the ones that don't turn out to be that way.

Tom was in the garden, binding twine around stakes, creating pyramids for the snow peas to climb. Mina was watching cartoons, lying sideways on the couch; then sliding to the floor; then flopping on to her stomach. All done without taking her eyes from the screen — her body itching for movement, while her mind was enthralled by the television. *She's inherited that from me*, thought Eve, sitting at the kitchen table, idly flipping pages of the weekend newspaper, aware of all the other things she should be doing, such as clearing the breakfast dishes, mixing the museum's soundscape of a parish hall (a racket of stamping feet, exuberant shouts, and the calls of a Saturday night dance in the early 1960s), wrapping the present for the birthday party Mina was to attend that afternoon.

Lotte was still asleep, of course. Despite the reassurances, she had not turned up as arranged for dinner last night, and Eve's heart near burst for Mina's disappointment. Mina in her red dress, white polka dots scattered over its ruffled skirt, going to check the study again and again. Pulling Lotte's own red dress from her suitcase, draping it over the sofa bed in readiness of her big sister's arrival. But no big sister to be seen.

You can wear your red dress again tomorrow for the party, sweetie, Eve had promised, putting Mina to bed and cursing Lotte's thoughtlessness. Pausing briefly at the door of the study to check Tom wasn't looking, Eve stepped into the room and draped Mina's dress over Lotte's where it lay on the bed. It had turned into a long night: there had been tears and a tantrum,

Mina unwilling to relinquish her dreams of the evening, and Eve unable to forgive Lotte her absence. The lasagne waited in the oven, pasta sheets curling at their edges, until Tom had served it up, accompanied by excessive compliments and the comment that Lotte didn't know what she was missing out on. It was almost eleven o'clock when Lotte did get home, Eve and Tom both alert as they listened to the scrabbling of a key in the front door, the clomping footsteps down the hallway. Eve braced herself for Lotte's breathy apology or vague excuse, but it didn't come, the footsteps turning into the study, the door closing.

I'm going to bed, Eve said, leaving Tom in front of the television, annoyed at Lotte as much as herself. In bed she had fumed, going over their earlier conversation in her mind. Surely Lotte had seen the excitement in Mina's face; surely she knew how her absence might be felt?

Over an hour later, unable to fall into sleep and distracted by the murmur of voices, Eve got up. Tom had not come to bed. Inching up the hallway, tense and hoping the floorboards wouldn't creak, an interloper in her own house, she paused at the entrance to the kitchen, confused by Tom's sniggering laughter.

I can't believe I thought they looked good!

Everyone must have been wearing them, said Lotte. What about Mum's poncho — remember how it had those tassels and the orange fringe? All my friends thought she was the most fashionable mother. We must have a photo of her wearing that somewhere, she loved it.

There *was* a photo, Eve knew, one where Helen was standing with her hands on her hips, smirking at the camera, the poncho spread square across her chest. Eve strode into the kitchen, flipping the light on.

There it is! Oh God, she loved that thing. It's hideous!

Tom and Lotte were crouched over the dining table, photo albums strewn about them on the floor.

Eve, sorry, did we wake you? Tom looked up, a smile still on his face. The kind of smile he usually reserved for Mina. Unabashed.

No, just getting some water, she said. She took a glass from the cupboard. What are you looking at?

Just some old family photos, said Tom.

You haven't shown me those before, Eve said. Not wanting him to know how many hours she had spent looking at them herself; that she had followed Lotte's childhood, Tom's marriage, from page to page.

I didn't think you'd be interested.

There was hurt in his voice, but she shrugged it off, aware of Lotte's eyes, watching. Always watching.

You never asked me.

It was a childish argument, and she hated the way she fell into it.

Come and see, said Lotte, moving over to make space. I'm sorry about dinner, Evie, I completely forgot. I ran into this man Mum used to know. We were reminiscing and I lost track—

It doesn't matter, Eve said, cutting Lotte off. Goodnight.

Head down as she marched back to the bedroom, careful not to slam the door. Lying in bed, listening out for their voices, itching with annoyance the provenance of which she couldn't face. She had pushed herself into this family; she was the one who deserved to be on the outer.

And the next day — the ordinary-seeming day — Lotte had slept in. Mina had discovered the abandoned photo albums as she ate her breakfast, flipping through them, enthralled by the mysterious little girl and confused about Eve's absence.

234

Where's you, Mum? Is that Dad? Who's that?

And Eve had gathered up the albums, ignoring Mina's pleas, and tried to distract her with pancakes and television, tried to return the house to what they knew, ignoring Lotte's invisible presence. Tom had begun to build his pyramids in the garden, winding wire around the base, giving the vines something to cling onto.

It was Lotte who started the argument. Eve had just let Mina into the back yard when she heard the door of the study open, and she dove towards the table, yanking her headphones on and pretending to be absorbed in her laptop, though every part of her body was attuned to Lotte's movements around the kitchen. It had sometimes been like this when they'd lived together. An argument about late rent payments or Lotte's inability to wash dishes would result in a stand off; early morning frost, the two of them overly polite and extra careful, apologising for being in the way in a tone that implied they weren't sorry at all. There had been the disagreements about Nate and then Eve thinking Lotte was stringing Vin along; the times they grew tired of the other's indecision about a situation that seemed so clear-cut from the outside. It was almost always Lotte who would crack first, reaching over to give Eve a back rub, or depositing a cup of tea on her desk with a smile, and soon they would be back to normal. It seemed like an ordinary day.

I am sorry, you know, Lotte said, pulling out a chair and sitting opposite Eve. I didn't mean to stand you up last night.

Eve tugged her headphones from her ears, tried not to catch Lotte's eye.

It doesn't matter.

It does matter. You don't believe me.

Eve sighed, making a show of closing her computer.

I don't have to believe you, she said. Mina believed you. She thought you would be there for dinner.

Even as she said it, Eve recognised the facade for what it was. Mina cared about wearing a pretty dress, about getting attention from someone new. It was Eve who'd thought Lotte would be there for dinner, who'd been disappointed when she was not.

I'm not just thinking about myself, Eve continued. I've got other people to think about now. You're not used to that. There are repercussions.

She was horrified at how easily the words came out, desperately hoping Lotte wouldn't hear the patronising tone of them.

Well, what would I know? Lotte smirked. I've got no one, that's what you're trying to say. You've got my father, and you've got Mina, and I've got no one else to think about.

You know that's not what I meant. It's just that Mina was really looking forward to you being there when we invited you, and then you didn't turn up. She was disappointed.

I'm just a guest, mused Lotte. I'm someone who gets invited to dinner. In my own house.

It's not your house, snapped Eve, tired of the game.

Lotte laughed, looking around the room. Mina's toys scattered everywhere, photos of her plastered all over the fridge.

No, I don't suppose it is. Don't you think it's a bit strange, Eve? That I end up with no home, and you end up with mine?

That's not fair! Eve could feel the tears pricking at her eyes. It's not like I meant for any of this to happen, Lotte. You left!

So you thought you'd stay?

Eve shook her head, pushing her chair from the table.

We invited you back. You wouldn't come. What else were we supposed to do? You know I didn't plan any of this. And I tried to talk to you about it. I called you, I emailed you. But you weren't here. You were off making all your big scientific discoveries, as though you're doing something more important than the rest of us.

I never said that. Lotte gestured dismissively at the room, and, once again, Eve saw her life through her friend's eyes. The smallness of domesticity, the minutiae of everyday life — undeniably insignificant in comparison to the machinations of the universe.

Do you think you can bring her back by working harder? asked Eve.

Don't you dare.

She's gone, Lotte. She's not here, and you've got to stop treating me as though she is.

You don't know anything about my mother. She was an incredible woman.

She was just a woman! Eve felt her anger ricochet about her chest. You think she was so perfect? Helen wanted out of the marriage. Did you know that? She wanted out of the family. Nothing you could have done would have made her stay, don't you realise that? You've been chasing this career, thinking it's what she wanted, and she couldn't have cared less. She was having an affair, Lotte. She had left Tom; she'd left you.

You have no idea what you're talking about.

She only came back because of the cancer, said Eve, horrified by the words coming out of her own mouth, but she kept going.

She knew she couldn't cope on her own. But until then she was seeing some man for years, that's what all her nights out were. *Years*, Lotte. It was nothing to do with astronomy. You think she was perfect, she was everything, but she was just like us.

Stop it! You have no idea what you're talking about!

Ask Tom. Ask your father. Eve stood up from the table, throwing a glance over her shoulder. Tom was bent over in the garden, reaching for something. She shouldn't be saying any of this; it wasn't her story to tell. But Lotte needed to know; Lotte who always prided herself on knowing everything.

She would have told me, Lotte said. Something like that. Or Dad would have said.

Why would he? You're never here. You couldn't give a toss about him.

That's not true. Lotte's face was red, tears forming in her eyes.

Helen's not even here any more, Lotte. Who are you trying to prove yourself to? Even Vin didn't want to stick around, you're so selfish, you're so obsessed with your work.

Lotte shook her head.

Vin's happy. He's happier now than he ever could have been with me. Is that selfish?

And I suppose you're happy, too? Is that why you're here, hanging around with nowhere to go?

I was visiting my father. Is that so wrong? Did you ever think maybe he likes me to be here? That he likes being able to remember Helen? Dad loved her like nothing else, Eve. You can't love like that more than once. But you know that, don't you? You know he's doing all of this for the second time; that he's just trying to fill the gap Mum left.

Lotte stalked out of the room, into the study. Eve felt her chest tighten, the distress pushing at her skin, searching for a way out. In that moment, she rued their years of friendship. Lotte knew everything about her; how much they had observed each other all those years.

Eve walked across to the hallway. From the side table she picked up the key, the pineapple keyring tickling at her palm.

Take the campervan, she said.

In the spare room Lotte stood with her hands on her hips,

looking at her bag, the red dress that lay across it.

You can have it; it's yours, said Eve. Take it wherever you want. Just as long as you leave. You shouldn't be here right now. We can't have you here.

She held the plastic pineapple, dangling the key in front of Lotte like a carrot.

No.

Lotte sat back down on the bed, like Mina when she was tired, claiming her ground.

Yes, said Eve, dropping the key in Lotte's lap. They both watched it slide to the floor.

For fuck's sake. Eve bent down, picking up the key. Get your stuff.

The flyscreen door banged shut as she thumped down the steps to the garage. She hauled up the roller door, the dust coming alive in the sunlight. The campervan was faded, a memory of itself; the stickers on the bumper showed the kind of things people used to care about: *Keep Australia Beautiful. Be Safe, Be Sure. Give a Damn, Vote Democrat.*

Squeezing into the narrow space between the wall of the garage and the van, Eve eased the driver's door open and pulled herself into the seat. Vinyl cool against her bare legs, with a towel handy to sit on — it will burn hot if the van is parked in the sun for a few hours, she must remember to remind Lotte of that. No, it doesn't matter. She doesn't actually expect the battery to start, but when she turns the key, the engine coughs into service.

Lotte will leave, and everything will return to normal. The little family: one, two, three. Releasing the handbrake, Eve put the van in reverse. Threw her left arm over the jump seat and looked back at the driveway. After the dark of the garage the bright sun flared, and she clenched her eyes shut, put her foot to the floor. The van leapt backwards, she didn't want it to stall. Gave it some more petrol and pushed out into the day.

And then everything stopped.

•

On Len's couch, Eve curled on her side, sobbing. Mina's face as it was that day: eyes closed, as though she might be sleeping, but also looking a little cross. Eve struggles to draw ragged breaths, her hands clasping at her head as if to stop the thoughts from pooling there. For over six months her mind has not been able to dredge these moments up; she has not even allowed herself to try. But now.

Mina was asleep. Her breaths were quiet. Eve tried to breathe in time with her daughter, small breaths, small lungs. Tom, bending down over her, tipping back her head. Puffing air into her body, her chest big, then small again. Already filling with blood, already the bruises forming beneath her T-shirt.

Eve breathed with Mina, and Mina kept breathing. Mina, so small on the stretcher that Eve did not know how to look at her. Her own heart swelling, too big for the shell of her body, so that she just wanted to excise it, throw it away. She did not deserve to feel that way, to feel at all. She had caused this.

The paramedics spoke calmly to each other; they did not seem to work fast enough, but already there was a tube forced down Mina's throat, her tiny shell teeth clamped around it. And that's how Eve knew it was too late, because if Mina was still there she would be fighting it. *I do it myself!* How many times had she told Eve that? How proud had Eve been of her daughter's determination, even as she was infuriated by it? The thought came at Eve with complete clarity. I have stopped my daughter being able to do it herself. I have stopped my daughter being.

She knew as soon as she felt it. A bump, a small resistance. No, it wasn't a bump, not really. It was a dull misgiving. As though the air behind the camper van had suddenly solidified. A wall built just where the camper happened to be. No crash or impact. One second everything was flowing, the next a bell jar of still. It just all stopped, with the lightest of touches. And Eve floundered about in this broken world, stamping down on the brake, fear jolting through her. Jerking the handbrake up. Flinging the door open, but the van was not quite out of the garage, the door hit the brick wall and banged back towards her, slamming her elbow. Did she feel it then? Or did she only know because her elbow was sore for days, a mockery of Mina's absolute pain? She pushed her way out, running to the rear of the van. Didn't want to see her. Knew that she would. How could she know what had happened and still have let it happen? Mina, lying on her back, arm flung up as though she was protecting her eyes from the sun. Body too loose, too small. Too still.

No!

She screamed. She was bending over Mina, she was lifting her, she was putting her down. Too limp. Too broken. Her shoulder jerked back, Tom was there. Tom would make it alright, he would fix it.

Mina? Mina, can you hear me?

Placing her arm by her side, tipping her head to the sky.

Call an ambulance!

She yelled it, didn't she? Standing, kneeling, reaching for Mina, unable to touch her. Her eyes closed, her hand loosely splayed open.

•

The tube had been removed. There was a white sheet pulled up over Mina's chest, and Eve knew that if she lifted it, she would see her Dora the Explorer T-shirt cut away, her bare chest exposed. Mina's hands lay on top of the sheet, the fingertips stained red and purple with texta. It was not possible, and yet it had already happened. Her daughter had died.

How long did they stay in the room with her? Tom was holding Eve's hand, and then he wasn't. He went to stand up, but then seemed to collapse further into the seat. He was crying, and he was trying not to cry, holding the sobs up near his shoulder, swallowing furiously.

I'm so sorry, Tom. I don't know what happened.

How many times would she utter that phrase to him in the coming days? Comprehending that it had no meaning, accepting that his eyes would scoot away from hers before she could finish speaking.

She didn't see Mina. She thought she was in the backyard; she had sent her out to Tom.

I thought she was with you. Eve whispered the words.

Eve had opened the sliding door, combed Mina's hair with her fingers, and sent her out into the backyard to Tom. Mina needs a haircut, thought Eve, recalling how her fingers had snagged at Mina's hair and her daughter's head had tossed impatiently. The morning struggles to comb her curls — why didn't they just chop it off? They could go to the hairdresser's on Tuesday, before story time at the library. The thought registered, then fled.

No, she wasn't with me, Tom said. I thought she was inside, watching TV.

But I sent her out. To you. You waved at me.

He had waved at her, at them, she was sure of it, his hand high as she had pulled Mina's hair back from her face then let her go, hearing the door of the study opening, steeling herself for Lotte's presence. But maybe Tom hadn't been waving. Maybe it was twine in his hands, pulling it back as he tied the stakes together.

Mr and Mrs Wren?

Two police officers, a man and a woman were standing in the doorway. Eve felt a rush of thanks. They were the picture of authority; they could help.

We're very sorry for your loss.

She did not know what they were talking about. Yet she did. She was glad when they went on.

We need to ask you a few questions. It's just a matter of policy.

Of course, said Tom. He took hold of Eve's hand and she melted toward him, seeking the comfort he offered. But it wasn't comfort. He was making sure she did not run away. It made Eve want to run away.

The police officers stared at their pads. They took notes, asking questions that Tom answered in his calm and certain voice. Eve hoped they were writing down the right answers. The ones that would make sense.

Mrs Wren, can you come with us a minute, please? The woman's ponytail bounced as she looked toward Eve then back to her partner. You'll be able to come back; it won't take long.

Tom let go of her hand, and Eve followed the policewoman down the corridor, into a room that had been divided into cubicles by plastic curtains. The officer whisked each one aside. Only one cubicle held a bed and they sat down next to it.

From her belt, the policewoman took a small unit, then reached to a pocket of her trousers and withdrew a straw. She ripped the plastic from the straw and attached it to the unit. It was as if she was giving Eve a juice box.

Can you take a deep breath and slowly breathe into this?

Eve did as she was told, eyes closed. There was a droning bleep from the machine, and the policewoman nodded.

No reading. You hadn't been drinking, Mrs Wren?

No. It's the morning. Eve was incredulous.

Yes.

The policewoman took a deep breath. She was sitting on a chair that had small wheels, and it nudged backwards when she shuffled about.

Now, can you tell us briefly what happened, Mrs Wren?

Eve waited for the thoughts to arrange themselves, but all she could see were Mina's eyes.

I don't know. I was just ... Her voice trailed off. The big, dark pupils of Mina's eyes.

Can you tell me what happened? What you saw.

Eve looked at her watch. Eleven o'clock. Exactly. Precisely. It was not any other time. She should have been cutting up an apple for Mina, adding a scoop of yoghurt. Sultanas dropped on top like skiers sliding down a mountain. Mina had always wanted to go skiing.

Mrs Wren. Please, take your time.

The officer's leg was bouncing up and down; she was crouched forward as if to protect herself from what she might hear.

What did you see, just before the accident? Where was your daughter?

One past eleven. It was impossible that a minute had passed. An hour, almost two. That she was not back in the living room, just after breakfast, fuming with Lotte.

I didn't see anything.

Dark. Then light. Then nothing at all, until right now. The officer was writing. She didn't stop writing when she asked the next question.

So you didn't see your daughter come out of the house?

No.

And you didn't know where your daughter was at the time?

At the time. Back then, two hours ago. But what does it matter, because now we are here? All that mattered was now.

Where is she now?

The officer looked at her.

Your daughter is just in the other room. With your husband. The officer swallowed. Eve could see her throat contract. She licked her lip. Mrs Wren? You do know your daughter has died, don't you?

Eve let the words lay between them. She waited for the officer to smile, to show that she was joking. But she was not joking.

Yes.

I'm sorry.

They sat in silence for a moment, and then the officer tried again.

Mrs Wren. I know this is difficult. We just need to ask you these questions while the events are still fresh in your mind.

In the days to come, Eve would learn that there was no urgency because 'the events' would only grow fresher, like time-lapse photography of fruit ripening on a vine, of flowers opening for the sun. That her brain would seemingly split: she would be in two places at once, the then and the now. That time would roll forward and back into that moment when Eve got in the van. There was the dark of the garage, and then the light of outside. Again and again, she would see her own hand reach up to the handle above the door, pulling her weight into the driver's seat. The familiar feel of the vinyl of the passenger seat under her hand as she reversed. Then nothing. The questions continued, Eve astounded at her inability to answer them, feeling that she was failing the officer in a way that could not be redeemed, until finally the woman led her back to the other room. To Tom, to Mina.

In the corridor, Eve looked at her feet. She had thongs on; when did she put those on? She had kicked them off in the footwell of the van. She never drove in thongs — it was too dangerous. You couldn't have enough control; you couldn't stop in time. Lotte had put them on the ground in front of her, told her to put them on before she led her to the front door of the ambulance. But Mina, Mina was in the back. With Tom. She was safer with Tom. Eve watched her feet, her thongs, one, two, one, two, on the shiny linoleum of the corridor. Yet she was sure she was not touching the floor, she seemed to be too high up. Above the head of the officer; she could see the part in her own hair.

Her daughter is dead. She killed her daughter. Eve experienced every moment twice. First, accompanied by the realisation that Mina was dead. Then by the knowledge that she was responsible. When they arrived home, she saw the door to Mina's room was closed. She wondered what her daughter was doing in there. It was a beautiful, sunny day; why wasn't she outside playing? Mina is dead. She killed her daughter.

The day passed or it didn't. Eve and Tom lay in bed, and he curled against her back, his face at her neck. Or she fell asleep on the couch, her arms wrapped about a cushion. At some stage, Lotte was there, sitting at the kitchen table. Lotte, who should have been driving away in the camper van. Whose fault it was. Whose fault it wasn't.

Morning.

The next day, Eve made her face look towards Lotte's face. She made her head nod. She made it look away. She did not see Lotte. Did not see the camisole strap looping her upper arm, a red mark where the elastic waist of her boxer shorts had pressed too tight in her sleep. All these signs that she was alive. She was the daughter who had not died. Eve saw, and she did not want to see.

I think you should leave, said Eve.

Yes. I'll go this morning.

Eve sat down. Tom came into the room.

I'm going to go, said Lotte.

Eve watched Tom's face when Lotte said this. His face did not do anything. All of their faces had forgotten how to do things.

Yes, he said. He pulled out a chair. He sat. They all waited. They wanted something to happen. Eve looked at Tom; he looked at the table. Lotte looked at the table. They had all forgotten their lines.

But where will you go? Tom asked Lotte.

Their vocabulary had been broken down into small pieces. Children's building blocks. There were no children.

I'll go to a hotel. I'll stay there. Until …

Finish it. Finish what you're saying. It's what Eve would say to Mina when her daughter's words trailed away and neglected to make a sentence. Lotte waited for one of them to nod, to murmur over the top of her. To do anything that meant she did not have to say it. No one said anything.

The funeral.

There was only this one thing to talk about, and no one wanted to talk about it.

No, said Tom.

Eve looked at him. His eyes were sunken. She had never understood that expression before now. His eyes were deep in his face — his skull circled them like the edges of a volcano. Nothing was spewing forth; he was spent. His face was ashen.

No, you can't go to a hotel. You will stay here.

Eve knew this was right. The alive daughter can stay. She was family. This is her family, the only one she had. Lotte was looking at her. She was beseeching.

Yes, Eve said. She was benevolence. She had so much to give because she had nothing to care about. She was for everyone except herself. Yes, you must stay.

It was too late to send her away. No one could remember any more of their lines. They stood from the table but they had nowhere to go.

I'm sorry.

Lotte in the doorway. Eve lying on Mina's bed. She was wrapped in the doona, but she kicked it off.

For what?

For everything, said Lotte. For being here.

It's not your fault, said Eve.

I feel like it is. If I wasn't here, you wouldn't have tried to get rid of me. You wouldn't have been driving the van.

It is exactly what Eve has been thinking. How dare Lotte be right? How dare she know?

It's not your fault, said Eve. But Lotte continued talking. She wanted a part of this, thought Eve, that was all.

It's no one's fault. Eve repeated the words of the grief counsellor who had arrived at the house earlier that afternoon, sent by the hospital. Eve had put the kettle on. The counsellor was the only one who drank his tea. He was in his forties. He was wearing sandals, the sporting ones made of black rubber and velcro. While he sipped his tea he reached down and pulled the velcro tab open. Sand sprinkled on the floorboards. He had been called back from his holiday at the beach for this emergency. It was very important to attend to the bereaved while the trauma was fresh, before things got too settled. Did he tell them that? He smelled like sunscreen. He spoke very softly, so Eve had to lean in closely to hear him. She didn't want to hear him, so she got up and put the kettle on again. He waited until she sat down again before he continued speaking.

No one can understand what you're going through right now. It's probably very difficult to process. But that's okay.

He waited for her to nod: go on. He waited for her to process. He slurped his tea.

There is no right way to mourn, he said. Whatever you feel is the right thing to feel.

He paused again, ripped open the other velcro sandal.

Tom coughed.

Thank you, that's very helpful.

Everyone nodded. Lotte was sitting at the end of the table. She shouldn't be there; she knew that. So she sat at the end, as though she wasn't there. Eve couldn't stop looking at her.

Sunlight tickled at her hair. She would be feeling it, warm on her bare shoulders. There were freckles there, from incidental moments in the sun over the years.

You're probably feeling a whole range of emotions right now, said the counsellor. It might be hard to know what to preference.

He didn't use words like 'loved one' or 'happier place'. He said 'your daughter' and 'Mina'. He didn't tell them what Mina would have wanted, because it was obvious that no one wanted any of this.

I don't feel anything, said Eve.

She would not be that person. The difficult mother who refused to acknowledge what was happening around her. She would not be in denial. But it just could not have happened. There must be options, avenues of recourse. She wanted the grief counsellor to have all of the answers, and she would listen to them, take them in. If she followed the rules, everything would be okay. She only wanted for there to be one way to feel, and she would make herself feel that way.

That's understandable, said the counsellor. He went to drink his tea, but then realised nobody else was touching theirs. Or saying anything. He was expected to go on saying something. He toyed with staying silent, with letting them fill the void.

You're probably still in shock.

Silence.

No, said Eve.

She was not in shock. She hated herself. She was revolted by what she had done.

I am disgusted at myself.

It wasn't your fault.

He said it with such conviction that she wondered whether he had been there when it happened. But then he would know. It *was* her fault. She was driving the van. The van killed Mina. Mina was not driving. Tom was not. Lotte was not. Mina was dead. Eve was not. Tom was not. Lotte most certainly was not. It was Eve's fault.

It was an accident, the counsellor said. You've done nothing wrong. It's no one's fault.

I killed my daughter. Don't you think that's wrong?

The counsellor looked down at his hands. He was probably wishing he was back at the beach. That if he left within the hour, he could get there while it was still light. She should tell him this.

Yes. It's not the way things should be. But it's no one's fault.

No one would let her take responsibility. Not out loud. She would be the same, if she were in their situation. These were things she would say to Tom if he'd been the one driving. And she would be right to say those things. And yet it was wrong. She was responsible.

The grief counsellor told them not to clam up. Not to be afraid of anger or tears. He spoke about emotions as though they were places to be visited. Holiday destinations with guidebooks, recommended lengths of stay, and things to do while you're there.

When he stood to leave, Tom stayed seated. So did Lotte. It was Eve who led him to the door and let him clasp her arm in a professional hug. She wondered if they were instructed to touch their clients to transfer their shared humanity and warmth. *The poor woman*, he was thinking. That's what he would say to his wife when he got back to the beach and their children played totem tennis on the lawn. She would pass him a beer, give him an understanding look. What was she like? she would ask. The mother? She would be thinking how glad she was that it was not her. But also that it would never happen to her because she was very careful.

When Eve closed the front door, she went to Mina's room and lay down on the bed.

It can't be no one's fault, Lotte.

Eve's voice is stripped of emotion. That must be because there was no emotion to be voiced. It did not even sound like herself. She wondered what it would be like to be mute, to never say anything again.

Later, they would pick out clothes for Mina to wear. The funeral director would come to the house, and Eve would sit in the back yard, eyes on the abandoned snow-pea pyramids. One lay flat on the lawn, another leaned against the railway sleeper border of the garden, looking as though it was ready for take-off. Terrifyingly, those days would be the easiest, as if such a word still existed. Later, Tom would put together a slide show of photographs, which Eve could not watch. The doorbell would ring, again and again, with the delivery of flowers. Lilies, gerberas, tulips, sunflowers. The damp smell of green florist's brick, the crackle of plastic cellophane. Later, they would brown and wither. The lily stamens would sprinkle fetid orange powder on the table. She would have to tell Mina not to touch, that it would stain her clothes. She would not have to tell Mina.

Later, Eve unrolled the newspaper from its plastic wrapping as if she was going to read it. Mina's face was on the front page. It was an old photograph, taken on her third birthday, and she proudly smiled with her teeth, her chin thrust forward. Eve knew the photograph well, because it decorated the header of her own Facebook page. She wondered if the newspaper had phoned her to ask permission to use the photograph. She wondered if she'd given it. The newspaper report was breathless. The journalist seemed to think he was there in the front garden, standing on the driveway. *It was a beautiful summer day*, wrote the journalist. *He got that right*, thought Eve. *A little girl had chosen her favourite dress to wear to that afternoon's birthday party. Her mother had wrapped the present.* But the present hadn't been wrapped, thought Eve. It still wasn't. What followed was a call to action. Comments from a child-safety expert. *We must be more careful. There must be a new policy.* Eve put down the newspaper and went inside.

The easiest days. Later, she put on clothes; she went to the funeral. There was no gathering afterwards, or at least if there was, Eve did not go. She did not want to eat, or sleep, but she did both of those things. The police visited, the same officers. There will be no charges, they told her. It was an accident. Yes, she told them. It was an accident. She thought that there still should be charges. Later, Tom would call the childcare centre, the kindergarten, and the gymnastics club. Later, he would water his garden for hours, the water turning the lawn to slush. Later, they would lie beside each other in bed, holding hands. Later, she would roll over to reach for him, and his pillow would be wet, and he would not be there.

•

There is a knock on the door, and light from the kitchen floods the room.

Jordie, just wait in there a minute.

The light disappears as the door closes and Len crosses the room.

Shall I help?

Eve can't answer, and he lifts the waist of her T-shirt. She raises her arms obediently, and he pulls the shirt over her head. Takes her hands and pulls her to her feet, as though he might ask her to dance. Instead, he tugs the jeans to the floor, holding her hands as she steps out of them. Formal as a valet, he offers a dressing gown, and Eve turns away from him as she inserts one arm and then the other. They both take pause, before he folds the lapels of the gown over one another and ties the belt.

Wait.

He goes out and then comes back in again. Crouching, he instructs Eve to lift her foot, and she holds his shoulder for balance as he pulls Explorer socks onto her feet. She thinks of

Nate, walking ahead, his socks rolled over the ankles of his boots. He had sent a card, after Mina.

Are you sure you don't want a shower? Len looks doubtful. Eve shakes her head, cannot imagine being wet again.

Come and have some tea.

Jordie is bent over a colouring book, his fist bunched around a green texta. A milky bowl of cereal has been pushed aside. He watches her sit, and then returns to his work. The kitchen table is edged in yellow foam, gaffer tape winding around the tubular steel legs and holding the foam in place. Prodding the foam with her finger, Eve watches the beds of her nails pinken with the pressure.

Jordie has haemophilia, says Len. We try to make sure he doesn't bump anything, because we won't know if he's bleeding inside until it's already done some damage.

Runny blood, says Jordie, matter-of-factly. And when the runny blood runs out, I get top-ups from other people.

That's what I brought on the bus with me, wasn't it?

Jordie shrugs. Probably, he says.

Len sets down a cup of tea in front of Eve.

That's Mum's, says Jordie sharply, looking at Len. The mug is decorated with a picture of a teddy bear holding a red, heart-shaped balloon. The image is scratched and faded from much use, but Eve can clearly see the letters written on the balloon.

Mum's at work, says Len. Eve can use it, Mum wouldn't mind.

Jordie's face flirts with thunder and Len sighs, picking up the mug and taking it over to the bench. The tea dribbles over the side then sloshes forth in a wave to a new mug. Jordie nods.

Is there someone I should call? asks Len, as he sets the tea down again. A husband, a friend, a sister?

Lotte: the name comes immediately. But she shakes her head at Len. They haven't spoken in months; not since it happened. Even a few months ago, when Tom told Eve that Lotte was sick, Eve had not picked up the phone. Lotte wouldn't want to hear from her, she was sure of that.

·

It was the first truly autumnal day of the year. The wind was cool, skating across the surface of the lake, but the trees were bursts of warmth, burnished oranges and glowing reds as the leaves fell, earlier every year, distraught from the heat rather than in readiness for the cold. Tom and Eve had walked with their hands in their pockets, matching each other's pace, moving aside to let other walkers past, or stepping around the children who were frozen in trepidation, holding soggy bread toward a flock of honking swans. They had taken to walking around the lake once a week on Sunday mornings, just as they had taken to watching DVD box sets of TV shows on Saturday and Sunday nights. Establishing routines that failed to expand into the hours of time suddenly available to them.

Lotte is going in for surgery this week.

Tom had glanced across at Eve, waiting for her reaction.

They found two small tumours in her breast in December. That's why she came back to Australia, to have the operation.

That's no good, said Eve. She knew she should have more to say.

I can't believe she didn't tell me when she arrived. She must have felt so alone. It's the same as what Helen had. Tom's voice cracked. She has the same gene, apparently, he said. She just found out.

It's a mutation, said Eve. Everyone has the gene; Lotte must have the mutation.

Did you know about this?

Tom's question was sharp. He stopped walking.

She had the test years ago, said Eve. Before she went to Chile. She's probably known for a long time.

Why didn't you tell me?

Eve was confused. How does she know this thing? How does Tom not?

I didn't know. I knew she had the test. I didn't know the result; she didn't tell me.

They walked on in silence.

Eve willed herself to lift her hand to his arm, as though she might have any comfort to offer. But her arm stayed in her pocket.

I was thinking we could go and see her, said Tom. After the surgery she has to have chemo. It's just the same as Helen.

There was terror in his voice. *Both my daughters* — she could almost hear the words that must have been echoing through his mind.

You should go, said Eve. Spend some time with her.

It wasn't the answer he wanted. Tom refused to leave her alone, and Eve could not offer to come. How do they pass so many days and end up in the same place as the first? Every day, Eve felt like she was sitting on the bottom of the sea-floor, and it wasn't like in a movie: she couldn't peer up to see him swimming just above, the sun piercing through the surface, illuminating his flagging clothes. The water was dark: it stung and pushed at her eyes; her hair grabbed at her face, her open mouth. And now she is here, and he is there, and she knows that she must let him go. That if she just creeps a little bit further away, he won't be distracted by her presence in the murky waters beneath him. He will be able to move on with his life, as he deserves to do. To concentrate on Lotte, the family he has left.

She has to leave him, because it is the only way to give him his life back. But the real sea, the actual sea, was icily hostile: it wanted no part in Eve's plan, demonstrating only how difficult it was to sink. Yet Tom hadn't come after her; he hadn't followed her to the coast. In Len and Jordie's small house, her skin prickling beneath the dressing gown, the blanket heavy on her shoulders, Eve takes hold of that thought, holding it close to her chest without examining it. Tom has not come to find her: he must be relieved that she has left. For once, she has done the right thing.

If you don't want me to call anyone, maybe you could phone, said Len. I think you should let someone know you're alright. That you've … taken a bit of a turn.

Len peers at her as he speaks, and Eve makes herself look back towards him. His bald head makes him seem older than he is: he is only thirty, or even younger. A boy, she decides, as if the years have deepened the gulf between them, removing all possibility of common ground. There are two wrinkles of skin at his neck, above the collar, as though he has spent a long time looking up at the sky.

I'll call Lotte, Eve says eventually. She's a friend of mine.

Len is relieved at this, nodding firmly.

That's good. You should do that.

He takes a sip of his own tea, waiting until Eve does the same.

Can I ask why you were down on the beach? Why you were in the water?

Would he understand? But how could he? And how could she ask him to? No parent should.

I just wanted to put my toes in, Eve explains. You know, to wake me up a little. And then I went a little bit deeper and the rest of me felt colder. So I dove right under.

Cold slamming at her body, chest seizing.

I meant to come straight back and have a shower, but I just felt so tired; I was resting on the beach.

You haven't, uh … He coughs. Bridget is better at these things than I am, he says. My wife, she's a nurse. But I feel like I should ask: you haven't taken anything, have you?

She sees then how it appears to him, how it would appear to anyone: lone woman, early morning beach, fully clothed.

No, I couldn't.

He thinks she could do such a thing. She's not allowed to do that. She promised Mina: anything but that. Eve knows she doesn't deserve to escape so easily; she must stay here so that she can be punished every day. It's Tom who should be free. He didn't deserve to be dragged down by all of this, but he refuses to step away.

No, I wouldn't do anything like that. It was just a mistake, I wasn't thinking. I think I just need to sleep.

She stands up, pushing the chair back.

Thanks for your help.

Len follows her into the living room, watching as she folds the blanket and puts it on the couch, picks up her wet clothes from where they lie in a pile on the floor.

I'll get this back to you.

She tugs at the dressing gown then flees out the door, thick-socked feet catching on the doormat so that she stumbles down the steps too fast.

Wait.

As she hurries past the toilet block Len appears by her side,

258

gently steering her back the way she came. At least let me put you in one of the cabins. They're mostly empty, and they've got heating. Wait here.

He jogs back to the reception office and disappears inside, returning with a key. Lets Eve into a cabin and prises the bundle of wet clothes from her chest.

I'll put these in the machine. There are blankets in the cupboard.

She sits on the double bed, watching him turn on the heater, the smell of dust filling the small space.

Just to take the chill off, he explains.

She's shivering again, but she doesn't want him to know. Plants her feet firmly on the lino floor, concentrates on the bunk beds on the far wall that reach all the way to the ceiling, their mattresses covered in blue vinyl. Like hospital furniture. Easy to clean. Only when he has left, pulling the sliding door shut behind him, does she take all four blankets from the cupboard, shaking them out before she lies down on the mattress and burrows beneath.

11

LOTTE

JANUARY 2015

Eve marches down the hallway. Lotte listens to the fly-screen door swing open and smack lightly back against the frame. She doesn't want to be here. Eve doesn't want her here. Her mother is no longer here. Yet she doesn't want to leave.

The scream comes in staccato gasps, a comical siren that hurtles through the house. Children whizzing past on bicycles? Dogs fighting? Lotte tries to make sense of the noise. She comes out into the living room. Her father is hurtling towards her, across the backyard, and then he stops at the glass door. They are both pausing; they both know something has happened, that something is wrong. The universe has split, and they don't want to step forward into it. He throws open the sliding door.

What's going on?

Lotte is about to explain — about Eve wanting her to leave, about her diagnosis and why she's come back. That she's sorry, she shouldn't be here. That she should have come back sooner, or not at all. But the scream is louder, it is more insistent, and she watches Tom's face unfold in realisation.

Eve?

He bolts for the front door, a second slam, and it takes Lotte

260

too long to follow. Emerging into the summer-bright day, she sees nothing but the blue campervan parked in the drive, blooming against the over-exposed sky. She has to drive away. And then Eve's shout, from somewhere behind the shrubbery and the van.

Call an ambulance, someone call an ambulance!

Eve stands behind Tom, one hand at her mouth, drawing it close and then away. Screams. Sobs. Lotte races into the house and picks up the phone. She urges the ambulance to hurry but they don't understand, they keep telling her to be calm, that everything is going to be alright.

Hurry, hurry, hurry!

She shouts it into the phone. She sees Mina's grubby feet; Tom is crouching over her. Eve is pacing, her body jerking back and forth. The van must have stalled when Eve pulled the handbrake on, but Lotte carefully opens the driver's door and pulls the key from the ignition.

Paramedics, the ambulance parked on the road. They run, one leaping across the deep gutter with a skip. They are polite; they take control.

And then the ambulance is gone, doing a harried U-turn in the street. The lights of the police car are flashing when it pulls up but there is no siren. Neighbours are in their yards, people standing close together. Two in that yard. Three in that one. Everyone is paused, their lives all momentarily in a balanced stillness; they had all been watching, relieved it was not them.

You called Emergency. The policewoman nods at the phone in Lotte's hand.

They've just left, says Lotte. They're on the way to the hospital.

A young girl, wasn't it? Both parents are in the ambulance? And this was the vehicle?

Lotte nods. They already know everything.

Are you a neighbour?

I'm her sister.

Whose sister? asks the officer. The mother's?

Mina's. The little girl's.

The officer seems to see her properly then.

I'm sorry, she says. Are you okay?

Lotte is fine; she knows this cannot really have happened.

We just need to ask you a few questions, says the officer. We'll ask the parents later. Who was driving the van?

Lotte looks down at the key in her hand. The officer follows her gaze. A pineapple in a hand. She pictures Eve, mouth agape, that short, bursting scream. And it was Lotte who should have been backing that van out of the garage. Who should have been getting ready to leave. The one with no home, no family. Nothing to lose.

I was ... I was meant to be leaving.

You were driving?

She could confess. It will be neat, finished. A written admission, a signature. A television crime drama, over within the hour.

It was Eve, she says. Mina's mother. The little girl's mother.

She is always saying the wrong thing.

Lotte sees her once, to say goodbye. Mina's body, too small for the machinery surrounding her, lies shallow beneath the blankets. She does not look as though she has died. Her cheeks are flushed pink, her face undamaged. She does not look worn down or broken, in the way Lotte's mother had.

Mina's hand is cool and soft, when usually it is twitchy and warm. Texta lines decorate her fingers. On the back of one hand is an 'M' marked out in love-heart stamps. Lotte had drawn it on after breakfast yesterday, using the pink texta with a felt tip shaped into a heart.

M for Mina? Lotte had asked. Or M for Mum?

M for Mum! Mina had replied.

Lotte kisses Mina on the forehead, something she has never done before. Until now she has always accepted hugs from Mina, arms high and tight around her neck, cheek pressed to cheek. She does this now, her cheek against Mina's lifeless one, afraid that if she holds her too tightly she will leave a mark.

A small side gate by the cemetery gatehouse is open.

Hmmm, let's see.

The woman in the gatehouse booth turns away and flips through a record book. Sweat trickles down Lotte's stomach and back.

Here you go, the woman says, handing her a photocopied map, a highlighter trail showing which way to go.

Now, no flowers, unless the headstone has a built-in vase. If it doesn't and you'd like to apply for one, you need to fill out a form. Not that it matters today — the flowers would soon be dead in this heat; it would be a waste of time.

They're dead anyway, says Lotte, taking the map. It hadn't even occurred to her to bring flowers; she isn't going to tell this woman that.

I beg your pardon? The woman peers at Lotte through the ticket-box railings, channelling indignation.

Cut flowers, Lotte says. They're dead anyway, even without the heat.

Well. The woman sniffs loudly. I was just saying.

Lotte walks along the path, thankful for the shade of

twisted oak trees that stand at a respectful distance, their roots interrupting the concrete, knocking it into tiny cliffs. She thinks she knows where her mother's grave is, remembers the road curving away behind the piles of clay covered in astroturf, but the map leads her elsewhere. How many people have been buried in the eight years since? In the end, she almost walks right past, her stride taking her forward even as her mind notes the familiarity. *Helen Jansone*. Her mother had kept her maiden name, while Lotte had been bequeathed her father's. And now Eve and Mina, too — as if they are all part of the one family. As if Helen had never intended to stay alongside.

Hi, Mum.

And she is back in those long days of summer, her voice unconvincing, her mother not answering.

Sorry it's been so long.

Lotte crouches down on the grass to get closer, then sits cross-legged, settling in, not wanting to seem as if she isn't planning on staying long.

I miss you. But I've always missed you.

She cannot keep it up, this talking into a void. It's strange to pretend you can talk to the dead just because you are in the vicinity of their bones. But if that's how she feels, why had she had the urge to come? She wants to tell her mother everything — yet if Helen could hear, she would already know.

The words on the headstone mean nothing to Lotte. *As it was in the beginning, is now, and ever shall be, world without end, Amen.* She sits quietly for some time. Ants crawl up her legs, their pincers sending sharp rebukes into her calves.

Yesterday, Mina's body had been cremated. The funeral director had asked about burial — there was a special part of the cemetery for children — but Tom had been appalled.

We can't leave her so far from home, he'd said.

The funeral was horrific, Lotte tells Helen. There were too many people. People who didn't know Mina, who just wanted to see. To see Eve. Pretending to pay respects as they gaped wide-eyed at the small coffin. Some held balloons. Mina didn't like balloons, she was scared of them.

Lotte digs a pen out of her bag, but all she has to write on is the map the woman had given her. She prints the words carefully — she will talk to her father about getting them added to the headstone, and she knows that he will understand.

With little warning, clouds crowd out the sun, shadow racing across the cemetery so that it is suddenly as dark as evening. Fat raindrops fall, splashing warm, and within seconds the heavens open, the rain hammering down, sending Lotte limping for the protection of the trees. A sign from the gods, she thinks, if only she could believe in such things. She thinks of all the phone calls she made last week to Helen's friends, and the stories they'd told. Of Lotte's meeting with Simon, and who he must have been. And she knows that she did know her mother after all, as well as anyone could; better than many daughters might.

Lotte looks at the note in her hands and smiles. *Per aspera ad astra*.

·

He comes to see her in the hospital. Floppy-haired, a T-shirt she doesn't recognise. He is holding flowers, and a pineapple.

I wasn't sure if you would be hungry, he says.

Vin.

He puts the flowers on the table that rolls across her bed. They obscure the view between them; all she can see is his all-too-familiar forehead, one of his shoulders. She pushes the table aside, and he stands to help.

Sorry, let me.

She wonders what he sees when he looks at her. Eyes deeper than usual; a streak of grey in her hair above her left temple. She's become quite fond of that.

How are you? How did it go?

Textbook, she says. Everything as it should. There were two small tumours, but they haven't spread. They don't think it will.

That's good.

She has already explained it to him on the phone. The preventative surgery, the treatment to follow. He was kind, concerned. Admonishing her for not having called him sooner. And now he is here.

He drops back into the chair.

I'm sorry I haven't been in touch.

No. She cuts him off, slicing her hand through the air. Please don't, she says. I'm only glad you came. It's nice to see you.

I was going to bring Janet, Vin says. But I wasn't sure how well you were doing.

Next time, says Lotte. I'd like to see her.

She is surprised to realise she is not lying, that the possibility of seeing Vin's sisters brings her a genuine lift.

She had a baby, didn't she? A boy?

They called him Jack, says Vin. He looks just like her. For the first six months, Cherry was jealous, she would bark so much they wouldn't put him down on the floor. But now they're the best of friends, and Cherry even sleeps beneath the cot, keeping guard.

That's sweet, says Lotte.

They talk through each of his family members, how well

everyone is doing. Lotte can feel the dull ache of the surgery across her chest. Mostly, the medication keeps the pain at bay; only the occasional twinge breaks through to the surface. A tube runs from below each breast, and she drains away the fluids when she gets up to go to the bathroom. She has not yet had to contemplate how much she has changed, and she knows that's all in the future. For now, her day is divided into processes initiated by the nurses — medication, meals, the bathroom, physiotherapy. Soon she will go home, to a flat she has rented close by, in Annandale. She hopes to be well enough to be back at work mid-year; she has already been making enquiries at the university.

I'm so sorry about what happened to Eve's little girl, said Vin. It seems like only yesterday she was born; I remember Eve sent a photo.

Lotte realises she must still have all of Eve's emails tucked away in her account, all those photos of Mina growing up over the years.

It was awful, Vin.

And she cries as she tells him. About the accident, about her broken friendship with Eve, about witnessing the impossible grief of her father.

I shouldn't have even been there, says Lotte. I should have stayed away, not even come back to visit. Not until after all of this.

She gestures at her body, the hospital bed.

I should have waited until I was better. I didn't realise how unstuck I was; I was awful, acting as if they owed me something.

I'm sure they understand, says Vin.

It hardly matters, says Lotte.

He holds her hand as she cries, and, for the first time since Mina's accident, she lets the tears come, not worrying that she should hold them back, that there are others more deserving of grief. She had left Ballarat after the funeral and flown straight to Sydney. From the airport she'd gone straight to the appointment with the specialist. Two weeks to find a flat, create a new space for herself, and then she was booked in to hospital for the surgery. She had caught up with some friends, some old colleagues, but not told any of them why she was back. Embracing her loneliness like a punishment, not wanting any sympathy; she was too undeserving for that. She had called Vin only yesterday, and here he was.

Tell me about Jen, Lotte says when the tears stop, her eyes small and tight.

Are you sure? he asks.

She nods. It is best to know. So he tells her about his new wife, about how they met, about the way his mother wonders why he couldn't have picked someone a bit more polished.

She's a sustainability officer, he tells her. She works mainly with the parks department. Last weekend, we went for a walk through Namadgi and she collected eight kinds of gumnuts — she's drying them out for the seeds, which she sells online.

She sounds nice, says Lotte.

Vin laughs.

She is, he says. You might even like her.

Later, Lotte will cry at this too; at having let go the one she loved. To what end, she would ask herself in coming months as her body determinedly put itself back together. But when Vin calls to tell her that they're expecting their first child, Lotte's heart swells with love for him, for everything he will have. She doesn't want it, not for herself, she is sure of that now. Or, at the very least, she does not regret letting him go, even as she wants to hold him close.

EVE

Sweltering. Her chest is slick with sweat, and she throws the blankets off, scissoring her legs free of their weight. Outside, the day has dimmed to evening, but the light above the cabin door has been switched on, throwing yellow back into the small room. A rolling landscape of lumpen shapes has materialised on one of the bunk beds. Another person? Then Eve realises it is her own belongings from the tent: her clothes, and the plastic shopping bags of canned food. Even her tent has been packed down and folded back into its bag, the sleeping mat and bag bundled up beside, her jacket hanging from the back of one of the chairs. *Why couldn't he leave well enough alone?* She rolls over to face the wall, its imitation timber shiny in the dim light. A chirrup, an impatient buzzing. Her phone. On the bedside table, plugged in. It will be Tom calling.

Lying on her back, staring up at the ceiling. How? How does one go on? All of these kind gestures, people willing to show they care and understand. But they don't, they cannot. She can see already the distress and pity that would appear on Len's face if she told him what had happened, what it is exactly she's running away from. Shock followed by the relief that always powers the

269

desire to help. *Thank God that didn't happen to me*; that's what they all think. She has even seen it on the faces of the other parents in the grief support group: people who had lost their children through illness, or accidents caused by others. By careless people.

The first time she went, in a meeting room in a community centre, she mentioned only that her three-year-old daughter had died. She was almost four, she had told the group. She had gratefully received the sincere condolences from people who were confident they understood. But the second time, standing by the hot-water urn and nursing a polystyrene cup, biscuit clinging to her teeth and refusing to wash down her throat, she mentioned to another mother what had happened to Mina.

It was an accident, Eve said. In the driveway. I was driving.

And she saw the horror in the woman's face, the barrier shooting up between them. *I am not like you*, the woman's body said, as she took a small step back, straightening her shoulders even as her words reassured Eve that she shouldn't hold herself responsible. And for a small moment, Eve felt pleased to have been able to provide this woman with such a feeling of superiority, however fleeting. She did not go back to the meetings.

She can barely recall the days after the funeral. Tom tossed the flowers in the bin before they had a chance to wilt, and late summer rolled on, unperturbed by what had happened. Eve didn't leave the house, sitting for hours in an armchair in the living room, looking at the crates of toys by the bookshelves, cataloguing their contents in her mind. In the evenings, Tom switched on the television, and they ate small bites of the food dropped off by friends and strangers. Odd, unfamiliar food: spaghetti bolognese that did not taste like their own; a Thai green curry that was accompanied by red capsicum and carrot that had been sliced into small spears and lined up in a ziplock bag, so they didn't go soggy in the fridge.

After two weeks, they both went back to work; clinging to routine, leaving the house at the same time each morning, promising to see each other in the evening as though it was something to look forward to. Neither of them mentioned that they could have left the house later than they used to, as they no longer had to go past the childcare centre; both of them arrived early at their desks. All day, Eve would surf the internet, losing herself in endless banality. She avoided Facebook and its showy reminders of the unblighted lives of others. She hungrily added strangers to her Twitter list, so that every time she looked at her feed her mind was pulled in a dozen directions. Then she'd delete them all, unable to bear their relentless march forward, the trail of thoughts that became the past as soon as they appeared. Three seconds ago. Eighteen minutes ago.

One day, Eve went to an appointment with a client. A philanthropic couple had bought a three-storey monolith — the old Mechanics' Institute library on the main street — and turned it into an artists' collective. Photographers set up desks where fiction had been; graphic designers were in the alcove for biography. They wanted to know how to quieten the space while keeping it open. They'd torn up the carpets and pulled down the curtains, and then wondered why the previously cosy building had become draughty, with melancholy sounds of the aching plumbing echoing up the staircase, footsteps rat-a-tatting like hailstones on the floor.

After touring the building, Eve had stood on the upper landing, unable to hear a word the man was saying. His mouth moving, his hand gesturing.

She could hear the building, but not the man. Windows

rattling in their cases; possums in the roof; the hum of loose wiring; the buzz of lights being set up for a shoot. She hurriedly gave them advice, waved away their offers of payment, and returned to her own office. Even there, the sound assaulted her. The sigh of the bar fridge as the motor kicked in; the stop-start traffic on the street below; the whoop and hurry of the pedestrian lights.

At home, she dug out her old minidisk recorder from the garage, shoeboxes full of the disks themselves. The words scribbled on them brought back few memories: *Orange, Jindabyne, Majura Pines*. But the moment she put on her headphones, she was transported. There was twenty-five minutes of the crackle and pop of red gum in a fireplace, the anticipation of the shifting and thud of the largest log as it burnt through, and suddenly, there it was, the coal sparking in response. Lotte had built that fire, Eve recalled — they were staying in a B&B in Orange, because some kids had smashed in every window down one side of the campervan. Lotte had forgotten to open the flue, and the room had filled with smoke, sending them springing to the windows, laughing, flapping their hands at the smoke detector that failed to squeal even when the smoke became so thick it made their eyes water.

There was a recording of cars rumbling over a plank-wood bridge: the rise and fall of the tarmacked planks — one, two, one, two — every time the same echo came as the back wheels chased the first. The bubble and slurp of a creek down by the coast, and she was immediately transported back to a long weekend spent camping with Tom, walking along the creek to the waterhole in the morning, then spending the afternoon at the beach, laughing as she threw up her arms, backing into the waves because she didn't want to be thrusting her pregnant belly before her, to be using the baby as a shield between her and the elements.

Tom would come home to find Eve in the armchair, headphones on, eyes open but not seeing anything, and he would pause by her, a hand hovering by her shoulder, her head. She would always return his touch, one for one, but could no longer initiate it, so sure was she that she had lost the right to assert her own needs.

I think ...

Tom stopped, folded the tea towel. They were wordlessly cleaning up after dinner, putting things back in their places only to pull them out again tomorrow.

What do you think about selling the house? he asked.

She felt another little bit of herself splinter, a crevice appearing where a hairline fracture had dictated it someday must. To be further from every single memory she had of Mina; to put her daughter so clearly in the past.

I think it's a good idea, she said.

Because it was not up to her to take part in these decisions any more. Just as she instinctually knew she didn't want to move, so she knew Tom needed it. The house held too many memories for him.

It would be a fresh start.

They bought a house on the fringe of town, in the foothills of the low volcano that disturbed the flat landscape. Their block was bestrewn with silver gums — beautiful, unworldly things, like lightning bolts speared into the ground, their white flesh peeking from ribboned bark. The house was only a few years old, a fortress of timber and steel that sidled into the landscape, large windows inviting the outdoors in. The master bedroom was up a flight of stairs, an eyrie amongst the whispering treetops, the blue-grey leaves politely carolling through night and day. She watched from the windows as Tom reconstructed his vegetable garden, ramming starpickets into the hard clay ground to hold the timber walls that would contain layers of soil, straw, and sand. She saw that he might be happy here.

Their bodies came together as easily as they always did. Afterwards, Eve settled herself in Tom's embrace, her cheek pressed against his arm.

Eve, I'm not going to tell you to get past this. But you need to stop blaming yourself.

She didn't say anything. He went on.

It was an accident. But I'm just as much to blame. I should have been watching Mina. I shouldn't have left the door open.

It was a discussion they had had many times, Tom desperately keen for her to accept his responsibility, as though that lessened any of hers. There was a door that led from the backyard to the garage, and Tom had left it open as he gardened. It was this door that Mina must have run through, perhaps pulling it closed behind her and frightening herself in the near dark until Eve lifted the roller door. Mina running down the far side of the van towards the daylight, and Eve reversing without a second thought.

I was driving, she said.

Why couldn't he understand that?

But that was one small moment in her life, said Tom.

He pulled his arm out from under her, sitting up in the bed.

Eve, I miss her. I miss our daughter, and I want to be able to talk about her, to remember her. But you won't let me. Every time I mention Mina I can see it in you: you're so angry at yourself and you just shut down. It's not fair.

Of course it's not fair!

She turned to face him, her thoughts clouding. How does he think such a concept even comes into it?

I killed our daughter. How do you expect me to react? Do you want me to just blather on about how wonderful she was, everything I miss about her?

Yes.

Tom's voice was small.

You need to forgive yourself.

How can I? Every time I look at you, I think about how I've ruined your life, what I've taken away from you.

Tom shook his head.

No. It happened, it was one tiny little moment, and it's done. But it's *now* that you're taking her away from me. You won't let me talk about her; you're shutting me out of your life. That's what I don't know if I can live with.

She had been waiting for him to say this. To let her know that she was no longer welcome in his life. It was as it should be.

I want you back, Eve.

Lying down, he reached out for her hand.

The next day, she packed her bag and took a train to Melbourne. A day later, she was on a bus to the coast.

She showers in the small bathroom, scrubbing at her scalp, the residue of sand stubborn beneath her fingernails. When she finally gets out of the shower, the hot water has hazed the air — she cannot make out her reflection in the mirror. She is crouching in front of the heater, drying her hair, when a shadow falls across the floor and there is a knock at the door.

I'm going to get some fish and chips for dinner — do you want me to bring you back some?

Len does not step into the cabin.

Eve glances at the food on the bunk. She hasn't eaten anything all day.

Yes, that would be great, she says.

He shuffles his feet, looking away across the park.

Look, Bridget's on a double shift. I could take Jordie with me, but he needs to rest. He can't run around as much as most kids. Would you mind watching him for a bit?

Her breath catches in her throat, fighting to get through.

Are you sure? I mean, I could, but …

That would be great. Just come by when you're ready. He won't be any trouble; I shouldn't be more than forty minutes or so and he's glued to the iPad, you know what kids are like.

I'll just put some shoes on.

She looks to her feet; she's wearing Len's socks.

No worries, come by when you're ready.

She pulls damp hair back behind her ears, squeezes her feet into runners. Trudging across the campground, she is conscious of how loud her shoes are on the gravel road. Between the cabins and the reception office there is an unlit expanse, the unpowered sites that would be crowded with tents in summer. Her footsteps are quietened by the grass and she stops, looking up to the sky, a pale umbrella above the campground hemmed in by cliffs and trees. She sees the brightest stars first, the yellow of Jupiter perhaps, and only a slice of cutglass moon. The smaller, duller stars appear slowly as her eyes adjust, and she remembers Lotte correcting her years before. They weren't necessarily smaller, those stars, just further away, many of them bigger than the sun itself. She had gone on in a long explanation of red giants and white dwarfs, the way stars become more unstable as they age, shrinking and cooling until the centre forms a black heart of dense diamond and ash.

How many of those black dwarfs haunt the heavens? Lotte hadn't known. She was more interested in the spectacular clouds of the planetary nebulae like Orion's Horsehead Nebula and the Cygnus Rift: the carcasses of dying stars that reflect and scatter starlight into glorious, billowing canopies. Every single star will eventually go out, Lotte had said, and with the last one will depart all possibility of life in the universe. She had laughed at Eve declaring it a miserable thought: after all, there would be no one around to witness it. The stars would continue as observant bystanders long after humans have taken their leave, just as they had played silent witness to the universe's slow becoming.

Len answers the door, letting himself out as he directs Eve in.

Jordie, you remember Eve.

Jordie briefly looks up, nods, and returns his gaze to the iPad in his lap.

I won't be long, says Len.

Eve sits down on the couch beside Jordie. He's not wearing his helmet, soft hair curling over his ears.

What are you watching?

Pluto. A spaceship has gone really close and taken photos of it. Look!

He tilts the iPad towards her, wanting her to see but not taking his eyes off the video. A gif flicks through the history of images of Pluto, from pixellated blocks of light to a densely detailed image of the planet, a distinct love-heart etched into its face.

It's the smallest planet, isn't it? Eve struggles to think of something to say.

It's not a planet. It's a dwarf planet. Jordie is full of scorn. It has a sister. One that's almost as big.

She knows this; it must have been Lotte who told her. Pluto, the lord of the underworld, and Charon, the ferryman of the dead.

It's very exciting, says Eve. And Jordie nods his head vigorously, presses the screen to start another video.

Soon, Len returns with two paper parcels held in front of him; the assaulting smell of chips claws at Eve's empty stomach.

Do you want to join us?

Len gestures at the kitchen. She wants to stay on the couch beside Jordie's warm feet, stuffing as many chips into her mouth as possible, not make polite conversation. But she nods, pulls herself up off the couch and follows him across the room.

Len unwraps the paper, piling chips and a potato cake into a plastic bowl, squirting it with tomato sauce and delivering it to Jordie.

We usually all eat at the table, Len apologises as he comes back to the kitchen. Don't tell your mum, he calls back over his shoulder.

The first chip burns the roof of her mouth, the second does the same to her tongue. They eat in silence for several minutes before Len gets up and puts a DVD on for Jordie.

They're delicious, Eve says.

Best fish-and-chip shop on the coast, says Len.

Is it the one by the roundabout? Or the one by the golf course?

You know the town? He is surprised. Near the roundabout, he says. The other one only opens in summer, for the tourists, and it's not as good. Have you been down this way a bit?

Not for a while. And only in summer. I was here a few years ago, with my husband, just before my daughter was born.

She breaks the battered flake with her fingers, jerking her hand back as the hot steam is released.

She must be around the same age as Jordie, says Len.

Eve shakes her head.

She's younger. About four years ago. She was almost four …

She waits for him to ask, before realising that he isn't going to. And she wishes he would.

She died, my daughter. Mina.

Mouth thick with oil, her fingers coated in it so she can't brush away the tears.

Len shakes his head. I'm sorry to hear that, he says. He wipes his hands on a tea towel and puts them in his lap.

What was she like? Mina? Was she a little terror? He smiles at Eve. I was hoping for a girl when Jordie was born but my wife reckons they're worse. That boys are straight up and into everything, but girls have got the smarts — they wind you around their little finger before you've figured out what's happened.

She was a bit of both, says Eve.

She licks the grease from her hand, wipes at her cheek with a sleeve. She used to be so bossy, always telling me, *Mum, sit!* every time she wanted company, though she couldn't sit still herself for five minutes. Eve nodded at the doorway. Every time we put a DVD on she'd be dancing around; she wouldn't sit like that and watch anything from start to finish.

As they talked, Eve could hear Mina's tuneless voice, picking up at the chorus, which always got belted out with due emphasis. She remembers Mina's initially wary then tragically besotted love affair with Peppa Pig; remembers the crumpled face she could pull the instant she was overcome with tiredness. And then she finds herself laughing, rolling her eyes at Len's description of Jordie's breakfast routine, comparing it with Mina's insistence of only eating her toast when it was cold and soggy.

There is a knock at the door.

Excuse me, must be a late arrival, says Len, getting up from the table. Won't be a minute.

All the good humour scoots away with him. Left with her own thoughts, not stories for a stranger, Eve can again only see her action. Hauling up the roller door, pulling herself into the driver's seat.

Eve.

Lotte has come into the kitchen, her cheeks flushed, just a scruff of hair visible beneath her woollen hat. Even beneath the knitted jumper, Eve can see she's thinner than she used to be, and her eyes dart to Lotte's chest, wondering. But all she can think is that she's here. She came.

Lotte.

Stumbling as she gets up from the chair, falling into Lotte's arms, hugging her fiercely, thinking her grasp is too hard — she's been sick, after all. But she doesn't want to let go, relief coursing through her, and something more, something close to joy.

I'm so glad to see you, says Eve.

Me too.

Eve looks up to see Len standing in the doorway, apprehension clear on his face.

I found her number in your phone, I called this afternoon, he says.

Thank you, Eve smiles at him, letting Lotte go. She cannot understand what she's feeling, except relief that she's feeling anything at all.

How are you? The surgery, everything, I'm so sorry, I should have—

Don't worry about it, everything's fine, says Lotte, cutting her off. I've come to take you home to Dad — Tom. I've been staying with him since you left. He's worried about you; he wants you back.

She looks like she is going to say more, but Eve just nods, relieved. Home. It's the only place she wants to be.

ACKNOWLEDGEMENTS

The Solar System Drive was conceived of by Coonabarabran astronomer John Shobbrook, and created by the Warrumbungle Shire Council and local astronomy enthusiasts in 2007. It consists of multiple drives beginning with Plutos in Dubbo, Birriwa, Merriwa, Tamworth, and Bellata, with all drives ending at Siding Spring Observatory.

The writing of this book was made possible through the assistance of the Australia Council, Creative Victoria, Writing Australia, and Varuna. Many thanks to Orange City Library and the Central West Writers' Centre, Jasmine Vidler, and the hospitality of Anne and David Hopwood.

This novel has been many years in the writing, and I want to thank those who have patiently given their time and consideration to reading early drafts: Rajith Savanadasa, Ian See, Naomi Saligari, Emma Wakeling, Alanna Egan, Myfanwy McDonald, Maria Tumarkin, Naomi Bailey, Leigh Hopkinson, Andrea Gillum, Jane Jervis-Read, Annette Joosten, Hannah Hogarth, and Stephanie Joosten — your kind and critical efforts are much appreciated.

This is a book about parents, siblings, children, and families of all kinds. I wouldn't be anywhere without mine, so thank you to each and every one of you for your support.

I am indebted to Henry Rosenbloom and everyone at Scribe for believing I could get this book written. In particular, my gratitude to Marika Webb-Pullman for her careful, assured, and intelligent editing — thank you for understanding exactly what I was trying to do and edging me that little bit closer. And thank you to Laura Thomas for the beautiful cover.

Finally, thank you to Rajith, who saw how difficult this one was to write and whose support never wavered. Writing love has nothing on living it; thanks for teaching me this. And for Mala.